Toppl

Toppling Miss April

Adrienne Dines

W F HOWES LTD

This large print edition published in 2007 by
W F Howes Ltd
Unit 4, Rearsby Business Park, Gaddesby Lane,
Rearsby, Leicester LE7 4YH

1 3 5 7 9 10 8 6 4 2

First published in the United Kingdom in 2005
by Transita

A CIP catalogue record for this book is available
from the British Library

ISBN 978 1 40740 532 2

Typeset by Palimpsest Book Production Limited,
Grangemouth, Stirlingshire
Printed and bound in Great Britain
by Antony Rowe Ltd, Chippenham, Wilts.

For Tim

ACKNOWLEDGEMENTS

I am so grateful to the following people:

to my husband Tim, and sons Kieran, Tom and Freddy for their constant encouragement;
to my parents Tom and Lall Phillips for their belief in me;
to my sister Caroline and friend, Sue Bohane, for proof-reading;
to my editor Marina Oliver for her astute editing;
to Sarah Pardoe for her inspiration.

A special thanks must go to Meg (Gardiner) Shreve for introducing me to the American Women of Surrey Writers' Group without whose advice and support Miss April might never have been toppled – Suzanne Davidovac, Nancy Fraser, Tammye Huf and especially Mary Albanese, who is forever Miss April!

CHAPTER 1

It wasn't just an old bed, its edges piled high with a confection of pink fluffy pillows and the mattress sagging contentedly – it was an altar – a pink, fluffy, marital altar. Monica Moran heaved a huge sigh and let the last of her tears fall. The salty drops slid down her face, over her heaving breasts and dripped onto what lap she had left. Opposite her, Imelda Hegarty watched sympathetically.

'Are you okay, Monica?'

Monica nodded. She looked around the room with a dazed expression and sighed again. Through the open wardrobe doors she could see bulging rails of clothes, every frill and flounce in wonderful shades of cream, cerise and violet and at the end of the rail, six or seven hangers with a man's shirt on each. Then she swung her gaze onto a photograph on the dressing table. A couple beamed at her – the wife glowing with pleasure as she lay back on a deckchair having ice cream fed to her by a small man wearing baggy trunks and a *Kiss me Quick* hat. 'He did look nice, though, didn't he?'

1

Imelda regarded the photograph seriously. 'Well actually, I always think a cap –'

'No – I mean at the funeral parlour! He looked nice didn't he, all laid out in his clean overalls.' She sniffed again. 'I always did like a man in overalls, all compact and packaged neatly in his little suit with only the one zip down the middle . . .' Her voice trailed off.

Imelda watched her, frowning.

Monica scowled. 'Don't look at me like that, Mel. I do like men in overalls, uniforms – whatever – and I used to have one.' She flicked the photo onto its face. 'And now I don't have one any more!' Then she threw back her head and howled.

As the noise rose to a deafening pitch Imelda rushed over to the windows to close them. The neighbours would think there was a banshee in the place with the racket Monica was making. Poor Mon. If ever a woman needed a man in her life it was Monica Moran and now she had none. Imelda peered out onto the street to see if the commotion had attracted attention. It had. Two fellows offloading ladders from a van opposite were watching the house and the window cleaner next door was leaning over so far he'd be the next one to be buried if he wasn't careful. Imelda shook her head. Monica's husband may have preceded her to the hereafter but her reputation was preceding her in the here and now. News of her widowhood spread like a rash and there were plenty of boyos willing to come round and rub cream on it. Crossly, Imelda glared through the panes and then pulled the curtains shut.

'Monica,' she said, 'we need to have a talk.'

Monica's howls subsided – slightly.

'I don't want you rushing into anything now that you might regret later.'

Monica lifted a foot gingerly. Even in the dim light her high black stilettos looked painfully tight and uncomfortable. 'I'd be lucky if I could rush anywhere in these bloody things! What're you talking about anyway?'

Imelda took a deep breath. 'You know, Monica – men. Now that your Fred's no longer with us you will need a bit of time to yourself, to get over it and all.'

From outside there was the sound of a ladder being positioned against a wall and someone starting to whistle. Monica smiled. 'Oh Mel – you're such a worrier! You don't really think I'd be interested in replacing my Fred as quick as that.' She prised the shoes off then limped to the window. Pulling the curtain open she watched the window cleaner as he bent and rinsed his cloths in a large bucket of soapy water. When he turned to go up the ladder again, he waved at her. Monica waved shyly back. 'Though I mightn't say no to an entirely different model!'

'Monica!'

'Only joking! Don't fuss, Mel. You don't think

3

I'd seriously be bothered with anyone around here, do you. They're all fly-by-nights anyway.' She sighed and flopped onto the bed again. 'My days of de-springing mattresses are over.' She sniffed. 'If I were to go looking for a new man he'd have to be someone really special. Someone unique.'

She shut her eyes and after a last few tearful gulps, fell asleep. Imelda waited till the sound of her snores filled the room before she opened the windows again. One blast of those snores and the hopefuls might think they were already too late and leave. Then she sat on the edge of the bed and watched her friend. Asleep, Monica looked so vulnerable; awake, the rest of the world was. Imelda could feel the knot of anxiety twist in her tummy again. What was she to do? If she didn't shift the grieving widow out of Dublin in the next week you wouldn't be able to breath for the pheromones. She patted her chest, it was already playing up with the stress. Monica couldn't go abroad after what happened the last time and she didn't have any relatives in the country as far as Imelda knew. She picked up one of the cushions and plucked at the fur anxiously. Dammit, where's your family when you need them?

As she twisted the cushion hairs around her finger and watched while the top went blue, Imelda thought about her own family. If she were widowed, she'd be fine. Her family was large and supportive and most of them married with families of their own, excepting Sean and Cormac, of course. Sean, for the last fifteen years Parish Priest of the small, if significant Parish of Tullabeg in Kilkenny and Cormac, estate agent, recently moved there from Dublin. Cormac, a fifty-two-year-old bachelor in a decent parish who had too little interest in altars and too much in altar boys. Imelda shook her head. There's another problem she'd have to give some thought to. If they didn't sort him out soon, the family reputation was at stake. Sean had said as much on the phone but she didn't know what he expected her to do about it. Cormac wasn't in Dublin any more so it's not as if the problem was on her doorstep; he was in Tullabeg, way down the country. Anyway, sorting Cormac was a huge task, always had been. He was a difficult case, a special case, unique.

Unique! With a loud snort, Monica turned over in the bed and landed Imelda, who had been perched on the edge of it, onto the floor. Imelda didn't mind. The solution was there. Cormac needed sorting and Monica needed a unique man, a well-sprung mattress sort of man, to keep her on the straight and narrow.

She clapped her hands in excitement at the brilliance of her idea – two birds killed with one stone, slung into the same bush, as it were. Monica would probably sleep for hours and by the time she woke, Imelda would have it all arranged. A quick letter to Sean outlining her intention to visit but without any of the details – men were so hopeless at subtlety and anyway, he and Monica always seemed a bit

5

awkward with one another. She'd say it was on account of their recent conversations and Sean could make what he liked of it. She'd just bring Monica to Tullabeg and unleash her on the needy Cormac. Nature would surely take its course and all their problems would be solved.

And everyone would be happy.

In the study of the priest's house in the parish of Tullabeg, two men sat facing each other over a tray. The priest's housekeeper, Miss Teegan, hovered by the door hoping to catch a glimpse of the errant speck of dust that would require her immediate attention. Beady eyes darted over the picture frames and she tutted in annoyance at the state of them. They were spotless. She tried the side table – spotless too. Aware that Father Hegarty was watching her crossly, she hovered a minute longer, willing to run the risk of a lambasting later about what he liked to call 'stickybeaking'. It might be worth it. The priest's visitor was his brother, Cormac Hegarty, one of the top estate agents in the county, wealthy by anyone's standards, handsome by hers – and unmarried.

'Ahem.'

'Father?'

'Was there something else, Bernadette?'

Miss Teegan inclined her head to one side and looked puzzled. 'Something else, Father?'

Father Hegarty spit the words through clenched teeth and she noticed that he was tapping the arm of the chair. 'You appear to be waiting for something.'

Miss Teegan threw her head back in what she hoped was a flirtatious toss of her newly released curls. 'Oh, not at all Father. I was just checking to see that you had every thing you wanted – is there nothing I could get for you. Maybe,' she patted the curls she could feel caressing the nape of her neck, 'a couple more sandwiches?'

Both men looked at the tray. There were two saucers with china cups balanced precariously on top, a milk jug, sugar bowl, and a silver tea strainer in a dish squeezed onto one end. The rest of the space was taken up by an enormous platter of sandwiches of every make and shape, with and without crusts. Father Hegarty stifled a sigh and spoke slowly. 'Bernadette, we have enough sandwiches.'

'Maybe some buns then?'

He looked at the plate of cup cakes balanced on the tray's edge; each decorated with white icing and a selection of either chocolate drops or melted fruit gums. 'No.'

Miss Teegan heard the note of finality in his voice barely masked by the tapping of his fingers. He always did that just before he shouted at her. With a quick glance of regret at the brother, she nodded. 'Right so, Father. Call if you need anything. I mean you might fancy a –'

'Bernadette Teegan!'

'Yes, Father, thank you Father.' She turned on

her heel and left the room before he had time to say any more.

As he heard the squeaking of Hush Puppies on vinyl recede down the hallway, Father Sean was aware that the room had become very quiet. Breathing a long slow sigh of relief, he lowered himself back into the chair. 'That woman,' he confided to his brother, 'will be the death of me.'

Cormac leaned forward and took his time choosing a sandwich. 'Do you know what your trouble is, Sean?' he said. 'She has you spoilt. Would you look at the feed she has for us here – ham sandwiches, egg sandwiches, salad sandwiches and look – fairy cakes! I love those!' He reached over and took one of the two fairy cakes, laden with cream that she had nudged onto the edge of the plate at the last minute. 'Positively sinful!' Licking the cream from round the sides of it, he smiled at his brother.

Sean tried to smile back but a complete lack of any sort of Christian feeling prevented his face from rising to anything more convivial than a grimace. He didn't know who was worse, his middle-aged coquette of a housekeeper who tried to feed every bachelor in the country to the altar or his soft-bodied brother who hadn't been near an altar for years. Two problems who deserved each other. He watched while Cormac's pink tongue caressed the confection as if food was due to go out of fashion and he wouldn't get the taste of it forever after. In and out it went, probing, licking and all the while Cormac kept his eyes shut to stave off any distraction.

Eventually the cream was gone so he popped the sponge into his mouth and raised an eyebrow. 'So, what did you want to see me for?'

Sean tried to look as non-committal as he could. 'Well, you're my brother, aren't you? Do I need to have a reason to see you?'

Cormac tapped the side of his nose and narrowed his eyes. 'Now Father,' his tone mildly disapproving. 'Would that be an example of withholding the truth?'

Sean was tapping the chair's arm again. 'For the love of God, what are you on about? Do you not think I have enough to be doing in a parish the size of this without wasting time getting to the point – if there was a point I was intending to get to, of course.'

'Of course,' Cormac was starting on the cup cakes.

Sean sat back in his chair. 'Anyway, as I was saying, Bernadette Teegan.'

Cormac peeled the paper carefully from the sides of his cake. 'What about her?'

'A fine woman.' Ignoring the shift of Cormac's eyebrow, he leaned over and let his index finger hover over the platter of sandwiches, pointing to each one in turn as if both of them didn't know that a sandwich was two slices of bread with ham and ham only between them. Eventually, he picked

9

up a ham sandwich and took a bite. 'Generous, god fearing, decent . . .'

'Irritating, nosey . . .'

Sean cleared his throat. 'God-fearing, decent, healthy and . . .' he took another bite as he tried to work out how best to portray Bernadette's most appealing credential. 'And . . .'

'And?'

'Available! For God's sake, Cormac! What do you want me to say? Don't you know it yourself? Available! That's what she is and you should be down on your knees thanking God for it!'

Cormac stifled a laugh. 'Ah now, Sean. You don't really expect me to consider a trip up the aisle with Bernadette Teegan, do you?'

'And why not?' Now that he had declared his purpose, Sean was feeling a little more confident. 'There are worse women qualified for burial in our family plot.'

Cormac pulled a sultana out of his bun and laid it carefully on the side of the plate. 'Oh, now if it's burying her you're planning, that's a different matter altogether.' His eyes were twinkling with merriment. 'For a minute there I thought you might be suggesting I marry her!'

Sean grasped the arms of his chair and counted slowly to ten. He opened his mouth but shut it again as a faint yipping nudged the edges of his consciousness. It sounded like someone trying to tiptoe on rubber heels so that they couldn't be heard. It sounded like someone not succeeding.

It grew louder and louder till eventually she appeared in the doorway.

'Father?' She raised herself onto the balls of her feet, framed in the doorway as if for flight should this be a bad moment.

'Yes, Bernadette.' Sean's voice was flat.

'This came for you em, recently, Father. I thought to bring it earlier but seeing as you had a family visitor already . . .' She held out the letter. 'There's a Dublin postmark, maybe it's . . . ?'

Sean looked at the envelope, one eyebrow raised. He turned it over carefully. Despite the fact that it was a fresh dry day outside, the seal was puckered where it had dried. 'Thank you, Bernadette, I've been expecting this. Whoever it was sent me this must have a powerful wet tongue, don't you think? It actually looks as if it's been opened and sealed a couple of times. When I get a chance, I might open it and read it myself. Was there anything else?'

'There was not.' Face reddening, she executed a perfect pirouette and made for the door.

'Shut it, please!'

She flashed a look of resentment at him as she pulled the door after her but they could both hear her humming her defiance down the hallway in time to her squeaking soles.

When he was sure that she was well and truly away, Sean looked at the envelope. There was a Dublin postmark on it right enough and below

11

that the meticulous handwriting they both knew so well. *The Rev. Father Sean Hegarty, P.P.* and underneath, *Parish Priest* written in bold and underlined. He held the envelope up for Cormac to see. 'Oh dear, is it that time of the year again?'

Cormac squinted across. 'Who is it?'

'Imelda.'

'Our sister Imelda?' Cormac put the bun down and wiped his lips with the linen napkin Bernadette had so thoughtfully placed on his side of the tray. 'When is she coming?'

Sean pulled the envelope open, trying to ignore the sticky seal. 'She's coming . . . let me see now . . . how are you, hope all's well . . . blah, blah, blah . . . hope to travel . . . *spend the* . . . Oh no!'

'What is it?'

'A fortnight – she's planning to stay a week with each of us. She'll call in a couple of days with further details.' The brothers looked at each other. Both had plans for the next few weeks and none of those involved having the air sucked out of every room they chose to sit in by the sombre presence of their sister. The prospect was dismal. Eventually Cormac spoke.

'Can't you put her off? Invent an epidemic or a religious festival or something?'

Sean turned the envelope over. 'Afraid not,' he sighed, 'though *I* will be very busy. Maybe she could be some help to you about the office, you know, a woman's touch?' The postmark was four days old. 'The kettle mustn't be working as well as usual. This was posted on Monday.' He folded the letter and put it into his breast pocket. 'And now it's Thursday. Chin up little brother and get your house in order. Like it or not, she'll be here Saturday.'

Bernadette Teegan opened the door of her green Mini Metro and adjusted the cushion on the driver's seat. Still smarting from the imperious tone Father Hegarty had used, she didn't trust herself to start up the engine straightaway so she closed her eyes and sat back in the seat for a minute.

He's a pig, God forgive me, she thought to herself, a man of God indeed. There's not an ounce of Christian charity or kind feeling in that one at all. She sighed deeply as she felt the heat of her frustration prickling behind her eyelids. He's not a bit like Father Barry, so he isn't. Before the heat engendered by the memory of Father Barry started prickling anywhere else she opened her eyes with a 'tut' and did the routine checks before starting the car. The steering wheel cover was unruffled, St Christopher centred on the dashboard and her skirt smooth. 'Right so,' she said aloud. 'Home for the tea.'

On automatic pilot the car reversed out of the driveway and should have turned neatly on the grassy area beside the gate, but suddenly there was a shout behind her and she slammed on the brakes.

A young lad of about eighteen was spread-eagled across the back window.

'Michael! What are you doing here?'

'Getting killed – did you not see me?' Behind the carpet of pimples, freckles and fluff, his face was white with fright. 'You nearly ran me over!'

'Well, in the middle of the gateway's a very stupid place to be standing when someone is trying to back out!'

'What? You weren't even looking!'

'Oh, you are a stupid boy.' She opened the door and climbed out. 'A very stupid boy.' She leaned into the car to readjust the cushion, which had shot forward when she slammed the brakes. The motion of stroking velvet calmed her. 'Why would I have to look when you weren't supposed to be there in the first place?' she asked him sweetly.

'But Aunty Bernadette . . .' He shut his mouth again. There was no point trying to argue. Bernadette Teegan did not indulge in arguments. Her philosophy on disagreement was simple and straightforward. She was right – always. And as an argument meant that she would have to spend precious time engaged in conversation with someone who was clearly misguided, ill-informed or just plain stupid, she would not indulge. He raised his hands, palms upwards and let them fall again despondently.

Seeing that he was not going to try and justify his unpredictable behaviour and was probably sorry for the distress he had caused her so late in the afternoon, Bernadette softened even more. She reached out and patted his shoulder. 'There you are, dear,' she said. 'Just be more careful in future. Now, what are you doing here? Did you want a lift home?'

Michael straightened and smirked at her. 'I don't actually. I'm here to see Father Hegarty.'

'Father Hegarty? You? Oh, Michael, you haven't been bad, have you?'

'I have not! Why do you always assume that I'm in the wrong?' There was that note of petulance in his voice that always softened her cough. His father had been the same.

'Michael, it's twenty past five on Thursday after-noon. I am just setting off home for the tea. When I get there, I expect to find you lounging on the sofa, your feet up and the paper crumpled on the floor beside you – testament to the fact that you've managed to rouse yourself long enough to turn to the three back pages and look at the pictures. And the reason I expect to find you there, is that I always find you there.' She peered at him closely. 'Because Michael, that's what you do. You lie on sofas and you lounge.' She threw her arms out and with a wide dramatic sweep indicated the driveway of the Tullabeg Presbytery. 'But you're not there, are you? You're here, on your way to see the priest.'

'It doesn't mean I've done anything wrong.'

'If you haven't the manners,' she spoke slowly and with great emphasis, 'or the guts to discuss

15

it with me first, then it's unlikely to mean you've done anything right.'

'Oh, for –' He swallowed as he tried to regain the self-control she had struggled for years to instil. 'I don't know what he wants me for. I haven't found out yet. He didn't say. He rang me up about an hour ago and asked me if I was busy. I said I wasn't. He said "good man, well I might have something for you, so." I said that'd be grand. He said, "well, could you come round?" I said I could. He said when. I said straightaway. He said "could you leave it an hour or so?" I said I could. So I did. I left it an hour then I put on my jacket and I came round. And then you nearly ran me over in the driveway but I survived and that's it. That's all there is to it. Are you happy?' He was breathless by now and his face was red with exertion.

For a minute she said nothing. That was a strange thing all right. What job could Father Hegarty possibly have for Michael and why would he not discuss it with her first? And why would he ask Michael to wait an hour? Only that she had stayed on to finish ironing the tea towels she'd have left ages ago and missed Michael to give him a lift home. As it happened, she'd only just missed him in the gateway. She'd have to give this one a bit of thought. Stalling for time, she looked Michael up and down. 'Well, you'd better calm yourself and go on in so,' she said. 'And straighten your collar and don't slouch when you're talking to him.'

He glared and turned away from her.

'And if he offers you a cup of tea, don't have it, I'm only after finishing tidying away and I have the best buns here with me anyway. You'll be getting them for your tea!' He didn't turn round. 'Oh well!' She shrugged her shoulders in resignation and got back into her car, muttering, 'that's young people for you. You do what you can to help but you really wouldn't want to be waiting for a word of thanks, you really wouldn't.'

She sat there in the growing gloom watching as he reached the front door. With the window open she could hear the bell jangle faintly in the distance and waited to see what happened when the door opened, though her view was mostly blocked by the trees on the drive. She couldn't be seen from the house and there'd be no point in her starting up the car now, drawing attention to the fact that she was there – the noise of it might muffle the sound of the bell. And anyway she had a sneaking suspicion that Father Hegarty deliberately arranged for Michael to come over when she had already left. She usually left at five on a Thursday and called in at the supermarket on the way home. He knew that. He'd often asked her to get things for him. And it wasn't as if he hadn't seen her to mention it either. She'd gone in to take the tea tray when he and his visitor had finished tea. She'd shown Cormac to the door and held it open while the two men said their goodbyes. Her cheeks burned at the recollection. 'Thank you, Bernadette, you don't have to stand there while I see my brother out the door. I'll be able to manage that one on my own.' The sarcastic way of him! Who did he think he was?

At that, a movement up at the house caught her eye. A light had gone on in the upstairs front room and through the opened curtains she could see Michael and Father Hegarty standing in the room looking all about them. Father Hegarty was pointing here and there and Michael was following his finger and nodding. They stayed like that for a few minutes and then the light went out. She waited but there was nothing at all. It was growing darker and though she had planned to get a nice head of lettuce from Supasave on the way home there really was no point now. Anything left at this stage would be limp and useless. She tutted crossly. Men and lettuces, wasn't it always the same? What a bother. Now she'd have to go shopping in the morning and she'd wanted to spend tomorrow at home.

Bernadette did not work Fridays. As it was a day of fast, Father Hegarty had little use for her on a Friday, but she'd left him a nice tin of salmon and a new potato salad for his lunch anyway. She'd made it fresh this morning thinking Cormac might come early and fancy a bit of lunch but then he was delayed and that put himself into a mood. There'd been more than enough and she scolded herself for not taking a bit home. Oh well, the best laid plans and all that. She checked her watch

18

– five past – where was the boy? Surely if Father had a job for him he wasn't expecting the lad to stay there and do it straight away? What could be going on?

She toyed with the notion of driving up closer to the house. She could always say there was something she's forgotten to get, or maybe she could remind him about the potato salad. That'd be the thing. Maybe when she mentioned it earlier he wasn't really listening and wouldn't know tomorrow that it was there and only bread and fish on a Friday would be a bit too frugal, even for a parish priest.

Her thoughts were interrupted by a noise from the side of the house. She sat up straight and peered into the darkness. There was a roar of mechanical origin as an engine was sparked into life, followed by enthusiastic revving. Bernadette's heart lurched. Around the side of the house two lights appeared low on the gravel and jerked their way along the drive. She knew what they were. As if the years were being peeled back, it all came into focus and Bernadette Teegan recognised the headlights of the late Father Barry's Volvo as it juddered towards her in the soft twilight. The exhaust belched as the car came nearer then stopped with a panicked jolt. Through a cloud of exhaust fumes she could hear the familiar swish as the driver's window was rolled down.

'Aunty Bernadette! What are you doing here still?'

With a shudder, she came down to earth. 'Michael? Is that you?' She leaned out and caught sight of the boy sitting behind the wheel as if it was his place to be there. 'What are you doing in Father Barry's car? Get out of it this minute!'

Michael's face pulled back into the car's dark interior. 'Father Hegarty said I could use it! He said it was okay!' He had his hand on the window lever as if ready to roll it up if the need arose.

'Did he now? And what do you need a car for? Haven't you me like an eejit driving you anywhere you need to go – and not a penny on you to go anywhere anyway.' The sight of anyone sitting in Father Barry's precious car filled her with rage, even if the anyone was Michael. Especially when the anyone was Michael.

'It's okay, Aunty Bernadette, honestly it is. I'm only having it for the loan, while I'm doing the job. Father Hegarty said it'd be okay and I can take as long as I like, two weeks at least he said.'

'You're going to work for Father Hegarty for two weeks?' She couldn't imagine anyone willing to entrust a job to Michael for one week, never mind inviting him to take two. 'What are you going to do?'

Michael puffed out his chest. 'Well, he said there were plenty of other fellows in the town who could do it but they were a bit quick and he wanted a fellow who would be prepared to take his time and do a really good job. I'm to start Saturday morning.'

'Start what? What is it he wants you to do?'

Michael grinned. 'He's going to have the furniture removed by tomorrow and then I'll be here at nine on Saturday. He said I'm to be well into it by the time the Dublin bus arrives.'

'Into what?'

'Nothing too difficult,' His newfound career, however temporary, was making him brave. 'Don't get your knickers in a twist. I'm his new interior decorator.'

She peered into the darkness in disbelief. 'Father Hegarty is trusting you to decorate his house? He doesn't need the house decorated.'

'He hasn't asked me to decorate the *whole* house.'

Suddenly she remembered the light in the upstairs front room, and earlier the letter she had delivered to Father in the parlour. The letter from his sister saying she was coming to stay. There was still a ghost of a smile on Michael's face and it rekindled as she beamed at him.

'Of course, you'd be the perfect person for the job, pet. Father Hegarty knows as well as the next man how carefully you'd tackle a job like that, and how you'd take your time over it. And he said you were to take two weeks, did he?'

He was nodding.

'And there's only the one room to do, isn't there?'

The nodding became more enthusiastic. She smiled back. Well, there was a thing. Father Hegarty, saintly man that he was, was leaving no stone unturned in preparation for his sister's visit – and leaving the eejit Michael in charge of the stones. With exaggerated care she turned the key in the ignition and signalled Michael to do the same. The Volvo roared into life, then spluttered, coughed and died. Bernadette sighed. The boy wasn't even able to drive the car to buy the paint. She gripped her steering wheel tightly and prayed for patience.

This was going to be a long job.

CHAPTER 2

The journey to Supasave took ages. 'Caution at all times,' was Michael's driving mantra and it seemed to him a foolish thing that a fellow in possession of only two feet should be expected to manage three pedals at the same time. It was all so confusing. He knew that the two on the outside went together – and never at the same time as the one in the middle – but how you managed to get your feet off one and onto the others at same time was a complete mystery. By the time they had turned out onto the road he had come to the conclusion that he didn't actually like pedals. Their potential for causing accidents worried him. So at snail's pace Bernadette Teegan drove into the evening with Father Barry's grey Volvo estate alternately crawling and lurching behind her.

On the straight things were fine; the turnings were more of a challenge. Approaching the first corner Michael eased his right foot off the accelerator and hoped the car got the hint and stopped. When it became evident that it hadn't, he hit the brake with his left. While the engine spluttered and attempted to calm its scrambled juices, he fumbled with the key and with a lot of pumping on the appropriate pedal, persuaded it to get going again. In front of him, Bernadette muttered a hasty prayer to St Christopher and pulled out as fast as she could. After the next corner she discovered that the safest place for both herself and her saint was somewhere along the road, pulled in but engine running. At the first sight of Michael clearing the corner, she revved the Metro into life and gave herself a head start, a sizeable safety margin. Soon, her head was throbbing with anxiety for the safety of Father Barry's car, never mind the boy in it.

After what seemed hours they reached Supasave. Seeing that Michael was aiming to park alongside the kerb outside, she drove around for a couple of minutes looking for a parking space. All around the car park, women in people carriers and men in Land Rovers struggled to squeeze into spaces that would allow cars to fit neatly but would not allow passengers to open the doors and get out afterwards. Bernadette was wiser than that. Even though the Metro was narrow, it was her pride and joy and she wasn't taking any chances. She whizzed around until she found what she was looking for – two lovely empty spaces next to each other. Then, lips pursed and face intent, she commenced her pilot-parking manoeuvre. Very carefully she turned the car and aimed it up the middle line – Aer Lingus style. She stopped, nodded acknowledgement at St Christopher and got out. With a quick check to ensure that she had enough space to fit a trolley comfortably on both sides and open the doors wide as well, she set off to look for Michael.

In the supermarket the smell of baking and soft strains of Abba's *Fernando* were comforting after a busy day. She picked up a basket and wandered up and down the aisles to see what there was on offer. No point actually filling the basket yet, she'd only have to carry it and the handles always pulled at the carefully mended Swiss embroidery on the sleeve of her cardigan. Up and down she went but there was no sign of the boy. She was just losing patience when she rounded the corner of a combined shampoo and conditioner display to see Cormac Hegarty standing there, his basket laden with an assortment of small boxes, lemons, honey and cloves.

With a quick pat of her curls, she was beside him in an instant. 'Oh, Mr Hegarty! Imagine seeing you twice in the one day!'

He looked up, startled, but said nothing.

'Are you away to do some baking?' She indicated the contents of his basket.

He shook his head.

'I use a lot of cloves myself, you know. Always think they give an apple pie a lovely flavour. Is it an apple pie you're thinking of making?'

Still there was not a word from him. They stood there looking at one another, she puzzled, he distinctly uncomfortable. Then she looked more closely at the boxes. They were remedies – for sore throats, coughs dry, tickly and chesty, and a large bottle of TCP.

'Oh dear me,' she said, 'aren't you the lovely man. Is somebody ill?'

This time his mouth opened and it looked as if he might answer when one of the young shop assistants, Lucy O'Donnell, came up with a crumpled list in her hand. Bernadette recognised his handwriting.

'Here you go, Mr Hegarty,' she said in a bored voice. 'That should be the last of it. Honey and Glycerine Linctus.' She popped it into his basket with the rest of his shopping. 'If that lot doesn't cure you, you'll just have to take to the hot whiskeys!'

'Cure you?' Bernadette looked at him closely. 'Are you ill?'

Lucy blew a bubble of gum and let it burst in a blast of lurid pink on her lips. 'He's dying on his feet. Spent the day in bed and only managed to get here because he's out of medicine and there's no one at home to look after him.'

'Is that right?'

He didn't have the chance to answer as the girl propelled him towards the cash register waving the note she had been carrying behind her. 'No point in asking him,' she said, 'he can't speak, throat all raw, no voice.' She took the basket. 'Come on, we'll hot rod you through the checkout and off home to your bed. Bye, Miss Teegan!'

'Goodbye, dear, goodbye Mr Hegarty.' Bernadette raised her hand and waved. Cormac's face had grown so red suddenly that he certainly looked as if he should be in his bed. 'I do hope you feel better soon!'

From behind a stack of washing powder Michael watched the scene. His heart was thumping loudly. By his reckoning he was standing only a stride away from where Lucy O'Donnell had been standing – right where her dainty feet warmed the cold supermarket tiles. Now that she had disappeared with Mr Hegarty, Aunty Bernadette was looking around for him. He braced himself for the tirade and stepped into view. None came.

'There you are, dear,' she said, thrusting an economy pack of Fig Rolls at him, 'help me carry this lot and we'll be away home.' She was smiling as she packed cream, serviettes and small bottle of sherry into her bag.

Michael looked at the selection. 'Did you not want a lettuce, Aunty Bernadette?'

'Oh no, if it isn't fresh it doesn't interest me.' She giggled. 'I thought we'd get something a little more exotic in tonight. We might be having a visitor.'

'Might we? Who?'

'Oh, now,' she touched the side of her nose, 'you'll have to wait and see.' And picking up her bag she left the shop.

Michael followed despondently. After that rumpus on the last corner he hadn't bothered with the car park at all. Instead he'd kept going, light on the accelerator, close to the kerb until he came to the place where the road started to go uphill. After that it was easy. You just eased off the pedal and the car stopped of its own accord. If he hadn't spotted the luscious Lucy O'Donnell near the window and sped up to impress her he'd have stopped ages earlier. Now he faced a walk of at least a quarter of a mile to where the car was, under the lamppost. Uphill.

Bernadette was not despondent. Even the sight of Father Barry's car being reversed slowly down the hill to a flat place where Michael could start it up again failed to dampen her spirits. She had seen the look in Cormac Hegarty's eyes as he was pulled away from her – the longing, the pleading. Lost his voice indeed! Hadn't she heard him herself not two hours earlier and he in full voice admiring her fairy cakes? No, there was nothing wrong with Cormac Hegarty that needed a range of cough medicines to cure. She smiled at the bag of shopping on the passenger seat. It wasn't germs he was suffering from, it was loneliness. He didn't need TCP; he needed TLC. Plenty of TLC.

And she the very one to give it to him.

It was eight o'clock before the doorbell rang. Michael jumped up to answer it but Bernadette stilled him with a glare. 'Sit down, you. There's no need to go jumping about the place just because there's someone at the door. You just carry on with your supper. We don't want you getting indigestion.'

Michael sat, muttering crossly to himself.

'What did you say? I'll have no undertalk at my table, speak up.'

'I said I'm more likely to get rust than indigestion! For the love of God, Aunty Bernadette, we've been having our supper for the last two hours!'

'We have not.' She picked up a plate of fig rolls and held them out to him. 'Have another.'

'I don't want another, I haven't room for another. I haven't had room for any more since we –'

The doorbell rang again, strident and insistent.

Bernadette looked at her watch and a faint colour brushed her cheeks. Two hours. 'Well, if you've had enough to eat what are you doing sitting there like a gormless eejit? It's a freezing night to be left stuck on a doorstep. Answer it.'

Michael didn't bother to reply. He pushed back his chair, bellowed the loudest belch he could muster, and for which he was sure to pay later, and left the room. As soon as she was alone Bernadette did a spot check on her appearance. Her curls were still bouncy and the lipstick she had been careful to reapply at intervals during supper, pink and inviting. As she swept a few errant crumbs off the table, she realised that some of the buns still left might be recognised as having put in an appearance at the presbytery earlier. If the visitor had been in the presbytery earlier, that is. A supper of leftovers was not the impression she had set out to achieve when she laid the table so she quickly whipped them off the plate and flung them into the drawer. Wincing momentarily at the thought of the state her money-off coupons would be in spattered with cream from the fairy cakes, she shrugged. No time to worry about that now. Needs must.

'Aunty Bernadette!' Michael's voice crackled from the hallway. 'We have a visitor.'

She dabbed her lips with a napkin embroidered with violets, her favourite flowers, and called back. 'A visitor, dear? At this hour of the night? Goodness me, is somebody ill?' The notes of gentility and concern in her voice were perfectly balanced.

'No, it's –'

There was the sound of a man clearing his throat and before she had a chance to get up, Cormac Hegarty appeared in the doorway. 'It's, em,' he coughed. 'It's me, Miss Teegan.'

'Mr Hegarty! You poor soul! Out on a night like this and you dying on your feet! Come in, come in, will you have a cup of tea?' He was shuffling from foot to foot, his face scarlet. 'Or maybe something cooler, you certainly look flushed.'

He shook his head. 'I'm fine, Miss Teegan, really.'

'Well, I'm glad to hear it. And you have your voice back and all.' She smiled at him sweetly. 'Fig roll?'

'No, no, thank you. I don't want to disturb your supper.'

'Not at all.' She pushed a plate and knife towards him and indicated the still-laden table. 'We were just sitting down to eat, won't you join us?' And noting Michael's eyebrows disappear completely into his fringe, 'Michael, put the kettle on.' While the boy fumbled with the tap, she gestured Cormac into the chair and started piling his plate with slices of pork pie. Then she sat and smiled at him beatifically. 'Was there something you wanted to see me about, Mr Hegarty?'

Cormac shuffled in his seat and glanced briefly over his shoulder to where Michael was standing by the sink, barely stifling belches. He opened his mouth to speak but the intensity of her smile stifled his resolve and he shut it again. For a minute he sat there, looking at her hopelessly until Michael eventually emitted a howler and she glared up at him.

'Michael Teegan, have you no manners in front of our visitor! I'm mortally ashamed of you. Leave the room this minute!' As he left, she turned her gaze back to Cormac, about to apologise, but instead of looking offended he seemed to have relaxed. 'I am sorry about my nephew's manners, Mr Hegarty.'

'Think nothing of it, Miss Teegan.' He was smiling now. 'Actually, I'm grateful to him, I was hoping to speak to you alone.'

'You were?' It was her turn to blush.

'On a private matter.'

'Oh!' Her hands were shaking so she slid them

onto her knees and found they were shaking too. 'What sort of a private matter?'

'Well,' he took a bite of the pork pie and chewed it ponderously. 'I must say this is delicious.'

'Thank you.'

'Absolutely delicious. Did you make it yourself?' He took another bite.

'N – that one? Oh, yes, I made that one.'

'Umm . . .' he was chewing ever so slowly.

Fizzing with impatience by now, she was sorely tempted to smack what was left of the slice out of his hand before he could occupy his mouth with it again. 'You had a private matter you wanted to talk to me about.'

'I did.' He put the pie down and wiped the corners of his mouth delicately. Then he sat back in the chair and spread his fingers out on the table as if to read his lines from them. 'It's about that – incident in the supermarket.'

'The supermarket. You wanted to talk to me about the supermarket.' It was not a question

'Well, not quite, Miss Teegan. It's more the embarrassment of you seeing me there, like that, with the assistant and all.'

'Mr Hegarty, what are you talking about?' By now the edge in her voice had become a precipice and he was very close to falling over it. 'What possible concern could your liaisons with Lucy O'Donnell have to do with me?'

Somehow the conversation had taken its own path and he definitely wasn't on it. He wasn't even sure what Lucy O'Donnell was doing on it. 'My dear Miss Teegan, I was not having a liaison with Lucy O'Donnell.'

'You just said you were.' She was slipping off it herself.

'No I didn't!'

'Then what did you say?'

'I said I was with her!'

'There you are then. You were with her – liaising!'

'I was not liaising.'

'What were you doing then?'

'For heaven's sake! I was buying flu remedies!' She looked at him blankly. 'What's wrong with that?'

The vacancy of her gaze calmed him and he took her hands in his. 'That's what I came to talk to you about, Miss Teegan.'

She made a mental note to use Vaseline hand cream daily from now as she felt his hands round hers, smooth and warm. Her voice grew smooth and warm. 'Call me Bernadette.'

'Bernadette.' With a quick glance to ensure Michael wasn't coming back into the room he leaned closer and whispered, 'I don't have a cold.'

Cormac Hegarty was not ill, but standing there with him so close and her hands encased in his made Bernadette's temperature rise. She shut her eyes and leaned closer. It was difficult to breathe. The room felt sultry and there was a whirring, or perhaps a singing, in her ears. She couldn't think straight.

'Miss Tee – I mean, Bernadette?'

'Yes, Cormac?'

'I think your kettle's boiled.'

She opened her eyes to find the room full of steam. As usual Michael had overfilled the kettle and so it hadn't turned itself off. There was a puddle of water on the sideboard and a steady drip onto the clean cork flooring. Cormac let go of her hands and, taking a large handkerchief from his pocket, started to mop his brow. The spell was broken.

'Oh, for goodness sake, can that boy not do a thing right?' She pulled a cloth from the cupboard beneath the sink and started wiping. Behind her, Cormac had started on the pork slices again. She dabbed at the water crossly – if that eejit of a nephew of hers slipped on it and broke his neck it was no more than he deserved – and turned to the table. She cleared her throat delicately. 'You were saying?'

'It's all very embarrassing.' He looked embarrassed. 'I am not ill, Miss Teegan. In fact, I am in the pink of good health. You saw me yourself earlier this afternoon. Positively in the pink.'

Perish the thought. She shut her eyes and started to nod slowly.

'However, as you witnessed, I was later in the supermarket buying a range of cold remedies – for an illness I do not have.' He sat back in the chair and lowered his head in shame. 'I have come to beg your forgiveness.'

The thought, unperished, was put on hold. She looked at him quizzically. 'Why do you need my forgiveness? You haven't wronged me, have you?' It was almost more than she could hope for.

He threw out his arms in a gesture of dismay. 'But I was lying. Miss Teegan, and you witnessed it! Lying, being dishonest, and I an Estate Agent!'

'My dear Cormac,' if he had inadvertently re-instated formalities, she was not going to play along, 'I have every faith in you. I'm quite sure that whatever reason you had for – for misrepresenting the truth – it was a good one.'

He took her hand. 'You are such an under-standing woman.' Her eyes were closing again. 'And so I have come to ask you a favour.' She nodded. 'I would like you to be my – my – partner of sorts.'

Her eyes shot open and the steamy kitchen filled with the sound of wedding bells and the smell of violets. 'What sorts?'

From the back of his mind there came a flash of the conversation with Sean earlier. Something about family plots. He felt the blood drain from his face. He let her hand drop. 'In crime, Miss Teegan, my partner in crime.'

Half an hour later, with a final delicate wave into the night, Bernadette shut the front door and went into the sitting-room. Her whole body glowed with the knowledge that in entering a conspiracy with the county's most eligible estate agent, their relationship had moved to a higher level. They were no longer nodding acquaintances; they were co-conspirators. They were partners.

'Michael! Would you come here a minute, pet!'

Pet? In his bedroom above there was a quick flurry as Michael leapt off his bed, readjusted his trousers and stuffed his magazine under the mattress. Pet? What could he possibly have done right?

'I want to talk to you.' Her voice, high and girly, sliced the dark hallway with frightening accuracy.

With a quick check that all the necessary adjustments had been made, he edged his way into the sitting-room and onto the armchair. 'Did you call me, Aunty Bernadette?'

'I did.' That appeared to be that. She was sitting bolt upright on the sofa, smiling. Every so often she smoothed the velveteen cushion by her side but seemed unable to speak. For a minute he wondered if she was having some sort of fit. Her eyes were glassy and she was taking short, shallow breaths that made her chest rise, bringing Swiss-embroidered violets ever closer to her chin. Higher it rose and the smile grew wider but there was still not a word from her. Toying with the notion that she might be choking and the smile merely a reflex, he was about to leap up and give her a thump between the shoulder blades when she suddenly exhaled. 'Sit down, you, till I tell you the news.' He sat. 'Mr Hegarty, I mean Cormac – to me not to you, still Mr Hegarty to you, for the time being – Cormac and I have reached an understanding.'

An understanding? For a brief, disloyal moment Michael marvelled at the idea. He had lived with Aunty Bernadette all his life and knew her better than anyone yet never, ever, had understanding been an issue. Hers was not a mind to be understood. It was a whirling dervish of moveable goalposts and only Aunty Bernadette knew where they were at any time. And only she was allowed a shot of the ball. She was nodding at him now, confident that she had scored.

'Isn't that grand?'

He nodded too. 'It is.'

'We're going to be partners, of a sort.'

'Are you?' He remembered Cormac's nervousness when he arrived. Good God! Suddenly the beatific smile and rising violets assumed significance. 'What sort?'

'Oh,' she clasped her hands together and giggled, 'isn't that the very question I asked him myself! The very question. Oh my . . .' Her voice trailed off and the smiling started again.

Michael was not smiling. His face had the gaping expression of a stunned mullet and he was shaking his head from side to side. 'He wants to marry you?'

She tutted impatiently. 'Marry? Goodness me, Michael, aren't you the romantic? Whatever put a thought like that into your mind?' Lest he reach the mistaken conclusion that such a forward thought might ever have occurred to her, she picked carefully at some flecks on her skirt. 'We're just going to embark on a partnership.' The fleck picking intensified. 'And it's vitally important that you play your part.'

Michael caught his breath. At last! Eighteen years in the care of a woman who, though known as 'Aunty' was actually some sort of distant relative to a mother he'd never known, who had reared him and never wanted a penny in return, and now she was going to ask him to move out. What self-respecting suitor would want to take on an eighteen-year-old charge when he could have Bernadette Teegan all to himself? He stood up slowly, trying to keep his voice steady. 'When would you like me to pack?'

'Pack, Michael? Where are you going?'

'Don't know yet.'

'Then why are you packing?'

'Moving out.'

There was a look of panic on her face. 'Michael Teegan, don't you dare! You'll not set foot outside this door. I need you.'

'You do?' His shoulders fell. 'I thought you wanted me to move out?'

'Why would I want that?'

'Because you and Mr Hegarty are going to be partners.'

'In crime, Michael, in crime.' Before he could repeat everything she said she caught his hand and pulled him towards her. 'Michael, you are very dear to me.' His eyebrows took flight again but she ignored them. 'And so I am going to help you. In return, you will say not a word to a soul. Understood?' Completely perplexed, he nodded. 'Now here's what we're going to do . . .'

CHAPTER 3

When Father Sean came into the kitchen at eight o'clock on Saturday morning, he was disturbed to find that he was not alone in the house. The back door was open and there was an alarming amount of shuffling and rustling coming from somewhere. For a minute he thought of burglars but the kettle was on and the table set. Burglars don't usually have breakfast. Identifying the larder as the source of the noise, he picked up a can of fly spray for protection and padded as quietly as he could across the kitchen.

'Oh there you are, Father! Good morning to you!' Bernadette came out of the larder, her arms laden with cans. 'My my, don't you look very cosy in your pyjamas?' She dropped the cans onto the table, her eyes travelling down his stripes and back again with lightning efficiency. 'My, my indeed.'

'Miss Teegan, what are you doing here?' He pulled an imaginary dressing-gown around him and knotted the belt, tight.

'And don't you look well rested. The bit of colour in your cheeks suits you.' She was smiling now.

'Miss Teegan, it's barely eight o'clock on a Saturday morning. You don't work on a Saturday morning.'

'This isn't work, Father.' She turned into the larder again and though her voice was muffled he thought she said something about preparations.

'What did you say, Miss Teegan?'

She stuck her head around the corner. 'For the visit, Father. Did you not say your sister was coming to stay?'

He didn't. 'No, Miss Teegan.' He smiled at her innocently. 'I don't believe I said anything to you about a visit from my sister.' With a click the kettle turned itself off. 'What gave you the idea that I was having a visitor?' His eyes lingered on the steam, triumphant.

She came out of the larder and crossed the kitchen. Without a word she rinsed the teapot and dropped in two spoons of tea leaves. She added an extra few leaves for luck, gave it a quick stir and set the pot on the table. As she glanced around the room for the tea cosy, her eye caught his and he was surprised to see just the twitch of a smile. '*You* didn't say a word, Father.'

He raised an eyebrow.

Setting three cups on the table she bent into the fridge for milk. Again her voice was muffled but the tone was dreamy.

'I couldn't catch that.'

She straightened up. 'I said Cormac told me.'

'Told you what?'

41

'About the visit, the poor man.'

He opened his mouth to speak, though he knew already that nothing would come out but a repetition of what she had said. She was a step ahead.

'And he right as rain on Thursday! I couldn't believe it when I saw the state of the poor man. If he's out of that bed before the end of the month I'll be surprised.'

With a great sigh of resignation, Sean lifted the tea cosy off the pot and started to pour himself a cup of tea.

Pausing long enough to sit opposite him and indicate that she liked hers milk first, she took a breath and continued. 'And as he said to me himself, or should I say, whispered, given that he can barely get his poor voice past a whisper, isn't it an awful tragedy that this should happen to him at this time and he looking forward to a visit from his sister. He'd been hoping she'd stay with him but now . . .'

Sean's teeth closed on the rim of the cup.

'The flu is a terrible thing, a terrible affliction.' Her voice was warm with affection.

'So my brother has the flu?'

She put her cup down and stared at him in mock horror. 'Oh Father, did you not know?'

'No, Miss Teegan, I did not know.' He had started tapping the table. 'I was of the impression, the distinct and well founded impression, that my brother was in perfect health.'

'Isn't that the most extraordinary thing? That's exactly what I would have said. One minute right as rain, the next, struck down. Are you feeling well yourself, Father? I must say, you are looking a little flushed.'

Before he had a chance to reply there was a knock on the back door. The two of them looked up to see Michael standing there, his painting overalls crisp, his curly hair scraped back.

'Oh there you are, Michael. I wondered where you had got to this morning. Did you want me for something?' She hoped the inflection hit the right note, politely inquisitive, not at all rehearsed. For a minute Michael looked confused. He looked from one to the other.

'Well, did you want me for something?' She was nodding at him, prompting him to continue.

The light came on. 'Oh, hello, Aunty Bernadette. No, I am here to see Father Sean about the job.' He finished with a gulp, looking pleased.

'A job, Michael? Is Father Sean helping you to get a job?'

Sean finished the tea and stood up. He wasn't quite sure what was going on but he knew that whatever it was, it was out of his control. 'He's going to work for me, Miss Teegan.' He indicated Michael's carefully ironed overalls. 'He's going to paint my spare room.'

'Well isn't that lovely?' Then, as if the thought had just occurred to her. 'But – what are you going to do about your sister? I thought she was going to stay with you? She can't stay with poor Cormac, with him so ill and all.'

Sean shrugged and turned to leave. 'I really don't know, Miss Teegan. I really don't know at all. What do you suggest?'

She added a hot drop to her cup and raised her eyes heavenward in contemplation. 'Oh dear, what a dilemma, now let me think . . . em.' As she slowly stirred her tea, the two watched her patiently, waiting. Suddenly, 'I've got it! What a great idea.' She smiled at Sean benevolently. 'It just came to me, like that!' She pinged the spoon off the side of the cup. 'It's obvious really. Your sister, what did you say her name was?'

What was the point? He was doomed. With a sigh, 'Imelda.'

'Well, Imelda can't stay with poor Cormac,' her chest rose slightly, 'as he is so ill. And now it appears that she can't stay with you either, given that you'd made arrangements to have the work done and Michael all ready to do it. So . . .' The suspense was stifling. 'She'll just have to stay with me!'

'What?' He knew his jaw had dropped. She was totally expressionless and for the briefest moment his feeling towards her bordered on Christian. 'You'd be willing to have them stay with you?'

'Oh yes, Father. More than willing. Anything to help out.' She was leaning over the table pouring a cup for Michael when his actual words struck her. 'Excuse me, Father, did you say *them*?'

It was his turn to smile. 'I did.'

'But you meant *her*?'

The smile broadened. 'No, Miss Teegan. A shame I didn't get a chance to tell poor Cormac, he could have passed it on to you. She's not coming on her own.'

'She isn't?' Maybe Cormac was wrong. Maybe Imelda wasn't coming to Tullabeg to sort out his life at all. Maybe she was just taking a holiday with that weed of a husband of hers, and staying at the Teegan's. Oh Lord. 'So she's bringing her husband.'

'It's not her husband. She phoned to say she's bringing a friend with her. An old friend.'

As the light dawned on Bernadette, Sean tried to keep his eyes averted. Bad and all as she was, he couldn't help feeling sorry for her. Too late now to retract her offer. Bernadette's eyes shot wildly from Michael to Sean and back again. He turned to leave her to it. 'Aren't you very kind to offer and I'm delighted to go along with your suggestion. Thank you. Won't it be lovely company for you, I'm sure you'll have a lot in common. You, Imelda – and Monica Moran.'

'Damn and blast and damn blast and bloody blast!' Bernadette threw her duster onto the floor and stamped on it. What was the point? What was the blasted point? According to the clock on Michael's windowsill – which was the only thing that seemed to function in his room, even when he was in it, especially when he was in it – it was nearly a quarter to. The bus might be late of course but that was unlikely to happen on the one morning she could have done with a few extra minutes. She looked around the room and sighed heavily. Too late now. There was no way she'd be able to make decent shape of it this side of Sunday. With a final dramatic sweep she hauled the duvet cover off and flung it on the floor. Ignoring the range of screwed up socks, she grabbed at the bottom sheet and tried to wrench it off the bed, knocking her glasses off in the process. Oh, that impossible boy, she muttered as the sheet came flying, bringing with it a pile of magazines that seemed to have been wedged under the mattress. Why would he leave them there when he had a perfectly nice bedside cabinet that she'd painted for him herself? Groping around in the mess for her glasses, she caught a fleeting glimpse of the advertisement on the back of one of the magazines – Marlboro Lights The Sign of a Man. Huh! What was that boy up to? If he was smoking there'd be hell to pay and no mistake.

From downstairs the clock chimed the quarter hour. No more time to spend in here. She'd have to finish making up the bed later. She picked up the bedding and kicked the magazines under the bed. Nobody would be looking under there surely. If Monica Moran was anything now like the girl she used to be, there wouldn't be much chance

46

of her spending time on her knees over the holiday. No indeed, on the flat of her back is more that one's style, God forgive me, she said aloud to the empty bedroom.

At the bottom of the stairs she caught sight of her reflection in the hall mirror and stopped. She dropped the washing and stood for a minute examining herself. Her cheeks were flushed with the exertion of trying to get Michael's room into a fit state for a visitor and even if she had only herself to admit it to, she did look nice with a bit of colour in her cheeks. She smiled coyly, thinking what a pity it was Cormac wasn't here to see it. She broadened the smile and leaned forward to get a better look at the effect of it. In its smiling state her face really was most pleasant. The dimple that was so endearing was still there. She let the smile fade slowly. The dimple flattened out but left behind it a thin line to mark where it had been. In horror Bernadette leaned closer and tried again. Smile, dimple, straighten – wrinkle! And today of all days! With the sun glinting harshly from a watery sky and the Merry Widow arriving any minute on the Dublin bus! Blinking furiously at the unfairness of it all, she picked up her load and made for the scullery. Widow she might be and that was sad, and merry she might appear and that was fine but there was no way that Monica Moran was going to get her greedy fingers on Cormac Hegarty. And that could

47

be the only reason why she would turn up in Tullabeg after all these years.

By twelve o'clock Bernadette had regained her composure and was sitting in her car across from the bus stop, on the lookout for Father Sean. He said he'd start Michael off and then go and meet his sister; there was no need for Miss Teegan to come. He would explain to the visitors about the unfortunate timing of his redecoration and Cormac's illness and bring the ladies over to the Teegans' later in the afternoon. Ladies, huh. Bernadette might have the body of a whippet and the constitution of a horse, but she had the memory of an elephant. It was twenty years since she last set eyes on Monica Moran and she hadn't forgotten a thing. Sean's first year as a curate in the parish and no sooner was he unpacking his suitcase than that one had hightailed it down from Dublin to see him. She'd stayed the summer, even after Imelda went home, ingratiating herself in the presbytery with little offers of help. To give him his due, Father Sean was not at all impressed but poor Father Barry wouldn't see badness in anyone even if they had it printed on their foreheads. By the time she left, the poor man was exhausted with finding things for her to do and it took Bernadette no end of time getting him relaxed again. Her cheeks reddened at the memory. Twenty years of peace and quiet and now Monica was back again, newly widowed and no doubt with a notion of the grand home waiting for whoever was lucky enough to catch the eye of Tullabeg's esteemed estate agent. Well, she wasn't having him.

At twenty past, the bus rumbled over the bridge and Bernadette woke from her reveries. There was an impatient crowd around the bus stop and she could just see the top of Father Sean's head peering over the top of them. She slid down in her seat and picked up her shopping bag to have a little rummage. It was just the right height for putting on your lap, and keeping there in front of you, without being seen. She didn't want him thinking that she was there to be nosey or anything. She wasn't the interfering type. No indeed but it was early closing this afternoon and who knows what extra she might need what with two visitors coming to stay and all. And if she happened to be across the road when the bus came and caught sight of those visitors that couldn't be helped, could it? It was always well to be prepared.

The bus spluttered to a halt and the doors whooshed open. Peering over the top of the shopping bag, Bernadette watched them disembark. There were the Hynes girls back from boarding school for the weekend; Tom Flynn who had gone for an interview according to his mother but Miss Teegan had her doubts about that; a couple of strangers who might be related to the new people at the Lodge – she'd check that later; then nobody.

Across the road, Father Sean was craning his neck to see into the bus and the people waiting to get on picking up bags and children and pushchairs. The first of the queue made for the step but moved back at the last minute. Bernadette could feel the tension in her shoulders as she waited, eyes squinting for a better look. Slowly a figure edged down the steps of the bus. At first it appeared to be a short, unwieldy person, but as she watched the shape began to make more sense. At the bottom there was a pair of spindly legs with sensible Hush Puppies and at the top, Imelda's face, thin and harassed. In between there was an inordinate amount of luggage, bags and boxes. Father Sean moved forward to help her just as she tripped off the last step. They set the luggage on the ground and turned to greet the last passenger. Bernadette found she was holding her breath. This was it – her first look at that hussy Moran in twenty years. As if she had timed her appearance for maximum effect, Monica Moran appeared on the top step. Bernadette took one look at what time had done and nearly swallowed the collar of her cardigan in the process.

Monica Moran was not the woman she used to be. Or rather, she was not just the woman she used to be. She was at least one other woman as well and their combined weight sat heavily on her overburdened bones. Where her breasts had been generous twenty years ago, they were now magnanimous, munificent. And her hair! Without thinking, Bernadette touched the curls resting neatly on the back of her neck. What was the woman thinking of – at her age? Bernadette's hair was light brown, tawny with a hint of honey, especially on the first Thursday of the month; Monica Moran's was brass, pure unadulterated brass. It sat on the top of her head as if it had landed there and was only held down by the two chandelier earrings that dangled nearly to her shoulders. Her lips were lurid and protruded as if she's blown them up with the same gust that caused her eyelashes to stand an inch proud of her face. With her coat flung open you could see her breasts, hoisted together and straining for release from a lacy spangled top. As she leaned forward to negotiate the bottom step Bernadette couldn't help clucking in disapproval. The woman was a disgrace. If that cleavage was any closer to the ground you could stand a bicycle in it.

Tossing her shopping bag onto the seat, she jammed her key into the ignition and started the engine. She'd seen enough. In her kindness and Christian generosity she had offered to accommodate the priest's sister in her spare room and now Michael had to move out of his room to let that slut have the use of it. She thought of all the work she had put into it that morning, and her intention to go home and finish off now. Well, she wouldn't bother. If they were happy to put upon her like that, they could finish the room themselves. She wasn't risking her back making up beds and hoovering under them. She'd leave the clean bedding on the top and Miss Roly-Poly Slut Face could do it herself.

At the thought of Monica Moran having to exert herself, Bernadette smiled. Then she remembered. The dimple. She slowed the car and headed for the emergency-parking bay in front of the chemist. She'd treat herself to some of that miracle cream designed to plump up your ailing collagen and a nice new lipstick. She allowed herself another faint smile. Watch out Monica Moran. You might think you're on to a good thing here but until you've seen Bernadette Teegan in action, you ain't seen nothing. No Ma'am, the show ain't over till the fat lady sings. Or gets the bus – home.

'Well, isn't it just lovely in here? So bright and fresh, you can still smell the paint!' Monica wandered around the presbytery kitchen touching the surfaces as she went. 'It isn't a bit like I remember it, except for Father Barry's table, of course. I couldn't forget that.' She let her finger slide into a notch in the old pine table and rubbed it gently. 'I remember this one well. So smooth it's like caressing a belly button, isn't it Sean?'

'I wouldn't . . .' Across the table, Father Sean struggled to keep from choking on a scone. 'I really wouldn't . . .'

Monica leaned forward and wiped a stray crumb from his lips. 'Of course you wouldn't, pet, and you a holy priest.' She gave another circle of the notch. 'Ah, those were the days, all right. You, a fresh faced curate, and the lovely Father Barry – and me.'

Imelda put her cup down and looked from one to the other. Sean was flushed. She hoped he wasn't coming down with the bug that had Cormac incapacitated. She tutted in annoyance. Just their luck that he should fall ill this week. It would have been so perfect. She would have had plenty of time to talk to him. And if a fortnight of Monica in full flight didn't stir the loins, never mind the heart, of a lonely country bachelor, there was no hope. Now it looked as if they would be spending both weeks at the presbytery. That suited her personally, of course, but it'd be well nigh impossible to keep Monica in check. She'd always maintained there was something about the presbytery that made her – unsettled. She sighed and looked at her friend. Monica was smothering scones and then licking the jam off her fingers one by one. It wasn't today or yesterday that she had seen forty and she still wasn't housetrained though it was good to see her lively. Fred's death must have been a terrible shock. At the memory of the funeral, Imelda felt a tear come into her eyes.

'Are you all right, Imelda?'

'Fine, fine.' She cast a glance at Monica. 'I was just thinking about your dear departed Fred. God rest him.'

As Monica let her finger slide out of her mouth

with a plop Sean leaned forward sympathetically. 'It must have been a shock for you, him dying in his bed like that.'

Monica took another scone. 'He died happy.' Then wetting the tip of her index finger, she carefully pressed the crumbs on her plate and licked them off slowly, one by one. When the plate was wiped clean, she raised her eyes and looked at them steadily. 'Anyway,' she said and she folded her arms under her breasts, 'it's all very upsetting. Will we stop talking about it now?' She grabbed hold of the table and hauled herself up onto her feet. With a last nostalgic caress of the notch, she went to the mirror by the sink and leaning over it as far as she could, started to reapply her lipstick. No sooner had she slathered the top lip than the door opened and Michael came in. His overalls were spattered in paint and he was looking flustered.

'Oh, sorry, Father, I didn't realise your visitors had arrived.'

Monica turned around, her lipstick in mid-air, her mouth open. She looked as if she had seen a ghost.

Michael wiped a grimy hand across the backside of his overalls and proffered it. Imelda shook, gingerly. Then he turned to Monica. She was motionless. Though her top lip was rigid with lipstick the bottom one quivered. 'Michael? Michael Bar – ?'

She stopped and looked at Sean. He stood.

'Excuse me, I should introduce you. Actually. I should have mentioned earlier. Monica, this is Michael; Michael, Mrs Monica Moran.'

'Pleased to meet you.' Under her intense scrutiny, Michael reddened.

'Michael is doing some work for me. Em . . . Actually, it's rather unfortunate. He's painting.'

Imelda glanced at the trail of primrose that followed Michael from the hallway and raised an eyebrow. 'Painting what?'

'That's what I should have spoken to you about.' He sat down again, shooting a warning look at the boy. 'I'd arranged – some time ago – to have the spare room painted.' Imelda tutted. Her chest was bad enough without having to sleep with the smell of paint. She was about to say so when Sean held out his hand to stop her. 'I know, I know, the smell. You'd be smothered by it.' She nodded, gratified. 'And I couldn't bear you to come all this way and not be comfortable so I've made alternative arrangements.'

Imelda frowned. This wasn't working out how she'd planned at all. It was supposed to be a cosy holiday in the bosom of her family designed to get her still-unmarried brother to come around to the idea of incorporating some cosy bosoms into his – Monica's preferably. Now they'd most likely end up in some bed and breakfast and that didn't suit. It didn't suit her at all. She sniffed in annoyance. 'What sort of alternative arrangements?'

'Well,' he looked at Michael, 'Do you remember Miss Bernadette Teegan?'

Monica snorted, 'As if I could forget her! Prissy little thing like a whippet on heat and a mouth like a chicken's ar –'

Sean shot up and cut her off. 'That's her.' He glanced apologetically at Michael. 'Anyway, Miss Teegan, my housekeeper, has kindly offered,' he ignored Monica's barely stifled groan, 'to have you stay with her.' He held his breath.

'With her?' Monica said.

'With us?' Michael said.

'With you?' Monica looked at Michael. 'What do you mean with you?'

Michael shrugged. 'You're staying with us. Father Hegarty said so.'

Monica walked over and peered more closely into his face. There was the ghost of a smile playing about her lips and a twinkle coming into her eye. 'Do you stay with Bernadette Teegan too?'

Michael shifted uncomfortably. She was so close to him now that her breasts were brushing the front of his overalls, and her perfume so over-powering that it was becoming hard to breath. 'I have to,' he said. 'I'm Michael Teegan. Miss Teegan's my aunty.'

By now the smile had grown and Monica's lips had taken on a life of their own. She patted Michael gently on the arm. 'Your aunty?' she turned to Imelda. 'Well there's a turn up for the book, Mel. Imagine that.' She twisted her lipstick back into the tube and smacked her lips together. 'Just like the old times, all us girls together again. What a lot we'll have to talk about' She smiled at Michael. 'With Miss Teegan and her nephew Michael. Well, Well.'

Bernadette was waiting in the garden with her shiny new secateurs when the car stopped at the gate. She hesitated for a minute till she heard the door open before smearing a little soil on the front of her apron and rushing round to the front.

'Father Hegarty! Goodness, is it that time already! Oh dear, you'll have to excuse the state of me, I get caught up in the garden and completely lose track of time.' She slipped the secateurs into her pocket and bending into the car, brushed an imaginary strand of hair from her face. 'And who have we here? Is that your sister?'

Imelda opened the passenger door and got out. 'Really, Miss Teegan, it is so kind of you to have us.' She came round the side of the car and shook Bernadette's hand.

Bernadette blushed in delight. Kindness was one of her qualities that she was hoping would be noticed by the Hegarty family. 'Not at all,' she said, 'isn't it only a pleasure for me to be able to oblige.' She held Imelda's hand another minute. 'And you must call me Bernadette.'

The two women stood regarding each other in mutual approval when the back door of the car swung open. A strangled voice emerged. 'Give us

57

a good push there, Michael!' Strappy sandals, shiny stockings and a great deal of thigh later, the body of Monica Moran appeared, prostrate, from the back seat. She held out her hand for Sean to help her to her feet.

'Thank you, pet, aren't you the gentleman!' She grinned at the two women. 'Don't you think it's a lot quicker getting into the back seat of a car than trying to get out of it?'

Bernadette stiffened, 'I wouldn't know.'

Monica smiled at her. 'No.' She looked Miss Teegan up and down. 'maybe you wouldn't. But then . . .' She turned to watch Michael as he slid out the door behind her. He was red in the face.

'Hello, Aunty Bernadette.'

'Michael! You're home early. You're never finished a day's work already?'

'No, I . . .' He indicated a mound of bags piled onto the seat behind him, 'I was to give the visitors a hand with these.' He went round the other side of the car and opened the door. Bags and boxes spilled out. 'Will I carry them inside now?'

Bernadette looked at the mess. Some were bags she recognised from the bus but others had been added since then.

Monica waved a nonchalant hand over the lot. 'When we heard we were staying with you, we just had to rush out and get a few things on the way.' She quickly picked up one of the Supasave bags and held it tightly.

Bernadette looked puzzled. 'And you're – ?'

Father Hegarty put the bags he was taking out of the car down and stood between the two women. 'Excuse me, how remiss. Miss Teegan, this is Imelda's great friend, Mrs Monica Moran. You might remember her from my first year here when she and Imelda came to help me settle in?'

Bernadette leaned forward and squinted slightly into Monica's face. 'Monica Moran, well, goodness me.' She let her eyes slip a moment to where Monica's breasts and stomachs completely obliterated the legs below. 'I wouldn't have recognised you. You were a young girl in those days.' She edged her hand forward. 'How nice to meet again.'

Monica raised herself to full height and sliding her hands under her shoulder pads, she got hold of her bra straps and hoisted her breasts a couple of notches. Then, with a quick glance to ascertain that the only shape protruding from Miss Teegan's cardigan was that produced by the threads on the back of her Swiss embroidery, she smiled and touched the proffered hand briefly. 'Indeed,' she said agreeably, 'I was only a slip of a thing then. But thankfully,' she touched the gold pendant nestling in her cleavage, 'I've developed since.' She flicked an imaginary piece of fluff off Miss Teegan's shoulder. 'And look at you, you haven't changed a bit!'

The ensuing silence was broken only by the sound of Michael dropping the bags. He scrambled wildly to save them as they slipped from his hands and fell, scattering packets of biscuits and three Battenberg cakes onto the path. Bernadette struggled to keep from whipping the secateurs out of her pocket and ramming it up Monica's nose. The cheek of her! Stopping off to get a supply of food. As if Bernadette Teegan wasn't renowned for the generosity of her table and her indisputable skill at baking. She picked up the cakes and plonked them in Monica's outstretched arms. 'I suppose these are yours?'

'Not at all.' Monica smiled. 'They're all for you, dear, a thank you for having us.' When Bernadette did not take her hands out of her apron pocket, she handed the cakes back to Michael. 'Shall we leave the heavy work to the men then? With big muscles like that around we won't have to lift a finger. Isn't it great, Mel?' Then she linked her arm through Imelda's and headed for the house.

Bernadette glared after them. She could feel one of her headaches coming on and knew exactly who caused it. The strident sound of Monica's voice was still ringing in her ears and the overwhelming smell of cheap perfume assailed her nostrils as the other woman turned. She watched as they made their way to her front door, Monica tottering on her ridiculous heels and Imelda, dwarfed, beside her. An unexpected wave of sympathy for the small woman washed over her. Imagine taking a holiday to the bosom of your family only to be lumbered with the likes of that for the whole duration? A wave of anger followed. Imelda wasn't the only one lumbered. She cast a quick glance at Father Sean who was unloading the car and carefully avoiding her eye. As well he might. For a split second she was tempted to tell him to pack the bags and that cheap baggage straight back into his car and take the whole lot away out of her house, but as he lifted yet another Supasave bag out of the boot, a series of pictures flashed into her mind. She could see the desperation in Cormac's eyes as he looked at her in the supermarket. She could see his shyness as he stood at the threshold of her kitchen worrying that he might be disturbing her tea. And she could feel the warmth of his hands as they held hers and his soft voice asking her to be his partner . . .

'Aunty Bernadette, are you all right?'

She opened her eyes in surprise. Goodness! The mere thought of Cormac was sending her into reveries.

And bringing her to her senses. She shook her head to clear it and then smiled beatifically at Father Sean and Michael.

'All right? Indeed I'm more than all right. Haven't I the opportunity here to open my house to your family.' From the front doorstep, Monica's shrill laugh cut the afternoon air; Bernadette ignored it. 'And renew acquaintances with old friends at the same time.' Ignoring the look of amazement on the priest's face she took the bags from him and ushered the two of them ahead of her up to the house. 'Come along now and we'll all have a nice cup of tea.' She sniffed at the sight of the Battenberg cakes in Michael's arms. 'And some nice cake to go with it. Home made.'

CHAPTER 4

By the time Bernadette had wiped her gardening boots on the bristle hedgehog, swept the step and found her slippers under the stair cupboard there was quite a crowd in the hallway. Imelda hovered in the kitchen doorway, ready to put the kettle on if that would relieve the initial awkwardness. Monica hovered by the sitting-room door, ready to sit down if that would relieve her pinched feet. Michael hovered in the middle of the hallway ready to be told where to take all the bags if that would help relieve the congestion. And Father Sean hovered by the front door, hoping to relieve himself by flying out of it at the earliest possible opportunity.

'Ah, here we are,' Bernadette said, backing out of the cupboard as elegantly as she could in limited space, 'let's all get comfortable and have a nice cup of tea.'

She turned and surveyed the scene. Everyone shifted a little but in the absence of choreography, it was difficult to decide who should move first.

Monica broke the silence. She reached over and took one of the cakes from Michael's arms.

'Thought you'd never ask!' she smiled. 'My stomach thinks my throat's been cut.'

Don't tempt me, Bernadette thought to herself as she turned back into the cupboard to hang up her gardening apron. The weight of the secateurs in the pocket was somehow comforting. She felt unarmed without it. Closing the door, she motioned everyone into the sitting-room. 'We'll have our first cup in here,' she said, 'then I can show you around and let you make yourself at home. Michael, leave those bags there for the minute and help me in the kitchen.' She took the cake from Monica's outstretched hand as she passed, 'I have some lovely treats just out of the oven but thank you, I'm sure this will be handy to have in the cupboard, in case there's ever an emergency and we're really stuck. Father, are you not coming in?'

Father Sean was already out the front door. 'I won't, thank you. I have some pressing parish business to attend to so I'll leave you ladies to it.' When Michael made as if to follow him, he held up his hand, 'No, no, Michael, you stay here. I'm sure your aunt could do with the help. We'll carry on with the painting Monday, there's no hurry to get it fin –' he caught Imelda's eye, 'to finish it today. I don't want you rushing through and having to come back and finish next week. See you all later!' And he was gone before anyone could stop him.

Michael stood in the hallway staring after him. It was bad enough being left alone with Aunty Bernadette but now there were two others as well. The little one was glancing at him as if she was afraid the paint smell from him was going to leap off and attack her. Every time he came near she held her breath. The other one was worse. All the way home in the car she sat right up against him picking the primrose spots off the knee of his overalls and then patting him and saying, 'We'll have it all off soon, pet, don't you worry!' She'd insisted on putting the bags on the outside and him in the middle of the seat – something about it not being safe to have workmen too near windows – and then practically sitting on top of him.

He looked around. All three women were watching him expectantly.

'Em, I'd better go up and change first, Aunty Bernadette. I'm a bit splattered.' He was about to mount the first step when she called him.

'Where are you going?'

'Upstairs, to my room.'

'Not to your room, Michael, dear. Go change in the scullery. I've left your clean clothes there.' Seeing him about to protest, she raised a hand. 'You can't go into your room at the minute.'

'Why not?'

She ushered him out into the hallway and lowered her voice, 'Because we've got visitors, you silly boy!'

'I don't –'

'And we need your room.'

'What for?'

She looked at him in despair. 'How is it that a person in whose veins blood flows can have a brain in which nothing moves at all?' When he didn't answer, she explained. 'They need to sleep in there, of course.'

Sleep? As the blood drained from his forehead, Michael had the quickest flashback. Sleep – his bed – the mattress – oh no!

'Are you all right, dear?' She was looking anxiously into his face.

'I'm fine, Aunty Bernadette, fine really. I'm . . . I'm just thinking that it's not very tidy and maybe I should go up and give it a quick tidy round before anyone else goes in there.'

She smiled. 'That's quite okay.' She pulled the sitting-room door shut and raised her voice. 'I've done it already.'

The blood drain had reached his neck and his heart was thumping wildly. 'You have?'

'Yes, dear. And I don't need to tell you what a shock I got. The state of it! All those magazines under the mattress –'

'Oh my God!'

'Don't blaspheme, dear, please. Really, Michael, I was most disappointed to find them there.' The

66

pounding in his ears was deafening by this stage. He thought he was going to faint. He held the banister to steady himself. Bernadette came forward and patted his arm. 'How well you might look ashamed. Did you not know I'd find them?' She raised her eyes to Heaven. 'After all the time I spent painting that lovely bedside table for you, and all!'

He looked confused.

'Yes, Michael. The one you promised to keep your books and magazines in. The one you completely ignore and make a mess on the floor instead.'

Michael felt the ground solidify beneath him again. 'And you didn't read them?'

'As if I had the time! Now would you please go and change.' She turned on her heel and headed for the kitchen.

'Aunty Bernadette?'

'Oh for goodness sake, can't you see I am an extremely busy woman? I have tea to make and people to look after.'

'I just wondered – where are they now?' His voice was steady, if strained.

With a look of exasperation she gestured towards the sitting-room. 'They're where I left them.'

'You left them in the sitting-room? My magazines?'

With a pleading glance towards Heaven, she walked over and placed a hand on his arm. 'Michael dear, in my sitting-room there are two thirsty women waiting for a cup of tea. In your room, under your bed, there is a pile of magazines waiting to be picked up. The first need is immediate, I will see to it now. The second can wait, you can see to it later. Is there anything there that you don't understand?'

Michael shook his head.

'Good. So can you now go and change your clothes and make yourself presentable.' He turned to leave. 'And Michael, don't think I don't know all about the temptations young boys are confronted with.' She was opening and rearranging her kitchen apron as she spoke, patting it neatly over her skirt. 'And if I ever catch you smoking . . .'

Monica sat by the dressing-table, trying to persuade the plastic wrapper on a packet of Kimberlys to open without making too much noise. Not that she was hungry, but an hour listening to Bernadette Teegan explain the best way to finish embroidery off neatly at the back was enough to give a saint the need to sink teeth into something. And you're no saint, Monica Moran, she smiled to herself in the mirror. That young Michael was a dote, she wouldn't mind sinking her teeth into him. The way he'd sat there, every nerve in his young body quivering throughout the tea as Aunty B. ran through the sleeping arrangements.

'I've put you in the guest bedroom now, Imelda, you'll find it very comfortable.' She turned to

Monica. 'I'm afraid we have only the one guest room. You'll have to go in Michael's.'

'That's fine, Michael and I won't mind sharing, will we, pet?' She didn't know which of them looked more shocked.

Monica chuckled to herself as she popped another Kimberly into her mouth. As her tongue probed the sugary coating to the soft mallow beneath she felt the old familiar stirrings she always associated with holidays in Tullabeg. It might be a small backwater to some, but even after years away it still had the power to move her. And if those particular movements were the ones she had in mind, she'd need all the energy she could muster. She popped another Kimberly into her mouth and stared at herself in the mirror. A tanned fleshy woman with a confection of hair stared back. Monica turned her face to the left and to the right to see which was the better angle. Hard to decide really. With skin like that, a woman is ageless – though maybe if her hair were down, the agelessness might appear to have started earlier. She raised her arms to unleash her tresses and smiled with delight at the effect. There she was, bathed in a waterfall of blonde shot through with gold in the light. And good for at least twenty-four washes.

Suddenly a movement outside the door caught her eye. Somebody was watching her! As quietly as she could she let the clips clink onto the dressing table, all the while keeping her eye on the door jamb. The other person was standing there, trying not to be seen. Angling the mirror, Monica watched back. She'd give them a minute to get comfortable and then she'd strike. As the final few clips were removed she slowly slid her leg around and just as the last one fell, she leapt up and pulled open the door.

Caught off guard, Michael fell into the room.

'Michael Teegan! What were you doing?' It was very hard to sound cross when every nerve in her body was jingling at the sight of him there, flat on the floor. 'You weren't watching me?'

'No! I . . .' He scrambled upright, suffused in scarlet, 'I needed to get something out of my room and I didn't want to disturb you.'

Having been released from their moorings, Monica could feel the soft tresses fall onto her shoulders. She lifted her arms and ran her fingers through. 'Ah. That's better. So much more comfortable when you've come all undone, isn't that right?'

Michael didn't answer. She sat and patted the side of the bed for him to sit beside her. 'Sit up here and tell me all about it. What was it you needed?'

'I . . .' Michael leaned forward and cast a quick glance under the bed. 'I have some books I need to read. They're just here. I'll get them now and leave you in peace.'

70

In a flash, her hand shot out to restrain him. 'Ah, don't hurry away,' she said, aware that her voice, softened by endless cups of tea and the few quick Kimberlys, had taken on a husky note. 'I'm glad of the bit of company.' She increased the quiver. 'It's been very lonely since my husband passed away.'

'That's terrible.' Michael said, sounding very grown-up and concerned all of a sudden. 'Have you family?'

Monica slid her hand down his arm and let it rest there. With her other hand, she followed the path her curl had taken towards the cleft of her cleavage. Then she sighed. 'I have no one.' She leaned in a little closer. 'I'm all alone.'

Accustomed only to the lightweight Michael, the mattress strained under Monica's more generous proportions and Michael found himself sagging forward till his chin was almost resting on her bosom. She could feel his breath warm on her skin and smell the marzipan on it. She smiled broadly. 'Michael Teegan! I do believe you've been at the Battenberg.'

He shot up. 'How did you know?'

She stroked his cheek affectionately. 'I know things about you, young Michael, that I don't think you even know about yourself.' Under her fingers his cheeks burned and she shut her eyes at the feel of them. God, he was a little pet all right, the nearness of him, the smell of him, the very heat off him caused her instinctively to roll forward as the years rolled back and she was nearly a girl again. Like the young girl she had been the first time she came to Tullabeg.

Beside her Michael's breathing was changing and as Monica felt him blow little puffs of air onto her décolletage she felt the passion rising and her life flashed before her – her excitement when she arrived in Tullabeg, her anger at Sean's indifference, her loneliness waiting at the bus-stop for the bus back to Dublin and all the world looking as grey and dreary as she felt. And just as she had given up hope and resigned herself to a lonely bus ride up to Dublin, out of the darkness came the headlights of a car and the rumble of a Volvo as it slowed. From the mists of her memory, came a new voice, Father Barry's.

'Are you away so soon, Monica. I don't think I had a chance to meet you properly at all. Would you not hop in here where it's warm?'

And she did hop in. And it was warm. It was very warm. 'Ooh Father . . .'

'Farther? But I'm nearly off the bed already!' Michael's muffled voice sounded upset. Monica opened her eyes to discover that in her reverie she had leaned right over almost wedging Michael's head between her breasts. Those soft puffs of air were merely attempts to blow the curls out of his mouth. As the rest of his body teetered on the edge of the bed he looked up at her imploringly.

'Actually, Mrs Moran, I'm not very comfortable here, do you think we might move?'

Monica threw her head back and laughed, simultaneously clearing his airways and landing him on the floor for the second time this visit. For a moment he looked stunned, then appeared to come to life very quickly. He reached out under the bed and grabbed a stack of magazines that were heaped there. Without a second's delay he was on his feet, backing out the door. 'Em, I'll just be away now. I . . . I have a few jobs to do for Aunty Bernadette.'

Monica shrugged. 'That's all right, pet. You run along now. I'm sure we'll catch up with each other later.'

With what looked like a sigh of relief, Michael turned and fled out of the room. Monica waited till she heard him reach the bottom step before she too sighed. Never mind. She got up and shut the door. Then she heaved her case on to the bed and started to unpack. She unloaded reams of underwear, swathes of viscose and an array of brightly-coloured dresses. Tossing the lot onto the chair she repacked the case with her supply of supermarket bags and lifted it back onto the floor wondering where she might put it. The wardrobe was too high and there wasn't enough other floor space so under the bed looked like the best bet – if it would fit. It did, just. As carefully as she could, lest Bernadette hear her and offer to store it somewhere else, she nudged the case with her foot. In it went, smooth as cream until suddenly it stopped. Something was in the way. From downstairs she could hear Bernadette's voice saying something about going for a little walk. Damn! She'd be up in a minute. As quick as her generous proportions would allow she whipped the case out and got down on her knees. She peered in under the bed and there it was. One of those books Michael was tidying up was wedged up against a discarded sock. Grabbing her hairbrush from the dressing table she reached in and coaxed the obstruction out. The sock was crumpled and crispy and the image of her departed husband flashed into her mind. She tossed it across the room and turned her attention to the magazine.

If her hair had been short enough it would have stood on end. She sat back on the floor and hugged the magazine to her bosom. And there she was thinking there was no hope left. Thank you, God, oh thank you.

Thank you.

In the sitting-room, Bernadette and Imelda were having the loveliest conversation. So lovely that they decided to have another cup of tea, out of the good teapot. By the time the tea leaves were strained, Bernadette was beside herself with joy to discover that they had so much in common. Indeed Imelda had remarked more than once that they could be sisters.

'Oh, we could, we could!' Bernadette lifted her

best porcelain pot and offered Imelda a hot drop. 'Wouldn't that be fun!'

Imelda smiled. 'You know, Bernadette. I don't know how we didn't manage to get to know each other better in previous years. They must have been keeping you hidden.'

Bernadette looked up sharply. 'What do you mean?'

'Well, take our first visit for example. Sean's first year here – do you remember it?'

Bernadette reddened slightly. 'Em, I think I do, vaguely. It was '83 was it?'

''84, actually. Monica and I were at a loose end and Mammy thought it would be a good idea for us to come down and give Sean a hand to settle.'

Huh, that Monica would give more than a hand and it would be anything but a settling experience. Without realising her own strength, she let her cup clatter into the saucer. She didn't want to think about Monica Moran's first visit to Tullabeg – or any visits thereafter. She wished Monica wasn't here now, though thankfully she had taken herself upstairs for a rest so at least the air in the sitting-room would have time to clear. The smell of cheap perfume was over-whelming. Bernadette didn't like to use perfume herself – too unsubtle, too provocative. A light dusting of talcum powder in those unmention-able places was more than sufficient for decent women. She smiled again at her new friend.

Imelda was a decent woman, a talcum powder type of woman.

'Aunty Bernadette?' Michael stuck his head round the door.

'You mean, Excuse me, Aunty Bernadette?'

Michael nodded. 'Did you need me for anything at the minute?'

Bernadette looked quizzically at Imelda. 'What would we need you for?'

'Nothing, It's just that I thought maybe I'd go and do some driving practice . . . in the car.' He had the keys to Father Barry's car in his hands and was already pulling the door behind him.

'Michael wait!' But he was gone already. Bernadette shrugged and raised her eyes to heaven. 'Boys! They don't listen to a word you tell them.'

'But Michael seems like such a nice boy, my dear. So polite and well mannered. Has he lived with you long?'

'All his life – I mean, apart from when he was born, of course.'

'And he's your sister's son?'

'I don't have a sister.' Seeing Imelda's confusion, she smiled. 'He's the son of a cousin, a second cousin, once removed, em, on my mother's side. He was orphaned early and so I offered to take him in.'

'How sad. Aren't you marvellous?'

Bernadette lowered her head till it was at just the right angle for indicating humility. 'It was nothing. I mean what else could you do, the poor child in need and me with a steady job in the presbytery.'

'Father Barry didn't mind?'

Bernadette reddened. 'Why would he mind?' She put her cup down and leaned close to Imelda. 'I can tell you right now; Father Barry was the kindest man. There wasn't a thing he wouldn't do for that child.'

Imelda looked surprised. 'Is that so? Well, I'm delighted to hear it. I never found him particularly friendly myself though Monica couldn't stop talking about him when she was here before.'

'Could she not?' Bernadette wanted to take another sip of her tea but she doubted she'd be able to force the cup between her clenched teeth.

'No. As a matter of fact, she was going to cut her holiday short only Father Barry persuaded her to stay on and after that, I hardly saw her. She was off helping him out with his parish duties every minute of the day.'

By now Bernadette was fit to take a bite out of the cup and to hell with the matching set. She remembered well how that slut had latched herself onto poor Father Barry as if she was his personal assistant – and Bernadette herself a fully-paid housekeeper! She was yes Father, no Father, three bags full Father, all the day. It was no wonder that poor Father Barry was exhausted by the time she left. She must have driven him to distraction with her goings on but you wouldn't hear a word of complaint out of him. Oh no. He just said she was a young girl in need of guidance and he would take it upon himself to guide her. And he did. The lovely man. And did she appreciate it? Not a bit. He might have been blind but Bernadette Teegan was no fool. She could spot a hussy when she saw one and Monica Moran was a twenty-four-carat brass hussy. She was all over him one minute then off back to Dublin without so much as a by your leave. Father Barry, used to looking after people who were lonely then noticed Bernadette, faithful, consistent Bernadette under his very nose and gave her a lift home in his car. And when he told her the awful things that one had done to him . . . she couldn't bear to think of it.

'Bernadette, my dear, are you all right?' Imelda was looking at her, her face awash with concern. 'You look upset. Are you thinking about your poor dead cousin?'

Bernadette looked at her gratefully. 'I am.'

Imelda patted her hand. 'Don't you fret now. You've done a wonderful job with the boy. There aren't many women who'd take on a responsibility like that.' Outside the window they could hear the sound of frantic revving as Michael flooded the engine. The two women winced. 'Oh dear, is he having trouble driving?'

Bernadette nodded, unwilling to break the sympathetic intimacy of the moment too soon. 'He will have, once he works out how to get it started. I'll have to get him lessons.' She sighed as she turned to the window. Michael had obviously figured out that something was wrong and so he was now walking slowly around the car looking for clues. 'It's not that he's unwilling to learn; it's just that, his lift, you know . . .'

Imelda didn't.

'It stops short of the top floor. Teaching him anything is quite an uphill struggle. You wouldn't want to lack energy or have a nervous disposition.'

'And I suppose you'll have to take on that as well?'

Another nod.

Imelda turned and looked out to where the engine was now threatening to fill the afternoon sky with great billowing clouds. She watched him for a minute and shook her head. 'I don't know,' she said. 'You have your work cut out for you all right. But don't you worry, my friend. Monica and I are here now and we are so grateful to you for letting us stay in your lovely house. We aren't going to be a burden.'

Bernadette dabbed her eyes and lifted them delicately towards Imelda. 'Oh thank you,' she said, mentally replacing the 'we' with 'I'. 'I'm sure you and I are going to be the best of friends.'

'We are, we are,' Imelda said. 'In fact . . .' she looked out the window again then came over and laid her hand on Bernadette's. 'I have an idea that we are going to be a great help to you.'

Suddenly, Bernadette had the impression that

the room was full of violets. There she was, hand in hand in friendship with Imelda Hegarty and though her hands weren't as soft as Cormac's they were nice all the same. Capable hands, clean hands, affectionate hands.

Like a sister.

CHAPTER 5

At six o'clock that evening Michael was standing at the front door of Cormac Hegarty's three-bedroomed, detached, neo-Georgian house, with off-street parking. On either side of the door stone cherubs held baskets overflowing with pansies and trailing alyssum. He looked around for a bell but there was none, only a brass cherub knocker. For a minute he let his hand rest on there nervously. What if this wasn't a good idea? What if Mr Hegarty thought he had a cheek coming to him for advice? What if he complained to Aunty Bernadette? He let the knocker fall gently and was about to go home again when a voice called to him.

'Michael Teegan? Is that you?'

He turned and looked at the house in surprise. The door was still closed and there was no movement from the windows on either side but the voice had definitely come from there. 'It is,' he said to nobody in particular.

'Up here!'

Michael looked up to see Cormac's very dishevelled head sticking out from a top window.

'Hold on there a minute, I'll be right down.'

When the door opened Cormac was standing there, resplendent in a cream and purple striped silk dressing-gown with matching slippers, his hair, darker than Michael remembered it, combed back. 'Come in, come in, you'll catch your death out there.' He ushered Michael into the house and waved him towards the sitting-room. 'Please take a seat. I'm afraid I'm not dressed for visitors.'

Michael looked around the room. He had been in Cormac's office before and thought it exotic but it was nothing on this. Two large cream sofas faced each other on either side of the fire screen, each one lined with an array of cushions in various ice-cream shades. On the glass-topped table in between little baskets held an assortment of sweets, Turkish delight, sugared almonds and a selection of marzipan fruits. Michael looked at the marzipan longingly.

'Would you like to try one?' Cormac pushed the basket in front of him and then sat on the sofa opposite, pulling the sides of his dressing-gown together where the act of sitting had forced them apart over his thighs. 'Now Michael, to what do I owe the pleasure of this visit?'

Michael had just popped a marzipan pear into his mouth and he let it melt slowly as he wondered how he was to explain his predicament. Mr Hegarty was an important man, a capable man. How was he to admit to him that at eighteen years of age, and given the loan of a car, Michael

82

couldn't actually drive it? Oh, he could start it sometimes, given a bit of a downhill slope and not spending too long on those pedals, but he just couldn't master the art of stopping the thing in the right place. Three times now he had positioned himself at the top of Bradys Hill, only a hundred and fifty metres from Supasave, and timed his descent to perfection. With Lucy O'Donnell coming off shift, he planned to pull up just as she got out the door and offer her a lift. He had a great supply of sandwiches in the glove compartment, and one of those lovely yellow cakes, and he had no doubt but that given the comfort of big leather seats, a bite to eat and soft music on the radio, they'd be an item in no time at all.

That is, if he managed to stop the car outside the supermarket. Three times now he had tried and three times now he had failed. Having yet to master the art of braking, he had succeeded only in slowing down enough to see her come through the door but was unable to do anything about it as the car sailed past and on up the hill on the other side. By the time gravity called it to a halt, she'd already got a lift with someone else.

He swallowed the melted mass of almond paste and looked at Cormac. 'I need your advice, Mr Hegarty, man to man like.'

Cormac's face opened up in surprise. 'Man to man, Michael? Did your aunt send you?'

'Oh no, Aunty Bernadette doesn't know I'm coming to see you. Nobody knows. I was hoping to keep it private if you know what I mean.'

Cormac loosened the belt of his dressing-gown slightly and leaned back in the chair. 'Just between ourselves, is it?'

Michael smiled gratefully. 'Yes, please, if we can.'

'Goodness,' Cormac said, 'now this is a turn-up for the books. So tell me, Michael, what's the nature of your dilemma?'

Michael took another marzipan and nibbled at the edge of it while he considered the best way to explain. 'There's actually two things and they're related. If I don't do the one I don't want to do, then I won't get to do the other.'

Cormac looked totally bemused. 'I see. Maybe you'd better tell me what it is you do want to do first.'

'Well,' a faint colour came into Michael's cheeks, 'there's someone I really like but I don't get to see very often . . .'

'And?'

'And now I have the loan of Father Barry's old car, I could get to see them on a regular basis – only the problem is, I'm not very good at driving so I keep missing the opportunity.'

Cormac leaned forward and tightened his dressing-gown cord again. 'So you want me to give you driving lessons, is that it?'

What a strange notion. Michael looked at him in surprise. 'No, not at all. I wanted you to give me advice. I've already got the offer of driving lessons.'

'Well, that's okay then, isn't it?'

'No! That's actually the other problem. I don't want lessons from her!'

'From your aunt?'

Michael shook his head. 'I nearly wish it was.' He licked the sticky sugar off his fingers slowly and wondered how frank he could be. Cormac was watching him almost affectionately so he decided to go for it. 'It's that woman, your sister's friend. You know they're staying at our house?'

'I do.'

'Well,' Michael looked around as if there might be spies watching them, 'She's a bit odd.' He tried not to think of how she had practically suffocated him in her cleavage and choked him with her hair. 'She acts as if she thinks I'm interested in her.'

'What sort of interested?'

'You know, sort of *I'm all woman, come and get me, Tiger* interested. And she's got these great big . . .' he demonstrated Monica's reason for having a short lap, 'and she tried to trap me in them – on my bed!'

'Good gracious! What did you do?'

'I ran away. She'd have had me pinned if I'd stayed there a minute longer.'

Cormac rubbed his chin thoughtfully. 'How old are you, Michael?'

'Eighteen.'

'And have you ever . . . been with a girl?'

Michael looked shocked. 'I have not.'

'And would you not . . .' Cormac seemed to be choosing his words carefully, 'consider that the experience with the woman might have been useful?'

Michael stood up horrified. The very thought of it. As if he would – on Aunty Bernadette's clean sheets and all! If that one lay on him he'd be covered in bruises for months and then what would Lucy O'Donnell say? 'Mr Hegarty, I am not interested in getting experience from women, thank you very much.'

Cormac gasped then the smile appeared, a slow and satisfied sort of smile. 'Well, well, well, I'm very glad to hear that, very glad indeed.' He looked at Michael, his face now glowing. 'And what exactly would you like me to do for you?'

Michael sat down again. 'Your sister, Imelda, thought it would be a great help to Aunty Bernadette if I learned to drive. Aunty Bernadette had told her it would take someone with great patience and energy to teach me so she asked her friend, Mrs Moran. I wanted to say no but I really want to learn.' His cheeks reddened again. 'If I don't get to see this person more I'm afraid that they'll think I'm not interested.'

'Oh, I'm sure they wouldn't think that.'

Michael looked at him sadly. 'They might though. Supasave is not the ideal place for a date, is it?'

'Supasave?'

'That's the only place we ever seem to see each other, in the aisles.'

'Any aisle in particular?' Cormac's dressing-gown cord seemed to be getting tighter again.

Michael indicated the bag of medicines on the side table. 'The medicine aisle was the last one.'

Cormac looked from the bottles to Michael and back again and then he leaned forward. 'Michael. What exactly do you want me to tell you?'

'Well, do you think, that I'd have a hope with – you know – the special person.'

Cormac reached over and took Michael's hand in his. 'Oh, yes, Michael, I do.'

Michael was surprised by the intensity of his response. He looked really moved. Michael flushed with delight. At last! Someone who really understood what it was like to be young and in love. 'And should I let that woman teach me to drive?'

Cormac turned his hand over and staring at the palm, considered the question. 'Why not?' he said eventually. 'You're not interested in her and judging by the strength in these hands,' he traced a finger down Michael's life line, 'you're a big strong boy, you'll be able to look after yourself.' He took a deep sigh and let Michael's hand drop. 'You learn how to handle that car as soon as you possibly can and then . . .' he looked earnestly into Michael's face and there were tears in his eyes, 'then your life will begin.'

'I can't wait.' Michael was about to stand up when he noticed Cormac was holding the sides of his gown and he certainly was beginning to look fevered. 'Are you okay?'

Cormac smiled broadly, 'I am more than okay, young man. I am rapturous,' and he patted his chest the way Aunty Bernadette did when the Pope or Daniel O'Donnell came on the telly. Then he winked.

Michael stood up and winked back. 'Thanks, Mr Hegarty. Thanks a million for the advice.' He went to the front door and let himself out. Outside the sun was shining and the air was full of life. He felt that if he took a good leap he'd be able to get into the air and fly. Instead he gave a little run and tapped his heels together the way he saw them doing it on that old film last Christmas. Whee! He was young and he was in love and soon he'd be flying through the countryside with Lucy O'Donnell in the passenger seat.

He turned at the end of the path to wave but Mr Hegarty wasn't standing at the window. As Michael watched, the curtains in the bathroom swept shut again. Another shower? Michael smiled. He'd have to tell Aunty Bernadette about that.

She liked people to be clean.

Bernadette Teegan got a sheet of paper from beside the phone and made two columns, *Things going well in my life* and *Things going badly*. 'Right,

Bernadette,' she said aloud, 'time to take stock and weigh up your options.' Then she started.

In the first column she listed everything she could think of in her own favour: her neat appearance and commendable personal hygiene; her eligibility – house paid for, steady employment and clean reputation; her ability to bake and garden without the after effects of either one impinging on the other; her new friendship with Imelda Hegarty. She paused there a while and then added *Mr Cormac Hegarty finds me charming, he's already spoken of a partnership*. She reread the list and smiled. It was quite impressive really. From the sitting-room came the cackle of Monica's amusement and the occasional deeper tones of Michael's reply. He sounded intimidated. Bernadette's smile faded. Then she started on the other side.

Monica Moran is here.

Monica Moran is staying here.

My house smells of cheap perfume.

That eejit of a nephew of mine is going to have driving lessons with her – in Father Barry's car!

The cheek of it. She put the pen down and re-read her lists while concentrating on breathing, deeply, from the diaphragm, all the better to rid her body of the various toxins she had inhaled in the course of the day. In-out, in-out. Slowly, she could feel herself calming. That was better. The light after-smell of her own cooking was always therapeutic. She leaned back in her chair and let her shoulders drop, momentarily, without undue slouching, as her eyes scanned the two lists again. Relax, Bernadette, maybe Michael will prove to be so awful a driver that even Saint Monica the Slut will give up on him after the first lesson.

Another cackle from the sitting-room cast doubt on that theory and Bernadette sighed. No point in sitting here brooding; she might as well find something useful to do. She breathed again and noticed that the lovely smell of her skills was being invaded by another, more acrid one. It was warm, sharp and organic. Sniffing the air as intensely as was ladylike, Bernadette rose and sliding one foot forward at a time so as not to disturb the wafts too much, she glided around the room. Near the cooker she sniffed – nothing. By the fridge – nothing. All around the cupboards – nothing, yet there definitely was something, somewhere. She returned to the table and sat down. It was stronger here. By now her sniffing had reached professional standards and without even thinking, her head followed her nose down almost to her lap. There it was! At that level the smell became sharper and more focused. She sat upright again. Oh bother!

She inched open the table drawer and there they were, the plateful of left-over fairy cakes she had flung in when Cormac came around the other night. In the heat of the kitchen, the cream had solidified on top but all that had been underneath was oozing out, stale and pungent, onto her collection of money-off coupons. She pulled the drawer fully out and lifted the whole lot onto the table. Nothing for it but to sort it out now. Unrolling a long wad of fresh j-cloth she offered up her suffering for the good of the souls in Purgatory and settled herself to the task.

'Oh dammit!' Under the force of her rubbing one of her fifty cent coupons came apart and she threw the cloth onto the table in disgust just as the door opened. The smell of perfume entered followed closely by Monica; pink-faced from the port she had insisted would settle her tummy before bed.

'Well, well, are you talking to yourself? It's a sign of madness.'

'I'm not mad.' Bernadette cursed herself for the speed of her defence. The woman was better ignored. She picked up the cloth again and bent down into the drawer to wipe where the cream had smeared onto the sides.

'Well, you know what they say, if it isn't madness it's probably age.' Monica chuckled, in her intoxication obviously harbouring the preposterous illusion that she was clever or funny or, God forbid, both.

'My drawer is sticky.' Bernadette said in her best measured tones.

'Is that right?'

'Yes, and I'm giving it a rub.'

Monica threw her head back, exposing the flesh of her chins and gave a great bellowing laugh. 'Sticky drawers, is it? Oh dear,' she wiped her watering eyes with the back of her hands. 'Well, you learn something new every day.'

Even the deepest diaphragmatic breathing could not control Bernadette's rage. The hussy! She opened her mouth but before she had a chance to say anything, Monica leaned over the table and took a bun. She held it up close to her face and sniffed at it gingerly.

'And what's this – are we guilty of hoarding little snackettes for ourselves in the night?' Her voice lowered to conspiracy. 'Not that it'd be a bad thing, you could do with a few extra pounds.' Very slowly, she slid her pink tongue along the side of the bun till it reached the cream and then she left it there a moment apparently considering the wisdom of swallowing the stuff. Eventually she decided against it and wiped the cream off onto her fingers. She sniffed the bun again. 'I wouldn't eat these though, they smell stale to me.' Then she dropped it back on the table. 'Anyway, I'm off to bed. I'll need to get a good night's sleep before our driving lesson in morning. Are you off to bed yourself?'

Unable to articulate a single word in her rage, Bernadette attempted a nod.

'You should too, you look all done in, to tell you the truth.' Monica went over to the sink and poured a glass of water. 'I'll just take this up with me in case I wake up thirsty.' She paused as she passed the table and reaching out her cream-smeared hand, patted Bernadette on the head. 'G'night now, Bernie. Sleep well.'

As the door shut behind her, Bernadette fought to breathe as she focused her eyes on the bun in front of her and tried to slow her heartbeat. It was no good. The bun which had once been an attractive cream-covered confection was now a doughy lump daubed in yellowing goo. It looked like Monica. Bernadette's fury rose like lava from the pit of her stomach. She felt like the Incredible Hulk's sister, about to burst out of her cardigan in rage. With strength that surprised even herself, she grabbed the j-cloth and ripped it apart in one go. Then, wrapping it around her fist she beat the bun to pulp on the table, all the while muttering, it's her head, she's dead. When the pulp was finally reduced to something that resembled the original uncooked mixture she stopped, exhausted, and leaned into the drawer again. Sliding her hand in, she pulled out a small envelope that was taped to the underside of the table. She sat down, fighting the emotion that was now threatening to turn into a sob and opened the envelope. The photo she pulled out was an old one and had all the lurid tones of an early colour camera. She smiled at it. Oh, you were posh in your day, Bernadette Teegan, all right, she said to the young woman in the photo who smiled back at her, slight but for the bulge in her embroidered cardigan. The man beside her smiled too, if a little nervously, and Bernadette let her eyes rest on him for only the shortest minute. Even that was enough to strengthen her resolve. The slut might be invading the sanctity of her house but there was no way she was going to slide her voluminous backside into his car. No way in the world. She smiled at the photo again as a plan formed in her mind.

'Don't you worry about a thing, Father,' she said. 'I'll not let that one besmirch your memory with her wanton ways. I'll look after you, the way I always did.' And slipping the photo into the pocket of her cardigan she got up and threw her apron onto the table with the rest of the mess. It could wait till the morning.

There were other things to sort out straight away.

Monica was tired. It had been a long and eventful day and though her body was ready to relax into a full night's slumber, her brain was whizzing. She had taken so many trips down memory lane since lunchtime that she felt qualified to give guided tours without an autocue. All the things she had forgotten were shifting themselves in the recesses of her memory and popping out to great effect in all sorts of unexpected places. And very nice they were too.

Turning to face the dressing-table, she started to strip. It was one of those old dressing-tables that have a large mirror in the centre and two smaller ones on either side. Monica liked those. For quite a few years now, she noticed that her reflection filled all the space in a single mirror and you couldn't see what was going on behind. That was a shame. Fred used to watch her undress, smiling broadly when he still had his teeth but later becoming crotchety and complaining that she was blocking out the light and couldn't she undress in the bathroom. This set-up was better. With the side mirrors angled, she had a big bird's eye view of everything.

She took a quick glance behind as she unbuttoned the front of her dress and let it fall to her hips. The cold air in the room hit her as soon as her shoulders were bare and she shuffled over to the radiator to check. The little dial was set to three, barely above starting temperature. Monica smiled. The whippet must have adjusted it after tea. Well, that was fine. It could be freezing outside and Monica still wouldn't be long heating up. She turned back to the mirror. Anyone would heat up at the sight of that. Above where the dress hung deflated on her hips, soft rolls of smooth flesh stacked their way between her bosom and where her waist used to be. She reached behind and undid the four rows of hook and eye fasteners that did the noble job of keeping her breasts at a reasonable height for resting on tables when she sat down to eat. Released, they slumped forward, nipples huge and purple, and her unhinged cleavage swung open. Monica breathed in the sweet warm perfume that rose from them, as they hung and rested, skin on skin, on the folds of flesh beneath. God, she was gorgeous.

As she bent forward to coax her dress over her hips, her breasts blocked the view of her knickers and Monica turned her head sideways, catching sight of the case under the bed. She'd forgotten the magazine. Imagine the likes of that fellow being in possession of such useful information? He seemed like such a timid thing. When Imelda announced at teatime that she had a solution to Michael's driving needs, she thought he was going to choke. He'd looked from one woman to the next and then hastily excused himself saying that he had business to do. When he came back an hour later, he was cock o' the hoop, full of beans, ready for action. Monica straightened up and slipped her silky nightdress over her head. She wouldn't mind a bit of action herself. Tired as she was, a night's sleep didn't have the same appeal.

Half an hour later, Monica was still awake. Down in the sitting-room, Michael had obviously turned in and she could hear the occasional snore. Imelda had gone to bed hours ago, determined to be up early for Mass in the morning, and she hadn't heard Bernadette come up. Probably still immersed in her drawers. She stifled a chuckle. The way the whippet had glared at her – fit to kill. Monica had seen that glare before. She shifted a little in the bed and shut her eyes. All in the past, all over now, all . . .

A noise from outside shook her out of her reveries and Monica sat up. Someone had started Father Barry's car! She rolled out of the bed and went to the window, expecting to see lights. There weren't any. Pressing her face up against the glass she squinted out, trying to make out the shapes in the darkness. At first there was nothing, then she saw it. A huge shape gently growled past the house towards the garage. Monica pressed her nose flatter against the glass until she was sure what she was seeing. That's right, it was the Volvo, being backed slowly into the darkness of the garage with the lights off. Who would be doing such a thing at that hour of the night? Monica smiled to herself. Maybe young Michael was going to get in a bit of practice to surprise her in the morning. But it couldn't be that, she had already heard him snoring soundly as she came out of the bathroom. She pressed against the window again, now smeared with condensation from her breath.

As the garage was at right angles to the house, she could just make out the shape of someone getting out of the driver's seat. It wasn't Michael. The hairs on the back of her neck were beginning to prickle. She wiped at the condensation, regretting for the first time that she had not succumbed to cotton nightwear. Silk, even synthetic, didn't absorb moisture and now she was having to bounce on her soles to see between the smeared lines she had created.

'Well, I never!' she said aloud. It was Bernadette. She was getting out of the car, in the dark, obviously trying not to be seen. As she watched, Bernadette closed the garage door behind her and then a thin strip of yellow along the ground showed that she had turned on the light inside. Monica chuckled and slid back into bed. The woman was a nutter. She was probably out there in the dead of night with her polish and her cloth about to assault the dashboard! Heaven forbid that a driving lesson would take place in a car with a speck of dust in it. Not that there was ever much dust in that car. She shut her eyes again, feeling as she did so the damp of condensation from the window along the sleeve of her nightdress. She smiled. There mightn't have been any dust but there sure was condensation. She rubbed her arm vigorously to warm it up. And there was heat too.

The sound of Michael's snores filled the stairway and slid under the door into the darkness in her room. Monica stopped rubbing her arm and moved her hands to her belly instead. In slow sensuous movements she circled the warm flesh that rippled before her palms. Between the snores she could just make out the sound of a voice from long ago whispering into her ear. *That's it, good girl, nice and slowly does it. Lovely, lovely, good girl.* She thought fleetingly of Bernadette below, vigorously rubbing a shine into the steel and plastic dashboard with her j-cloth and she laughed aloud as the memories flooded into her.

Good girl? Good girl? She panted into the darkness. I wasn't just a good girl, Father, I was the best!

★　　★　　★

In the garage outside Bernadette was not polishing the dashboard. Had there been a carpet of dust on the sills she would not have noticed. Instead, she was sitting quietly in the driver's seat reading her notebook by torchlight. It was very informative and she was grateful, not for the first time, for her wisdom in having undergone a six-month course in 'Practical Mechanics for the Modern Woman' in the local polytechnic. There were only two others on the course, young hussies who were under the bonnet of a car only with a view to working their way into the back seat of one, and they really didn't pay attention at all. Bernadette had listened to every word, removing her blue marigolds to make copious notes whenever the teacher made a point that she felt would come in useful. And now, as she reread those notes, she understood just how useful they might prove to be.

Skimming quickly over the chapters on *Where Things Are, What These Are For* and *How To Get Things Going* she eventually came to what she was looking for – *Scuppering the Works in Emergency*. And this was certainly an emergency. She could feel the rage begin to build again but she fought it. No way was Monica Moran going to drive around Tullabeg in Father Barry's car with anyone – and especially not Michael. No siree. She hadn't got all that education just to sit there and let other people take advantage. If anyone had a right to be driving around in this car it was Bernadette

Teegan. She put the notebook down briefly and ran her hand along the dashboard. Ignoring the dust on her fingers she caressed the steering wheel, its finger ridges flattened smooth by years of use. If she shut her eyes she could just see his hands, solid fingers with their short wiry hairs wrapped around the wheel in the textbook ten to two position as he drove through the dark lanes to her house.

Faster and faster she caressed the wheel as the memories flooded through her: the cold smoothness of the seats as she slid in and the way they used to warm up when he turned the engine on; the way they used to heat up even more when he turned it off half an hour later in some quiet place in the country; the way he would turn and look at her and hold her hand and thank her for being his only one true friend in the whole lonely world, his confidante, his soul mate. And then he would spill out his heart and her own would fill with compassion for this man, striving for spiritual perfection while tormented by his manly passions. Only she truly realised the extent of his struggle and when he finally confessed to her, after a lovely drive and a few sips of whiskey from his flask to warm her up, about the times he had lost the struggle, she understood completely. He had asked if she could ever forgive him and when, flushed with the warm spirit she said there was nothing to forgive, he had reached over and begged her to hold him like a mother.

Bernadette had never known her mother, having been raised by the nuns in the local convent so she wasn't quite sure what such a hold might entail. She took another quick slug of the whiskey for courage and leaned in close against him. For a moment it felt strange but in the folds of his arms and with his breath running like heated fingers through her hair, she quickly got the hang of it. It was actually very nice. Very nice indeed. She snuggled up to him and rolled her head from side to side as the feel of her hair seemed to be giving him great comfort altogether. After a minute or two he shifted a bit and when she asked him if he was all right he nodded but he didn't look all right. His face was flushed and a thin sheen of sweat was growing on his forehead. Bernadette felt a wave of panic. What if the poor man was having a heart attack what with all the stress he was under? It certainly sounded like a heart attack with his breath coming and going in great loud gulps.

'Are you struggling. Father?'

'I am, Bernadette,' he said, moving his hand to the nape of her neck.

'Is there anything I can do to help, Father?'

He paused for just the tiniest second, and then taking hold of her hand, guided it into the pocket of his trousers. 'In there,' he said, his breathing sounding even worse.

Though she'd not have admitted it to a soul, Bernadette actually felt a little bit embarrassed.

She hadn't ever had her hand in a man's trouser pocket before, except to remove the handkerchief before sending them to the dry cleaners. And certainly never when the man was still in residence. Still, this wasn't an ordinary situation. Poor Father Barry had just opened his soul to her and here he was now, struggling, and she the only one who could help him. But what was it he was actually expecting her to do? Suddenly, it dawned on her. Of course!

'Is it your heart tablets, Father?'

He mumbled something.

'Are they in your pocket?'

Another tiny pause. 'Oh they are, Bernadette – would you feel around for them?'

'I will.' And she shoved her hand further into his pocket. It was very deep and there were lots of things in it: scrunched up notes, a handkerchief, a few toffees, but no tablets.

'I can't find them, Father!'

'Try – again!' He shifted in the seat so that he was now turned towards her and the rubbing of her head and neck intensified. The poor man, he must be in a right state of panic. Maybe he had the wrong pocket. Bernadette considered how she was going to reach the other one. Father Barry was quite a substantial man and his belly overhung his belt by a considerably impressive amount. At the moment it was heaving with the exertion, up and down, up and down. There was nothing for it. If she didn't act quickly, he would probably die on her, right here and now. In one gulp she emptied the flask and then squirming up from her seat she flung herself astride him and plunged both hands deep into his pockets, scrabbling for all she was worth. It was difficult. Her head was wedged against his chest and she couldn't quite reach the bottom of the pockets what with his belly and all.

'Sorry, Father,' she panted, 'I'm not doing very well.'

He shut his eyes and smiled. 'You're doing fine, just fine.'

'It's just you have so much rubbish in your pockets and I can't reach the bottom.'

Without a word, he arched back and loosened his belt. The breathing was definitely worse now and Bernadette was in a right fluster. She was well into his pockets but there wasn't a tablet to be found. Instinctively sensing her panic, because he was a sensitive man, Father Barry helped. He moved her hands and probably realising that the gear-stick was poking into her, shifted her weight forward. There was another minute's scrabbling. Fingers and gear-sticks everywhere till you wouldn't know what was going where and suddenly he stiffened. His face went very red, his breathing stopped. Bernadette sat bolt upright and stared at him in horror.

'Oh, Father,' she said, 'You're not dead, are you?'

Very slowly, like a miracle unfolding, his eyes opened and a smile crept across his lips. 'Oh, Bernadette,' he whispered, 'I'm not dead at all.

Thank you.' He was looking at her as if she was to thank for his recovery.

Suddenly, she felt shy. 'But I didn't find your tablets.'

He raised his eyebrows. 'Were you really looking for them?'

'Of course I was! You don't think I'd leave you struggling like that and not try to help?'

'Goodness!' He lifted his hand and pushed one of the stray curls off her face. 'Bernadette, my sweet, I never doubted you for a minute.' Then he folded his arms around her and kissed her forehead gently. Bernadette almost had her own heart attack. She couldn't believe it. Here she was, in the dark, in Father Barry's car, sitting on his lap and he kissing her forehead and telling her she was sweet. She wished she hadn't finished the whiskey. Her throat was dry and she was finding it hard to breath.

'Oh Father . . .'

The sound of her own voice brought Bernadette back to the present with a jolt. She looked around in confusion as the cold of the garage crept in on her and she shivered. She wasn't sitting on Father Barry's lap feeling loved and treasured; she was sitting on her own, in the dark, with her mechanical notes on her knees, rubbing the steering wheel as if she could rub it hard enough and bring him back. She felt abandoned. All alone in the world except for Michael. At the thought of Michael she allowed herself a little smile. He wasn't a bad boy really, just a bit slow. Father Barry would be proud of him.

Then she remembered – Michael, the eejit, the one who'd agreed to driving lessons with a woman you wouldn't trust alone in a confined space even if you were armed with a pitchfork. Right, time to remedy that one.

She picked up her notebook and skimmed the page again. Drain the petrol? Remove the battery? Too obvious. Cut the wires? Pour sugar into the tank? Too harmful. It was Father's car after all and she had no intention of damaging it. No, it was safe here in the garage and here it would stay. She read to the end of the page and there it was: perfect! Pulling the lever she released the bonnet and got out. She lifted the rod, leaned in and with her blue marigolds she prised the cap off the distributor. Inside, the rotor arm lay peaceful, undisturbed.

You might look insignificant, she whispered, *but like myself, it'd be impossible to get along without you.* She pulled off the little arm and wrapping it in a bit of tissue, popped it in to her pocket with the photograph she had taken from the kitchen earlier. That's it. Now there was no way they'd be able to start the car. The driving lessons were well and truly disabled. She patted the spark plugs sympathetically. *Sorry boys, there'll be no sparks coming your way for the next few days.*

She thought of Monica above snoring in the bed.

'Nor yours either,' she said aloud, 'nor yours either.' Monica woke exhausted the following morning. Maybe it was the late night snacking or the copious amounts of port needed to wash it down, but she hadn't been able to settle at all. Memories of the past chased hopes for the future around in her head all night till she couldn't tell whether she was coming or going, or who it was that was going, or coming, with her. Also, even though there were plenty of covers on the bed, her fingers and toes were stinging as if she had frostbite. By the time Bernadette's voice 'coo-eed' up the stairs with a bright 'good morning' for everyone, her head was pounding.

'All right, all right, keep your hair on!' Monica struggled to the door, toes curling as her soles touched the cold floorboards. She hadn't noticed that Michael's carpet fell short of the skirting boards. Hell! It was freezing and her toes still hurt. Dancing on the balls of her feet she opened the door. 'Oh!'

Outside on the landing Bernadette and Michael were forming an orderly queue. Michael had obviously just been dragged off the sofa but Bernadette looked as if she'd just received an intravenous dose of the joys of spring. Unlike Michael who was still in crumpled pyjamas, Bernadette was fully dressed in a leaf-green twin set with pearl beading round the neckline and a neat A-line skirt that came to just above her knees. In honour of the Sabbath her jewellery was tastefully chosen, a pair of marcasite earrings in the shape of a crucifix peeped from beneath her curls, still tight and freshly released from the sponge curlers Monica saw in the bathroom yesterday.

'Well, look who it is, sleeping beauty! I hope you had a good night?' Bernadette's smile was generous in its proportion if more than a little frightening to witness at that time in the morning.

Monica felt uneasy. Not only was her negligee doing a bad job of keeping her warm out of the covers but her bladder was feeling the strain of being upright. If this really was a queue, she hoped they were backing out of the bathroom and not waiting to go forwards into it. She clamped her knees together as tightly as she could and forced an early morning sunlight watery smile.

'I had a wonderful night, thank you, Bernie,' she said, 'I always do.'

Bernadette pulled the edges of her cardigan together stiffly. 'I'm sure.'

Her moment of discomfort abated for the minute, Monica sidled closer to Michael. 'And what about the man of the house?'

Michael looked confused then realised who it was she was referring to, 'Oh, yes thanks, I slept fine.'

'I know you did, pet. Wasn't I above here in the bed listening to the snores!' She brushed a stray scrap of hair from his forehead. 'They were so loud that – d'you know what?'

Nobody breathed.

'I could have sworn you were there in the room with me!' When his face reddened she cupped her breasts and, hoisting them skywards, continued. 'Right there, in the bed, snoring away.' She sighed deeply as if reliving the memory. 'Oh, it made me feel *so* cosy. That's probably why I ended up having such a lovely sleep.' She turned to Bernadette. 'Did you get to bed early yourself?'

'Yes, thank you. I don't go in for late nights.'

Monica looked her up and down slowly. That was interesting. She'd taken ages to get to sleep and she was sure that even when she had eventually dropped off, Bernadette was still outside in the garage. And here she was claiming an early night. Well, well. So the vestal virgin wasn't immune to a little fib or two. For a moment she was tempted to pursue the matter to a glorious conclusion but it was cold on the landing and the call of nature was growing louder by the second. 'Oh, lord,' she moaned, grabbing Michael's pyjama sleeve, 'I don't know about you, pet, but I'm desperate!'

'Mrs Moran! If you don't mind!' Bernadette looked disgusted. 'This is a decent Catholic house –'

'Oh for God's sake,' Monica's patience was running out. She tapped impatiently on the bathroom door, 'this is a decent Catholic urge. Imelda, are you in there? Come out quick, I'm in need!'

With much undoing of locks and sliding of bolts the bathroom door opened and Imelda's freshly-washed face appeared. If she was confused by the sight of Monica clutching a terrified Michael by the arm while Bernadette looked on in disgust, she gave no indication. She brushed the three of them lightly with one of her shy smiles.

'Have I kept you waiting? Oh, I am sorry.'

Bernadette was just about to assure her that she, for one, wouldn't have minded waiting all day when Monica dropped Michael's arm and pushed through the doorway, ushering him aside as she went. 'You'll be sorrier if I don't get in there in this minute!' and she shut the door soundly behind her.

There was silence on the landing. Bernadette fumed at the insolence, the ignorance of that woman and the foolishness of Michael who stood there, gormlessly, letting himself be pushed around. She felt like giving him a good slap and telling him to get a grip before banging on the bathroom door and demanding that that horrible woman open up immediately. She took a step forward and was lifting her hand to rap on the door when it occurred to her that the only thing she was achieving was closer proximity to the bathroom and thus a greater earful of the sounds therein. Monica was obviously feeling better and had started to sing. As Bernadette stood poised, the sound was reaching its crescendo and what was lost to vision behind the door was not lost to the imagination.

'She always sings. That way you know she feels

better, poor dear. She suffers with her innards, you know.' Imelda offered, by way of explanation.

'We all suffer with her bloody innards!' Bernadette muttered as she dropped her hand and stuffed it tightly into the crook of her elbow. Then, realising that Imelda looked shocked, she added, 'I mean, I can't bear to see someone suffer. The poor dear, it breaks my heart, it really does.'

That worked. Imelda's expression softened and she smiled at Bernadette. 'She'll be okay, you know. You mustn't worry.'

'I won't.' But Bernadette's assurances fell on deaf ears. Imelda was now looking at her with an expression you could use to glaze buns. Bernadette returned the gaze and the lovely sisterly feeling she'd had yesterday began to wash over her again. Despite the dreadful noises behind her, she had to keep her cool. Imelda Hegarty was a guest in her house and this was probably the best opportunity she was going to get to impress upon her the suitability of a family merger. If that meant putting up with other certain inconveniences for the minute, then that's what she would do. A quick glance at Michael shifting uncomfortably from foot to foot only strengthened her resolve. For all that he had a faint look of his father about him, it was only a sideways kind of a look and there was none of that manly strength when you looked him square in the eye. She looked him square in the eye.

'Michael,' she said, remembering to keep her

voice steady and gentle. 'Why are you still standing here, pet? Should you not get yourself ready for Mass?'

'*But, Aunty Bernadette, I need to go to the –*'

She raised a hand. 'Now now, none of that crudeness in polite company, Michael.' Behind her Monica was now shrilling. 'And you don't want to make poor Mrs Moran feel under pressure to hurry. No, you just pop along and put your Sunday clothes on and let's get some breakfast. What would you like? I know how hungry you are on a Sunday. What about a nice runny egg?'

It was the word 'runny' that did it. Michael shot a contorted look at the two women and with a yelp turned and ran down the stairs as fast as he could. Remembering to keep her expression affectionate, Bernadette looked after him. Where was he off to now? He surely couldn't be that hungry. Behind her, the bathroom door opened and Monica stood there.

'Is he away? I thought he was in the queue?'

Bernadette glared at her. 'No,' she said. 'One mention of my famous breakfasts and he was off like a greyhound.'

Monica snorted. 'I don't doubt it. Well, if you'll excuse me, ladies, I'd better get on with it and make myself beautiful.' She smiled at Bernadette as she passed her. 'At our age we need all the help we can get, don't we?'

'I wouldn't know.'

There was silence as the two women looked each

111

other up and down. Monica was the first to speak. 'Ah, God love you,' she said gently, She reached out and patted Bernadette's curls 'I can see that.'

Bernadette shut the bathroom door behind her conscious that the joys of spring, and all other seasonal joys due to her had shrivelled up and died. As she reached for the soap she saw something that caused her to pause. On the shelf there were two alien toothbrushes. One was a regular, pale blue, soft bristle. She smiled at it. The other was obviously Monica's. The head was pink with curled-back bristles and the handle was the shape of an elongated Barbie doll – all exaggerated breasts and completely naked. Bernadette shuddered. This was the final straw. Blatant vulgarity left lying around where poor Michael could walk in any minute and see it. He'd be mortified. For all that he was eighteen now, Bernadette prided herself on the fact that she had got him safely through the trials of adolescence without once having to mention the facts of life or answer any awkward questions about alternative uses for front bottoms. Well, she wasn't going to have him start today. On a Sunday. Without a second thought she picked it up and stuck it straight into the toilet bowl. A quick swish around, a tap on the rim and back onto the shelf – the far end of the shelf, on its own. There! No more than that foul-mouthed hussy deserved.

If Bernadette had been a common sort of woman

112

she'd have a little whistle now. She unpuckered her lips and resisted the temptation to award herself a wrinkle-forming smile. No, Bernadette Teegan might be sorely tried by present circumstances but she would not give in. She remembered the little rotor arm in the pocket of her Saturday cardigan. The Teegans were made of sterner stuff.

At the sight of Michael's dinosaur toothbrush she shrugged. Well, some of them anyway.

CHAPTER 6

By the time mass was over, Bernadette was in a better frame of mind. The reading was one of her favourites, The Good Samaritan, and though she really couldn't see herself being so foolhardy as to go picking battered foreigners off the side of the road, she supposed temporary tolerance towards sluts from Dublin might clock up as many Brownie points in God's eyes. Or Cormac's. Certainly Father Sean had smiled and shaken her hand warmly.

'Sean, dear, you don't know what a treasure you have in Bernadette,' Imelda told him as they came out of the church. 'She really couldn't be kinder.'

Bernadette kept her eyes lowered, humble. 'It really is a pleasure.'

'And what are you ladies planning for the afternoon?'

'Well, I thought a walk over to the ruins of the old monastery might be nice,' Bernadette looked at Imelda hopefully. 'It's very picturesque and the air there is so fresh and bracing. Would you like that?'

'Oh,' Imelda practically clapped. 'That sounds

wonderful! There's nothing I like better but,' she looked doubtfully at Monica, 'what about it, Mon?'

'A bracing walk, up a hillside, to see a ruin? Let me think a minute . . . em . . .' Monica's eyes twinkled in merriment. With a dramatic sweep of eyelashes that had trebled in volume and length since her last trip upstairs after breakfast, she contemplated her décolletage. In the centre of a wide expanse of flesh, a huge bejewelled crucifix was wedged in her cleavage. She thrust her chest forward. 'Look at that. What can you see?'

Sean looked from one woman to the other in panic.

'Really now, what can you see?' Monica urged her breasts even closer. 'Look there.' She poked the pink flesh, leaving white circles all over. 'What would you call those?'

Sean's mouth opened but no sound came out.

Seeing that Michael, renewed by the blessings he had just received, was about to offer an answer, Bernadette snapped. 'Oh for the love of God, put us out of our agony!' Remembering her audience, her voice softened, very slightly. 'I mean, this is hardly the time or the place, is it?'

Monica's lashes flew upwards. 'For goose pimples? What better time would there be for goose pimples than standing outside in the cold? No pet, I'm sorry,' she laid one hand gently on Bernadette's arm and patted her own bosom with the other. 'Aren't you lovely to ask but I think I must decline the offer. You wouldn't know to look

115

at me, but my chest's quite sensitive.' She gave an obligatory cough and smiled at Sean. 'It reacts to the least little thing!' Another comforting pat. 'Honestly, any little thing at all.' And she turned and, limping slightly, headed for the car.

In her wake the Teegans and Hegartys stood in silence. Imelda looked affectionately after her friend, Sean looked embarrassed and Michael looked at the ground, trying to hide his relief that Aunty Bernadette had answered before he did. Typical that, and he'd been so sure he had the right answer and all. Behind him a few stragglers were leaving the church and as he moved aside to let them pass, his heart rose. Across the road Lucy O'Donnell and her mother were coming out of the newsagents, and like a slow clip from a Sunday afternoon film, Lucy was moving towards him. You didn't usually see the two O'Donnells on a Sunday. They didn't 'do' Sundays, not since Kathleen O'Donnell fell out with the priests over something years ago. Now here they were. The mother had the *News of the World* held in front of her and she was coming straight over to them as if she wanted to be sure Father Sean noticed it. She looked defiant. Lucy looked gorgeous. She had tight jeans that fell short of her belly button and an even tighter top with 'Babe' in rhinestone sequins across the chest. It looked as if it had been sprayed on and it was very flimsy. Michael's cheeks burned and he lowered his head.

'Morning, Father, Miss Teegan,' Lucy's mother greeted them, nodding at Imelda as she passed.

'Good morning, Mrs O'Donnell. Good morning, Lucy. How are you?'

'Fine, thank you, Father.' Kathleen gave a tight smile while Lucy shrugged. Michael shrugged in sympathy. He could see she was uncomfortable, what with Father Sean looking at her mother as if she should have been at Mass and her mother looking at Father Sean as if she dared him to say so and instead they would stop and have some silly conversation about the recently dead or the recently born. And all the while it was was obvious to him that, like Monica, she was feeling the cold. Those weren't goose pimples. He shifted uncomfortably from foot to foot. The proximity of her and the way her lips trembled when she shivered was making him feel hot all over. He could just imagine how it would feel to wrap his arms around her and have her snuggle in close and get all cosy and . . .

'I'll do it!' he said aloud.

The others looked at him.

'Do what, dear?'

'Em . . .' Lucy O'Donnell was looking at him too and there was a faint smile playing about her lips. Actually it looked a bit like a smirk but that was probably the cold. 'Have driving lessons. I'll have driving lessons.' He tried to keep his eyes off Lucy's rhinestones. 'Then I'd be able to give people – who were in a hurry – lifts home from Mass.' He gazed meaningfully at Lucy.

'How kind of you.' Imelda beamed. 'Won't that be lovely? You're just like your Aunty, kindness itself.'

'Yes indeed,' Mrs O'Donnell agreed.

'Yea, great.' Michael didn't mind that Lucy wasn't as enthusiastic as the others. She was probably shy. He remembered Cormac's assurances, and he was an intelligent man, an estate agent. As Lucy and her mother walked off, Michael smiled and pulled himself upright. No bracing Sunday walks around the ruins for him. He was a man with a mission. Leaving Sean and the two women on the church porch, he strode off towards Bernadette's car, calling as he went, 'Hey, Mrs Moran, about those driving lessons . . .'

Bernadette pulled her crochet beret closer over her ears. That settled it then. It looked like just herself and Imelda on the hills for the afternoon. Perfect! She'd loan Imelda those new furlined booties she hadn't even worn and her woolly scarf and the two of them would be like twins. In fact, if you were to meet them for the first time, you'd swear that they were related already. From the back seat of her car came the sound of Monica's guffaws and Michael's tittered response and she sighed. There was no point in her warning the boy against having anything to do with that woman. He had got it into his head that he wanted lessons from her nothing was going to change his mind. Well, they were welcome to each other. She could have him for the afternoon and a fat lot of good it would do him when the car failed to start. He wouldn't be happy at all. Bernadette knew from experience what a petulant little maggot Michael could be when things didn't go his way.

Offering Imelda her arm, she nodded her good-byes to Father Sean and hugged her hopes and her friend warmly. Things were turning out very nicely indeed. Michael would be sulky and truculent by the time they got home. Imelda would see what a burden he could be and how much in need of a father's guiding hand. Monica would be out of favour, having failed in her task, and Michael's mood would have dampened her spirits to the point where they should be going mouldy. And Bernadette? Bernadette would be as she always was, calm, kind and forgiving. Fragrant oil over all the troubled waters. Like a mother figure to everyone. Like family.

At precisely one-thirty Monica chuckled as she watched the two ladies, wrapped up like twin Michelin men, set off for their walk. In her fold-up shopping bag Bernadette had brought with her everything they might possibly need for the two-hour trek. There were slices of buttered fruit bread, two bars of Kendal mint cake and two flasks, one of tea, one of Bovril. There was also a small silver flask of whiskey but Bernadette did not mention that. While Imelda laced her feet into the boots Bernadette lent her, Monica watched through the sitting-room door jamb as their hostess filled the flask and slipped it into her breast pocket. Good on you, girl, Monica thought. She decided against saying anything to Imelda. Bernadette was definitely up to something and if Monica hoped to find out what it would behove her to keep quiet and let things take their course. She waved them off and went to get ready for the driving lesson.

With the sun now in a cloudless sky, upstairs was bathed in light. Monica stood for a minute in the warmth and let her body relax. Two hours in the passenger seat of Father Barry's car – even the thought of it was making her sweaty. In the bedroom, she peeled her top off over her head and flung it on the bed. It was altogether unsuitable for a driving lesson. She pulled open the wardrobe door and ran her hands over the selection of fabrics on display. Silk/polyester, too thin. Satin/polyester, too slimy. Merino/acrylic, ideal. Just warm enough to lie into and cool enough not to stick. Not for the first time she congratulated herself on impeccable taste. God's little gift to mankind, she whispered, as she slid the cosy jumper over her head. The wide neckline allowed for a good view of her décolletage while the rolling collar emphasised the generous contours of her breasts. Then she sprayed a fresh blast of perfume on the underside of the cowl neck and swished her head from side to side to see how effectively the hint of sensual aroma was picked up on the air. Perfect, absolutely perfect!

Then a quick pop into the bathroom to wash her teeth in case there'd be occasion to lean over and give the boy closer instruction. She picked up her toothbrush and after a quick brush, slosh and spit, reached over to get a tissue to wipe where the water had caused her lipstick to bleed. As she did so she noticed Imelda's toothbrush. The bristles were curling from vigorous brushing and Monica made a mental note to give her another one as soon as they got home. She still had a full box of novelty toothbrushes left that she'd taken with her after she got sacked from the chemist the Christmas before last. Maybe she'd send one to Bernadette too, as a 'thank you'. That'd be a nice thing to do. Bernadette, the dark horse, she was sure to appreciate that.

Downstairs, Michael was waiting impatiently at the front door.

'Goodness,' Monica said as she came down the stairs, 'aren't you the eager one?' She linked arms with him. 'Now, you masterful thing, where are you taking me?'

Michael looked confused. 'I'm not taking you anywhere! I thought you were teaching me to drive.'

'I am indeed. Lead on, Macduff.' And seeing his confusion, Monica took the keys from his hand and headed for the garage.

The door was open and there it was, dusty, a bit rusty but oh, so achingly familiar. She walked around it trailing her hands on the contours.

'Are you all right, Mrs Moran?'

Monica looked at him. 'Testament to lost youth, that's what it is.' And realising that he was probably about to correct her and say, no, it's a Volvo, she opened the door quickly and gestured him to get in. She climbed in the passenger's side, took one deep breath and then shook her head firmly. 'Right, what do you know about driving cars?'

Michael grinned. 'Actually, I know lots about driving cars, it's only stopping them I have trouble with.'

'Oh,' Monica felt a little disappointed. She'd hoped this would take some time. 'Start it up so and we'll see how we get on.'

Michael plunged the key into the ignition and turned it. Monica's heart leapt as the engine turned over and she braced herself for the familiar purr as it burst into life.

It didn't. Once, twice, he turned the key but the engine refused to do anything more than hum irritably at him. 'I don't think it's working.' There was a rising note of panic in his voice.

Monica smiled. 'I often find if a fellow has trouble getting going, a quick flick of a more experienced wrist does the trick. Here, let me.' Gently shifting her breast out of the way, she leaned right over across his lap and caught hold of the key. Panting slightly with the exertion, she turned it but to no avail. After a couple more futile attempts, she hauled herself upright and shrugged.

'It won't start, will it?' Michael said when the colour flooded back into his face.

'Not for the minute, it won't.'

'What's wrong with it? It was going fine when Aunty Bernadette tried it yesterday. Why is it not working now?'

'I don't know yet.' She patted his knee. 'Give me a minute to think and I'll have it all figured out. Did you say it was fine when your Aunty was driving it?'

Michael nodded. He looked like a little boy who'd just had his candyfloss stolen. Monica studied his profile and a wave of affection washed over her. He sat staring straight ahead, gripping the steering wheel, going nowhere. There was a look of his father about him all right. Suddenly, it dawned on her. Bernadette had no worries about harm coming to either of them during the driving lesson – and why would she? She'd been here in the garage last night. She knew already that they'd be going nowhere! She'd obviously fixed it somehow. There was no point in trying to figure out how. Monica's expertise in cars was confined largely to back seat gymnastics and apart from getting things started and stopped in time she had little other interest. However, here she was in the car, on a windy Sunday afternoon with a young man. It'd be a shame to waste it.

'Right,' she said. 'I know what it is.'

Michael said nothing.

'It's a sign.'

With all hopes of driving round to O'Donnell's and watching Lucy's rhinestones fading as quickly as the afternoon light, Michael slumped further into the seat. 'A sign.'

'Absolutely right. Now sit up straight and I'll explain it to you.'

For the next hour, with a patience that exceeded even Imelda's claims, Monica explained everything she knew about the front of a car. She told him how great the big wheel was for steering and covered his hands as he demonstrated how strong you'd have to be to turn a wheel on a car that wasn't moving at all. With his foot on the clutch, she guided his hands through the different gears and then she showed him how easily the seats could be adjusted if you were in a situation where you needed to change position for one reason or another.

Michael was fine up to this point but now he looked confused. 'Why would you need to change position if you're driving along?'

'Well, you mightn't be driving along, you might be stopped.'

'Surely you'd be getting out then.'

'Not necessarily.' Monica adjusted the folds of her collar and swished a little. The aroma rose. She leaned in a little closer to him. 'You might just want to sit a while . . . for a chat.' With her head now resting on his shoulder she started to stroke his arm. 'Or a little cuddle, or whatever.' Her hand travelled down to his leg and she started to caress it in tiny circles at first then bigger and bigger and all the while her breathing keeping time so that her breasts were rising and falling, rising and falling, and Michael was beginning to look seasick.

Suddenly he jolted upright and his voice was authoritative. 'You can stop that now! I know how to handle you! I have big strong hands!'

'Ooh!' Monica thrilled, 'I'm delighted to hear it.' The breast undulations were reaching pneumatic drill speeds. She rolled her sleeves up and started to tickle him. 'And what do you intend to do with them?'

It was a struggle for Michael not to laugh. He was sensitive to being tickled, so he caught her hands and held them tight. 'No, Mrs Moran, you're to stop that. Mr Hegarty told me I was well able to handle you.'

Monica let her hands drop. 'Mr Hegarty?'

'Mr Cormac Hegarty.'

Monica's eyebrows disappeared into her fringe. 'Cormac? What does Cormac Hegarty have to do with you?' She looked at him closely. 'You're not a –? Then she remembered the magazines. He couldn't be.

Michael puffed slightly. 'He's my friend.'

Monica sniffed. 'And he's advising you on how to handle women? That should be interesting. Why would he do that?' And seeing that Michael had that sulky look again, she sat back, hands folded in her lap. 'Come on, pet, there's obviously something on your mind.' Her voice took on a warm huski-ness as she held out her arms. 'Tell Aunty Monica all about it.'

That did the trick. So grateful for a sympa-thetic hearing, Michael leaned forward and nestled in the soft folds of Monica's bosom. He told her all about Lucy O'Donnell (Monica snorted inwardly – that toothpick, she'd not given her a second glance); he told her about his futile attempts to pull up outside the supermarket; he told her about Cormac's advice. She knew he was holding back on the last bit so she rubbed his head gently and assured him that there was no way she could help him if he didn't tell her everything, so he took a deep breath, and with apologies for any remarks that might be offen-sive recounted the conversation with Cormac as faithfully as possible.

By the end of it Monica didn't know whether to laugh or cry. Michael wasn't willing where she was concerned but after listening to him she realised that he was actually a complete and utter eejit. Not that she was choosy but whatever about being a sandwich short of a picnic, it was a poor state of affairs when the sandwiches you had weren't even filled. She gave a deep sigh of resignation and Michael whimpered in response, nestled cosily on his human pillow.

Eventually Monica spoke. 'Well, pet,' she said, 'I don't know if you want to hear this but I'm not sure that Cormac was really telling you what you think he was. There's something about him you need to know.'

Michael was silent.

'I've known Cormac for years, pet, and he'd never be able to advise you on how to handle women because, you see, he's –'

'*Snzzzzzz*'

As the crescendo of Michael's snore filled the car, Monica's shoulders started to shake with laughter. There was a surprise all right. Just when she had been about to cross him off for good he goes and does a thing like that. Falls asleep before the important bit. Just like his father, after all.

Cormac was having his favourite sort of a Sunday. He'd woken late, breakfasted long and was now resting to let the food settle before deciding what to eat next. He popped a Turkish delight into his mouth and followed it over his teeth with his tongue as he contemplated how good life was when all was going just the way you wanted it to –

A sharp knock on the door halted his reveries and he tutted at the disturbance. Four o'clock on a Sunday afternoon for God's sake. Who could want to see him at that time? He was already on his feet when the thought struck him. Hardly Imelda. It couldn't be. She was fastidious about germs and the idea of her visiting a brother struck down with flu was ludicrous. Pulling the belt of his smoking jacket around him and mustering up his best ailing impression, he ambled to the door.

'Well, hello, sweetheart!'

Standing in the doorway was a vision in cream merino with a soft pink polyester pashmina draped across her shoulders. It certainly wasn't Imelda.

'Can't I come in?'

He stood aside to let her enter and held his breath as she passed. Some things hadn't changed, he noticed. It was never easy to breath around Monica Moran for one reason or another.

'Still the same old perfume, Monica?'

'It is not!' She flicked his shoulder playfully.

Cormac smiled 'Well, the same amount anyway. Come in, sit down, I wasn't expecting you.'

Monica scanned the room appreciatively before backing onto a mound of cushions that left her perched on the edge of one of the sofas. She reached behind her and hauled a couple out. 'God help us, Cormac, is there anything in here that isn't padded? It's very plush.'

Cormac held out a tray of sweets. 'Oh, I've done all right for myself in Tullabeg. Nice and peaceful, the way I like it.'

Monica said nothing, just sat back and watched him closely for a minute or two.

Cormac started to look uncomfortable. 'What?' he said, 'What is it?'

Monica took a sweet and pressed her finger lightly onto the sugary coating. Then she put her finger in her mouth and left it there while she continued her scrutiny of him. Eventually she eased it out and leaned forward. 'Cormac,' she crooned, 'What are you up to?'

He puffed slightly. 'I don't know what you're getting at.'

Monica laughed. 'Sweetheart, you never did. Now come clean.'

Cormac knew he sounded peevish but she was impossible, really she was. He tried to glare at her but to no avail. Monica Moran had known him for over forty years and probably knew him better than practically anyone else. He gestured to the tray of medicine by the door. 'D'you mean that?'

Monica raised her eyes to heaven. 'No, of course I don't. Any eejit could work out why you'd claim to be sick with the prospect of Mel putting your recipe cards into alphabetical order and arranging your sock drawer in order of shades for a fort-night. I mean Michael.'

The hairs on the back of his neck began to prickle and Cormac shrugged. How did she do it? He hadn't seen her for twenty years and then she turns up out of the blue and goes straight for a gold medal in mind reading.

'I only encouraged the boy to learn to drive. He wants to expand his social contacts and I think it's a good idea, for a boy, as it were.'

Monica laughed. 'And I suppose you thought you might be seeing more of him if he had the freedom of the roads.'

Cormac cleared his throat. 'Well, I wouldn't deny

that'd be nice all right.' He straightened up a little. 'He's quite fond of me.'

'As a father figure, pet, as a father figure.'

Cormac shook his head. 'I don't think so. We've had a little chat you know.'

Monica leaned forward and pulled her pashmina down, revealing a strange marking on her chest. It was like a deep red indentation. 'Cormac, do you know what this is?'

He pulled back. 'Is it contagious?'

She patted the mark affectionately. 'In your case I'm afraid not, though I wouldn't mind a little more of it myself. Look closer. What does it look like?'

Cormac turned his head from side to side but he couldn't decide what he was looking at. It was familiar; all curved one side then curling up into a little . . . Good gracious! He sat bolt upright. 'Is that an ear?'

Monica covered the mark proudly. 'It's Michael's.'

'Goodness!' Cormac considered the implications of this for a minute. 'What was Michael's ear doing there?'

'Sadly,' Monica rearranged her pashmina over the mark again as if to protect it, 'it was only resting – the rest of him was asleep.'

Cormac laughed. 'Poor old Mon,' he said. 'Are you losing your touch?'

'Not at all,' she said. 'You know my motto, *softee softee catchee monkey*. And you, my friend, are not in the chase at all.'

'But he said –'

'He said women, pet – he's not interested in women. Did you think to ask him how he felt about girls?'

Cormac's face fell. 'You mean it wasn't me?'

Monica shook her head.

'Oh well, *c'est la vie.*' he said bravely. 'I'll have to look elsewhere so.'

He looked so crestfallen that Monica felt sorry for him. Swinging herself forwards on the sofa she rose and crossed to sit beside him. She held her arms out. 'Never mind pet,' she said. 'Tell you what, would you like another look?'

And leaning forward Cormac found some consolation in gazing at the fading mark on Monica's chest. There was surely some place in its owner's heart for him. Such a lovely ear. Ignoring Monica's protestations that it was tickling her, he traced its outline affectionately. Outside the sun was sinking rapidly and as the late afternoon shadows grew longer Cormac gazed forlornly at the disappearing ear.

Just as its memory finally merged into the soft pink of Monica's skin, he thought he caught a glimpse of something at the window but he didn't look up.

Shame that.

CHAPTER 7

Poor Imelda wasn't looking well. She wasn't looking well at all. As she tucked her up in bed, a hot water bottle on her tummy, Bernadette muttered all sorts of sympathetic noises and assured her guest that she'd find some medicine as quickly as she could.

'There, dear, I'm leaving you this nice bucket by the bed in case you need to – you know. It's perfectly clean so you mustn't worry about picking up any germs from it.'

'Thanks.' Imelda managed a weak smile between the waves of nausea that had been growing all after-noon. 'I don't know what it is, it just came on all of a sudden.'

'And I'm sure it wasn't something you ate.' Bernadette thought she'd better get that point in from the start. After all, she was feeling fine, Michael was glued to the television with not a bother on him and the slut had actually taken herself out for a walk so whatever it was, it was definitely peculiar to Imelda. 'Do you suffer from a weak tummy usually?'

Imelda swallowed. 'Not usually.'

Bernadette smoothed the sheet. 'Well, you try to sleep and I'll get something to help.'

'Thank you, dear. I'm sorry to be such a bother.'

Bernadette glowed beatifically. 'Now, now. Not another word.' She backed out of the room like the angel of mercy she was and shut the door quietly behind her. Blast! What was she going to do now? She was sure there were no indigestion remedies in the house. They weren't necessary given that she prepared everything they ate and her cooking simply didn't produce indigestion. If Michael ever claimed to be ill it was obviously as a result of something he had eaten elsewhere and she was happy to let him suffer the consequences – mute warning against foolhardiness that would serve him well in the future. But here she was with a sick Imelda on her hands and not a thing to offer her. She looked around in despair.

Suddenly she had an idea. If she was not given to weak innards thanks to a habit of clean living, the same could definitely not be said for Monica Moran. Bernadette had already seen the huge pink wash bag Monica was carrying around earlier. There were sure to be remedies for every complaint in it. She'd take a quick look, in the interests of research. She pushed open the door of Michael's room and there it was by the bed. Picking it up she quietly unzipped it. Inside there was an array of toiletries, a packet of batteries and, in a side pocket, one of the most extraordinary containers Bernadette had ever seen. It was fleshy-pink coloured and had buttons and strange bumps all over. Bernadette picked it up and turned it from side to side. No label. Wasn't that typical – not even a 'Use by' date. God knows what potions that woman was bringing into the house. Well, it was her house and she had a right to know what was going on under her own roof. Bernadette hoped it was legal. Gripping the neck she twisted the lid but to her surprise, instead of opening, the thing came to life! With a frenzied whirring it leapt out of her hands, gyrated and squirmed on the floor. Bernadette stared at it in horror. What on earth? There must be some type of little animal inside of it. Maybe it was some sort of vermin and by the contortions it was producing, she could only surmise that the poor creature was in desperate pain. She hoped it wouldn't escape.

She watched it for a few minutes till she felt safe that it hadn't any other surprises. It seemed to be happy to lie there, whirring and stirring so she took a deep breath, pulled her hanky out of her pocket and, picking it up, popped it back into the bag. There was a rustling and shifting while it settled itself into position at the bottom but Bernadette didn't wait. Turning on her heel she left the room as quickly as she could.

'Oh!' As she shut the door behind her, she almost collided with Imelda, ashen-faced. 'I didn't realise you were out of bed.'

Imelda traced a weak path over her tummy. 'I threw up. I had to get out to get to the bathroom.'

Then she managed a watery smile. 'I thought I'd give my teeth a quick freshen up and then try to sleep as you suggested.' She gestured towards the bedroom door. 'I thought Monica was back.'

Bernadette looked around. 'No, she's not back. I was just . . . just . . . opening the windows; get lots of fresh air through the house. In case it's contagious or anything.'

'Good idea.' Imelda stuck the toothbrush into her mouth and turned to go back into the bathroom. Bernadette followed her. She stood behind as Imelda swished and sloshed and spit and then held out a hand to escort her back to bed. As Imelda rinsed her brush and put it back on the shelf, Bernadette felt cold.

'Imelda! What's that!'

Imelda smiled. 'Monica gave that to me – couldn't you guess?'

As Bernadette looked at the Barbie brush dripping onto her clean sink the blood slowly drained from her forehead. Of course! No wonder poor Imelda wasn't feeling well. She put her hand under her friend's elbow, her voice now as weak as Imelda's. 'No dear,' she said, 'I can honestly say I couldn't.'

As soon as Imelda was settled, Bernadette put on her outdoor shoes and grabbed her bag. Her mind was in turmoil. What was she going to do now? Poor Imelda was probably dying from some awful disease she had picked up from having her toothbrush swished in the toilet after Monica used it and Bernadette would be blamed. How was she to know that the brush was Imelda's? She knotted her scarf tightly under her chin with scant regard for the springiness of her curls, cursing Monica all the while. It was all her fault of course. If she hadn't been so vulgar, this would never have happened in the first place. Now what was she to do? The chemists' were all shut on a Sunday and the doctor was away for the weekend. Where was she going to get medicine? She sat in her little green car and prayed for guidance.

Suddenly it came to her: of course! Cormac was sure to have something. Like all refined men he had a delicate constitution and she knew he's bought a range of cures from the supermarket on Friday. Maybe there'd be something there for Imelda. With a quick prayer to all the saints she knew, she turned the key and headed for the town.

By the time the car pulled up outside Cormac's she was feeling much better. She'd worked out her strategy en route. Obviously it was not necessary to determine the source of Imelda's illness – it could be anything and those Dublin coaches are known to be rife with airborne germs. That was it, all right, and the reason Monica wasn't infected was that she was immune to filth by her very nature. She loosened her scarf and ran her fingers through her hair. Composing her features into an attractive, windswept-but-capable-of-coping-in-emergency look, she tiptoed up the drive. Cormac might be taking it easy and she wouldn't want to disturb him unduly. Pausing at the front door she stood with her hand over the brass cherub. What if he wasn't in? What if he was upstairs in the shower? Michael had mentioned what a clean man he was. What if . . .

From Cormac's front room she could hear the sound of voices and her heart stopped. Even as the tips of her curls turned to dagger ends she recognised the raucous sound of Monica Moran. It was coming from inside! Clenching her fists she slid her handbag up her arm and sneaked over to the window. With a quick glance round to ensure she wasn't being watched, she pulled her scarf over her face. The sill was difficult to reach so she had to hitch her skirt and stand astride an array of assorted heathers to get into position. As her feet sank into the muddy earth, she stretched up and peered in the window.

And in an instant, her world came crumbling down around her ears.

There they were, Cormac Hegarty and Monica Moran, knee to knee on the sofa and she forcing his face into her chest! It was obvious from his sad expression that he wasn't enjoying a bit of it but that one wouldn't care. She had her head back and was smiling broadly, triumphantly, and all the while poor Cormac's face grew sadder and sadder. Bernadette fumed – the bitch! Well, she wasn't getting away with it this time. She might have broken poor Father Barry's heart twenty years ago and left Bernadette picking up the pieces and staving off his heart attacks but she wasn't going to do the same thing to Cormac.

With scant regard for the dreadful state her tights would be in, Bernadette unplugged her feet and leapt over the bushes back onto the path. She did a little jig to knock off the loose soil and with her handbag clutched to her side, marched to the car.

'It's a wise man knows his enemy, and an even wiser woman,' she muttered as she drove off and Cormac's house grew smaller in her rear view mirror. 'And I know my enemy all right.' Her heartbeat quickened and she fumed. 'I know my enemy, Mrs Monica Moran. Well, I'll tell you something – Cormac may be watching your front . . .' a tear escaped and trickled down her cheek, 'but he'd be better off watching your back. Someone'll have to, cause now it's war!'

It was long after tea that Monica finally arrived home, slightly tipsy and without a word of apology. Bernadette could not bring herself to look at her but made hasty excuses and went to her room. Ignoring the faint humming noise from Monica's room, she shut her door and stood in front of her mirror. After a minute she leaned forward and took a closer look.

Then, just like they did on rude films before she turned them off in case Michael should walk in, she started to undress. First she unbuttoned her cardigan and let it slip off her shoulders onto the floor. She lifted her chin and was about to toss her hair in that seductive way women do when they've discovered a silky new conditioner when she became aware of the cardigan, crumpled at her feet. Really, it wouldn't do. No matter how often you hoovered, there'd still be bits of fluff and fluff wreaks havoc with pure new wool never mind what it can do to your drains. She picked the cardigan up, patted it down carefully, and hung it in the wardrobe. Then she returned to her task. After the cardigan came her top, sliding sensuously over her lacy thermal vest and then straight onto a separate hanger. Last was her skirt. She examined it carefully as she unzipped – lovely tweed and all the autumn shades you could think of, with an overall effect of green that matched her twin set – and the zip was proper metal as well. When the skirt was neatly hanging, pleats straightened, she returned to the mirror and stood there, practically naked, except for her underwear. With her hands on her hipbones she swivelled from side to side trying to view what she was seeing with an objective eye. Eventually, she stopped and stood still. There was no getting away from it. No man in his right mind could possibly want the likes of Monica Moran with her swathes of surplus flesh when they could have Bernadette Teegan instead. She really was very nice. Lovely square shoulders that always gave a great hang to jackets and cardigans; a neat waistline so that you could tuck in your blouse and not have it hanging over your belt; no unnecessary bumps or bulges on front that distorted patterns or stretched fabric so that you couldn't match up the seams for ironing. And her legs were fine too, nice and straight with regular size five feet (or thirty-seven if you wanted to show off and be continental). It was handy having feet that size, you could always find something in the sales. She sighed deeply; grateful for the gifts she had been given.

Then she stiffened. Monica was coming up the stairs. Please don't let her come in here, she prayed, but Monica, hiccupping for all she was worth, went straight to her own room. For a while she fumbled about and then it went quiet. Bernadette waited, conscious of the sound of her own breathing and the faintest hum. Suddenly there was a shout of laughter and Monica called out. 'Ah, no, I'm too tired anyway.' And then the silence was absolute. Bernadette shrugged. Obviously insane. Surely no man could ever take the likes of that seriously.

But they did, you know, she said aloud. The finest man in the country was driven to his grave with her antics and now my lovely Cormac is having his head turned, or embedded in a slut's cleavage. Bernadette hushed her own breasts forward with the sides of her arms. It didn't make any difference. She let her arms fall again. No, that wasn't the solution. Cormac Hegarty was a refined man. He didn't like vulgarity, Bernadette was sure of that. And turning herself into a slut wasn't going to protect him. She rubbed her hands together and remembered the feel of his as he stood with her in the kitchen. So clean, so soft, so . . .

So bloody fickle if only two days later he was letting that one onto his couch! Bernadette whipped her vest over her head and reached under the pillow for her pyjamas. Well, he might have a faulty memory but she didn't. All he needed was a gentle reminder that it was Bernadette Teegan who had caught his eye first, and she wasn't about to give it up without a fight. As she pulled her tights down, folded them over the back of her chair and tucked her pyjama top into her pyjama bottom she winked at herself in the mirror and smiled. If Cormac didn't know what he was missing, he soon would.

Monday started badly for Monica. Imelda still wasn't feeling too perky and opted to spend the day reading. Michael had left early and though she had enjoyed visiting Cormac yesterday, her head was throbbing, her feet were stinging and she didn't fancy a rematch. Gulping down a glass of water to ease the sucked sandpaper feeling in her mouth, she frowned at her reflection in the spotless kitchen window. Damn that Cormac – he was a spiteful little hussy all the same. Any eejit could see he didn't have a hope in Hell with Michael but Cormac wasn't just any eejit. No fool like an old fool. He'd stared at Michael's ear

141

imprint until it disappeared and then sighed deeply as if someone had stolen his bun, his favourite bun, his only bun.

'Ah Cormac, pet, will you get a grip. A young fellow like that won't be interested in an old fogey like yourself.'

'That's what you think.' Cormac puffed out his chest. 'He and I had a good heart-to-heart and I think you might actually be very misguided.'

'He's not, do you hear me, *not* for you.'

Cormac stood up and poured sweet sherry for the two of them. Holding out a glass towards Monica he smiled. 'Do you want to bet?'

'A bet? Like the old days?' Monica took the glass and clinked it with his. 'The old hunting duo back in action?'

'Yep.' Cormac drained his glass and poured another.

Monica followed suit. And so the tone for the evening was set. Over the course of the entire sherry decanter and a couple of glasses of Riesling on top, they reminisced about the old days, mostly the Saturdays when the two of them, flushed with the power of adolescence, put on their finery and trawled the streets of Dublin looking for action. They were marvellously successful, a striking pair and made a great team. Having the same taste in men helped. Glass followed glass as the memories poured out and if it occurred to Monica more than once that Cormac wasn't as quick to drain his glass as he was to refill hers, she didn't want to halt the flow of the conversation, or anything else, by mentioning it.

Now here she was with a thumping headache, aching extremities, a sick stomach and not a remedy to be found. She might as well go back to bed. With one sweaty hand on the banister and the other palm-flat against the cool wall, she eased herself up the stairs and slowly lowered her body onto the bed. She tossed, slowly, and turned, gently, but she couldn't get comfortable. Life was too awful just at the minute – she wanted to opt out.

'Uggh,' Rolling onto her side as another powerful wave of nausea hit, her hand brushed the floor beside the bed and caught the edge of the magazine she had stuffed under the side-table. With one eye shut she hauled it out and peeped at it. The eye still open twinkled.

'Well, well, well. I'd forgotten about you.' She flipped over the cover and read the list of contents. Every item on the menu was accompanied by a small illustration to whet the appetite while leaving little to the imagination. Even a sideways half-view made her feel better. Twenty Tips to leave her Begging – page 12. Get Those Juices Flowing – page 34. What Women Really Want – page 41. She propped herself up in the bed and turned to page 41. The pictures were one thing but the article made her shake her head in dismay. Poor Michael, was this where he was getting his information, from a panel of twenty-two-year-old 'sexperts'? No wonder he hadn't had any luck with Lucy O'Donnell. Nobody in any of the pictures looked as if she weighed a pound over eight stone, and spread-eagled out like that showed little more on top than a ladder of ribs and a set of teeth that were obviously the result of years spent at the dentist's. She shook her head. He didn't stand a chance.

Throwing the magazine back onto the floor she lay down and shut her eyes. There was a need there all right and seeing as she was on her holidays and had time to spare it was only kind that she should fill it. With the car sabotaged she wasn't going to be able to teach him too much about getting from A to B, but she could always teach him everything else he needed to know. Soothed by the rightness of her conclusion she began to drift off to sleep. Just what the doctor ordered, a quick snooze and when she woke up she'd be ready for anything.

Cormac was in a similar frame of mind. His head didn't hurt too much as he was always careful drinking sherry to alternate it with a glass of something else, diluted prune juice or organic apple. And when he slipped out to the toilet, he had a drink of water to keep things flowing. He chuckled. Monica had straight sherry. She must be feeling awful, really awful. He plinked a vitamin C tablet into the glass and watched it fizz. She deserved it, moving in on his patch as if every man in the world owed allegiance to her. And flaunting those enormous breasts, yuck! He shuddered. She really was a vulgar woman and it saddened him, slightly, to see it. As teenagers they had been thrown together by hopeful parents but it didn't take her long to realise that those hopes would be forever unfulfilled. When she sucked the chocolate out of a Rowntrees éclair and slid the warm toffee into his mouth, he enjoyed sucking the toffee more than he would ever be tempted to chase the chocolate. Eventually they settled on a hunting partnership. No man in Dublin was safe when the two of them were in action. If one didn't bring him to his knees, the other was sure to. Now the breasts on her would have the poor man on his back – squashed.

He picked up the vitamin drink and sipped it slowly. Well, she wasn't getting her hands on Michael. He wasn't one of those sophisticated Dublin types. Cormac's heart gave a little flutter. He was a simple country boy, lonely and friend-less, needing an older, more mature person to give him some guidance. He took another sip. Bernadette wouldn't stand for it anyway, he was sure of that. He smiled broadly – that's what he should do. He'd talk to Bernadette and alert her to Monica's behaviour and maybe suggest that the boy would be safer spending some time with him. He looked around the pristine kitchen fondly. A few afternoons here with him would wipe all thoughts of Monica out of his head. He'd soon put him straight.

Put him straight, dear me. Cormac put down his glass and headed for the stairs.

Shower time.

CHAPTER 8

For the rest of that week, life in Tullabeg settled into a gentle routine. Bernadette, tight-lipped, performed her duties as requested in the presbytery and Michael painted; Monica and Imelda spent their days having gentle walks in the countryside. Imelda was still feeling queasy, though she was very diligent about drinking lots of Bernadette's homemade lemonade and washing her teeth carefully afterwards. She linked her arm through Monica's as she thanked her for her patience in keeping herself amused.

'And you have been lovely with Michael. Driving lessons every evening. I'm sure Bernadette really appreciates all the help you've been giving him. Is he learning anything?'

Monica flushed. 'Oh he is,' she assured her. 'I couldn't begin to tell you how much.'

So she didn't try.

Michael wasn't going to be giving away too many details either. As he loaded his roller and swished coat after coat of paint onto Sean's spare room walls, he found he was whistling to himself. Well, not exactly whistling, more blowing air through the gap in his front teeth in a tuneful way. Life was certainly looking up. From being the nervous, bashful, not-to-be-taken-too-seriously chap he had been just a week ago, he was rapidly becoming a man.

He shook his head in amazement at his own stupidity on Saturday when he had mistaken Monica Moran's kindness for anything other than what it was. She was not at all pushy, she was the kindest, most understanding woman he had ever met. After that first time when he (embarrassing now to admit it) thought she was actually interested in him, they had moved onto a level where, as she explained, they were friends. Real, true friends. As soon as she had opened her womanly arms to him and encouraged him to tell her all his troubles, life had changed. She understood completely the anguish of unre-quited love. She understood the pain of wanting somebody but not being able to reach the some-body because, a) the car doesn't stop in time, b) the somebody doesn't take you seriously. With the patience of a saint, she solved both his prob-lems. She explained in detail how to slow down and stop a car. With her hand cupping his, for encouragement, she went over the motions hundreds of times. 'Firm that thigh and press in the brake, firm this thigh and squeeze the clutch – slooowly,' she intoned like a mantra till he could do it with his eyes shut. And mostly he did have his eyes shut: she said it was better for concentration.

When he was confident that he had no more worries about the car and they'd practise doing it for real once it got started, she moved on to the second issue, the problem of Lucy O'Donnell. Here he paused and reloaded his roller. Oh Lucy, light of my life, not long now. Monica laughed when he confessed his fear that he just wasn't in Lucy's league.

'What!' Her eyes shot open so that her thick black eyelashes were practically wedged in her eyebrows. 'Not in Lucy's league? My dear boy, you are more than qualified to be in Lucy's league, in her arms, dare I say it, even in her knickers if that's what you want!'

Michael flushed a furious red.

Monica leaned close. 'That *is* what you want, pet, isn't it?'

He couldn't speak. Imagine admitting that to anyone, his deepest darkest desire?

Monica didn't need his admission. She was so astute. She just smiled and nodded and said, 'Of course you do and why shouldn't you? A grand healthy attractive lad like yourself.'

Michael stole a quick glimpse of his face in the rear view mirror. Curly ginger hair, spotty face and ears that stuck out. He shook his head. 'I'm not really all that attractive, am I?'

Monica patted his knee. 'You're gorgeous, that's what you are.'

He indicated the spots and the ears but she was adamant. She took a deep breath and linked her hands together in front of her as if she was praying. 'Do you know what, Michael, I'm beginning to think that I was sent here for a purpose. When Imelda suggested that I come down for a couple of weeks to keep her company I thought she was trying to cheer me up after my husband . . .' she dabbed at her eyes briefly, 'passed away so tragically, I thought it would be a waste of time. I haven't been here for more than twenty years and the only friend I had in this town has long since . . .' another little dab and her voice strengthened, 'but now I can see my purpose.' With a great swish of fabric under strain, she shifted herself round so that she was facing him. 'Forget the odd little spot, it's a sign of burgeoning manhood.'

'Is it?'

She nodded. 'You're awash, that's what you are, awash with manly testosterone. Imagine it, gallons of the stuff surging through your veins, throbbing through your arteries, all the way around,' and she traced the path of the aforementioned tubes all round his body so that he actually thought he could feel it. Then her voice lowered. 'What you have to do, what you *must* do if you are to win the heart of the fair Lucy, is to harness the power of that testosterone, contain it, so that the next time she sees you, she'll know there's something pulsing there, waiting to be unleashed.' She sat back and said in a very ordinary voice. 'That's all.'

150

Then she turned and caught hold of the door handle. 'Well, I'd better be off.'

Michael grabbed her sleeve. 'Don't go.'

'Why?' Monica asked. 'Was there something else?'

Michael could feel the sweat gathering around the collar of his shirt. 'I don't . . . I mean I wouldn't be able . . .'

She placed a gentle caring hand on his. 'What is it, pet, what's worrying you?'

He looked around to check for eavesdroppers. 'I don't know how to.' He whispered, fighting the tears in shame. 'I've never, properly, with a real girl, or with anyone actually.'

Monica gave a little shiver and her voice sounded clipped and a bit higher than usual. 'Haven't you? Goodness, that is a problem. Let me see . . .' Knitting her brows together she chewed at her lip for a minute or two. While Michael watched her intently, she appeared to be having a conversation in her head, an argument even. Eventually she gave a huge sigh and turned to look at him. 'Michael, do you trust me?'

He nodded.

'Right so,' she said. 'I'm going to propose something that might work but you must promise to keep it a secret – except of course from your Aunty Bernadette. I wouldn't ask you to keep secrets from family.'

Michael wasn't so sure about that. And a couple of minutes later when Monica told him what her proposition was, he was certain. Aunty B was funny about some things and he had the strangest hunch that this was one of those things she was likely to be funny about, but at least Monica's assurance put his mind at rest. Without her confidence he'd have thought it was a bit, well, unusual, but she was so relaxed. It must be okay. He quickly decided he'd not say a word because it wasn't anyone's business anyway. He was a man now and men don't have to discuss everything with everybody.

He flushed momentarily as he remembered how much she was selflessly prepared to do for him. In her kindness, she offered to teach him all he needed to know about testosterone harnessing. With saintly patience she explained there were several exercises he'd have to practise before he got it right but she was here for another couple of weeks and she was willing, as a gesture of thanks to Bernadette for her hospitality, to teach him.

'Wow,' Michael said when she was finished, 'you'd be willing to do that? Thanks!'

'Please,' Monica waved a bejewelled hand, 'I don't need thanks. A couple of weeks' tuition and you'll be the star of Lucy's league, I can promise you.'

Michael's grin was so wide that the spots on his cheeks flattened. Then he remembered. 'What about my ears? Might they put her off?'

Monica smiled. 'No woman in her right mind would object to those.' She patted his knee and winked. 'By the time I'm finished with you, pet, Lucy O'Donnell will be glad of those ears. All that surging testosterone, she'll need something to hold on to!' Then she threw back her head and laughed heartily.

Michael laughed too. He wasn't quite sure what the joke was but it was obviously a good one. His body tingled with excitement at the prospect of the knowledge he would gain in the coming week. Lucy was as good as his.

Michael's jauntiness unsettled Bernadette. He was permanently hungry and once or twice she'd caught him looking at her with just a hint of a smile on his face.

'Are you okay, Michael?' she asked.

He nodded, and clearing his throat brought his voice down an octave. 'Fine, Aunty Bernadette, just fine. Thank you for asking.' And then he went on chewing his sandwich.

Bernadette shrugged. He was in a funny mood all right but at least it was an improvement from his usual sullen self. He went straight back to his painting afterwards and every so often she could hear the odd discordant note blurting out from between his pursed lips. When she stuck her head up the stairs at five past four to offer him a cup of tea, he was already gone, his overalls discarded and without so much as a goodbye. She peered out the front window to see if he was waiting for her, propped up against the car looking at the pictures in some gutter newspaper, but there was no sign of him. Oh well, that was fine. She'd just have to drink the pot herself.

It did the trick. As the last dregs of tea trickled out her brain cleared. She took a look at herself in the mirror and was instantly cheered. The remnants of her morning's hairdo were holding up well and with a fresh flick of mascara and lipstick she'd be more than ready to face the world. She cleared the teacup and tidied the table. Father's supper, cold salad cobbled together from the remains of lunch, and a fresh scone, was on the side covered in muslin, with a note telling him what it was, how many of the ingredients were organic and GM free and how she hoped he'd enjoy it. She wasn't known as a pillar of the community for nothing.

Turning her car out onto the road, Bernadette's spirits rose. Nobody got too close, beeped or even shook fists at her. And the steering wheel wasn't clammy either. Encouraged by this universal pleasantry she decided to extend her drive, perhaps detour through the village proper to see what there was to be seen. If there were a couple of parking spaces, she'd maybe pull in and go for a little walk.

Luck was on her side. As she pootled along the street she noticed a delivery truck was pulling out, leaving her a nice big space to squeeze into. She turned her wheels and drove in in one – perfect! A car behind her beeped and the driver gestured her forwards. She glared at him disdainfully. What? Did he expect her to wedge in just so that he could squeeze up behind? No way. Bernadette Teegan's twenty-year-old car wasn't practically scratch free from taking chances. She knew the secret of perfect parking was to avoid manoeuvres at all costs and if she budged now there'd be all sorts of twisting and turning to do. Pretending to be deaf, she waved her hand gaily at the driver and mouthed, 'Yes indeed. Thank you so much.' She picked up her basket, locked the car door and hurried onto the pavement. A quick check in the window of the butcher's for reassurance and she was off.

She had just reached the end of the street and was about to cross the road when she heard a knocking somewhere. Though it was unlikely to be for her, she turned to check anyway and her heart rose. From the upstairs window of 'C. Hegarty, Estate Agents', Cormac was waving furiously. He confirmed that she had seen him and then disappeared. He was coming downstairs! With a quick pat of the hairdo, she pinched her cheeks for colour and arranged her lips into an ingratiating and attractive smile.

'My dear Bernadette! What a lovely surprise!' Cormac opened the door and beckoned her in.

'Well, good afternoon to you.' She nodded

majestically at the young assistants sitting in the front office.

With a hand on her elbow, he gestured to the stairs. 'Please, why don't you come upstairs to my private office. It's much more comfortable there.'

Bernadette could feel herself blushing furiously. Imagine him being so bold in front of those young men! People would get the wrong idea. The thought of it sent a shiver of excitement through her.

Once inside the office, a magnificent room with soft rose walls and a great mahogany desk, Cormac pulled over a chair for her. There was the sound of people in the rooms below but Cormac waved it away. 'I'm keeping a low profile for the moment, with my alleged illness and all.' He winked at her conspiratorially.

Bernadette winked back and tapped the side of her nose. 'Message received and understood, partner.' She covered her mouth to hide the giggle that was threatening to escape. Really, this was all lovely.

Cormac eased himself into his big leather chair on the other side of the desk. 'Now,' he said, 'studying her closely. 'Tell me all about it. How are things going for you? Are you exhausted with the visitors?'

Bernadette struggled for an answer. She had wrestled with this very question last night. Should she tell him the truth about that horrible woman and risk upsetting him, if indeed he was as weak as he appeared to be last Sunday; or should she be positive and loving, reveal her true self and hope he had the sense to realise it. She opted for the latter.

'I'm never exhausted, Cormac, and it's a complete pleasure for me to have such delightful company in my house.'

'Is it?' He looked surprised.

'Of course.' Bernadette unleashed one of her tinkling laughs that she knew men found so attractive. 'I just love having people to look after.' She batted her ultra-volume, clump-free eyelashes. 'I think it's so important for a woman to be more than merely decorative.' The image of Monica flaunting her laden décolletage at the poor man flashed before her. 'I mean, I'd hate it if people thought that's all I was good for.'

'My dear Bernadette, there is no way that you will ever be considered merely decorative.' He hesitated, grappling with emotion, probably. 'Though I must say, you are looking lovely today.'

The ceiling of Bernadette's world disappeared and she went floating off into the sky, carried along on the honeyed wafts of Cormac's words. He was working his way up to a full declaration of love, that was obvious, but what of the little scene she had witnessed? Struggling with the temptation to shut her eyes and just float free, she dragged herself down to earth. If she and Cormac were to have a future together, and she had no doubt but that that was what was in his head, then there must be honesty between them.

'Do you really think so? You surprise me. I thought you admired a different type of woman altogether.'

Cormac's eyebrows shot up. 'A different type of woman? What gave you that idea?'

Bernadette framed her words carefully. 'Oh, I'm not sure, really. I just though that maybe you'd like someone more . . .' She indicated a larger frame.

'Buxom?' Cormac offered.

'Yes, that's right, fatter, with hair more . . .'

Cormac waited.

'More artificial, perhaps. And jewellery, lots of costume jewellery.'

'Goodness,' Cormac looked disappointed. 'She sounds horrendous. What makes you think I'd like a woman like that? Where would I even find one?'

Bernadette took a deep breath. 'Mrs Moran looks a bit like that.'

Cormac slapped both hands on his desk and laughed loudly. 'Monica Moran! The only man who could ever be attracted to Monica would have to be a cannibal – a very hungry cannibal!'

Bernadette laughed too, delighted. He didn't love Monica. All her fears were unfounded. Relief made her generous. 'Mr Hegarty! What a thing to say. I'll not hear a word said against her. She's been such a help to me . . .' Cormac appeared not to hear, 'with Michael.'

Cormac stopped laughing.

'Oh yes,' Bernadette continued. 'Every evening she's been giving him driving lessons, only the theory mind,' she giggled, 'they've had difficulty in getting the car to go, but she's been going through the motions with him anyway.'

'I bet she has,' Cormac muttered. He cleared his throat and looked very serious. 'Bernadette, I know this is none of my business but I have to ask you.' He leaned over the desk. 'Do you really think she is the right sort of person to entrust with that sort of thing?'

'Do you mean driving lessons?'

Cormac nodded. 'She is a woman, after all.'

Bernadette bristled. 'I'm a woman.'

'Ah, yes,' Cormac's smile was warm and affectionate. 'But you are a different type of woman altogether. You are the type of woman whose influence can only be beneficial. Mrs Moran is vulgar. She is not the right influence on the boy at all.'

Bernadette nodded. That's just what she thought as well – another meeting of minds. 'Are you suggesting I teach him myself?' She asked, her voice quivering with concern and feminine fragility.

Cormac shook his head. 'The boy needs a man in his life.'

Bernadette clasped her hands together and sat bolt upright, looking around the room as if an army of male driving instructors had suddenly taken up position behind the houseplants. She looked at Cormac pleadingly. 'But where will I find one?'

Cormac came around the desk and took her hands in his (mental note: buy the Vaseline). Looking deep in her *eyes* and licking his lips greedily he asked, 'What about me? Have you considered me?'

Have I ever? Bernadette squirmed in her chair. Whether it was the passion of the moment or the fact that the pot of tea had finally hit home she wasn't sure. She leapt out of the chair and ran to the door. 'Yes indeed, there's a thought.' If she didn't get to a Ladies soon, there'd be no telling what sort of a woman he'd think she was. She rushed down the stairs as smoothly as her clamped-together knees would allow. Cormac followed her to the door. 'Call me?' he shouted after her.

'Oh, I will, I will.'

She raced to her car and leapt in, squeezing all the while. If she drove carefully and ignored the other traffic she should be able to make it home in a few minutes. She turned the key and the car hummed into life. She pulled out, crouching low over the steering wheel and headed for home. Damn, damn, damn her bladder. He was working his way to a proposal and she couldn't stay the course. She recalled his eyes, desperate, pleading, gazing into hers as he offered to be the man in her life. Well, Michael's actually, but she knew what he was getting at. Despite the discomfort and the tooting of other drivers as the roadhogs headed home for the day, she smiled broadly to

160

herself. So he'll have another couple of days to prepare his speech. That wouldn't do either of them a bit of harm. They were destined to be together, any fool could see that, so what were a couple of days to them. They would have the rest of their lives together.

From his window in the top office, Cormac watched her scuttle into her car and drive off, causing a near pile-up on the street. He chuckled. Imagine Sean trying to marry him off to a lunatic like that – one minute smiling in ecstasy, the other scurrying down the stairs as if her kneecaps were magnetically attracted! Ah well, at least he'd planted that seed about how good he'd be for dear Michael. He sighed as he heard the chaps down-stairs pack up for the evening. They were good enough but he found them dull now. A little bit of money in their pockets and their own calling cards and they thought they were cock o' the walk. He had no interest in their urbane, shallow sophis-tication. Michael's unsullied innocence was more appealing any day. As the sound of Bernadette's engine disappeared into the distance, he rubbed his hands in glee. She'd be back, begging him to replace Monica as guide in Michael's life. He smoothed the soft fabric of his shirt over his belly.
And think of the ear imprints then?

By the time that evening's theory lesson was over, both Monica and Michael were exhausted.

Although she prided herself on her altruistic motives in agreeing to his request for help, Monica had not expected to enjoy herself quite as much as she did. For all that he appeared dopey, there were areas where Michael was rapidly gaining expertise and Monica was not only pleased with his progress, she was euphoric with it.

He had started off gingerly enough and found it hard to hide his surprise when the raw material she presented him as a 'learning aid' bore little, or mostly no, resemblance to the sort of rawness he had seen in his magazine collection.

'Wow,' he said, when she unleashed a great swathe of flesh from beneath her underwiring, 'I though women were supposed to be, sort of flattish, there.' He reached out a tentative hand.

Monica was ready for him. She reached into the glove compartment and pulled out the magazine she had found under the bed. She ran her finger down the list of contents till she came to the article she was looking for – Men Who Like Tools. Opposite the title was a large glossy photograph of a young woman perched on a cliffside. She had wavy black hair stuffed into a hard hat on her head, rock-climbing boots, unlaced, on her feet and in between, she wore nothing but a smile. She was clutching a rock hammer. 'Do you mean like this?'

Michael flushed scarlet. 'Where did you get that?'

'Doesn't matter,' she said, 'and I don't mind, it's perfectly healthy. In some ways.'

'Is it?' Michael couldn't imagine Aunty Bernadette dishing that up with his daily porridge and vitamin pill. 'What sort of ways?'

'Well,' Monica declared, 'as a geographical guide to the general layout, these pictures are fine. But as an aid to the harnessing, or even unleashing of the sort of hormonal surges you're struggling with . . .' she paused and looked at the picture very seriously, 'I'm afraid they're no use at all.'

Michael glanced at Miss April and her rock hammer despondently. He said nothing.

'No, and it's a shame. She has such a pretty face.' She shut the magazine and took his hand in hers. 'Don't settle for anything inadequate, pet. Women like that are only useful as washboards – and that's only if you can get them to stand still long enough to work up a lather on their ribs. They're laundry aids, pet, not love aids.' She caught hold of a wad of flesh. 'Here, this is what you want to look out for. Forget the basics, here are the bonus bits. Feel that – isn't it lovely and warm.'

Michael reached his hand out and laid it gingerly on her proffered flesh. From the glow in his cheeks it was obvious that both the warmth and the love-liness were appreciated. He looked at her shyly. 'Ummm, I didn't realise before. I used to think that the skinny ones were nice but I can see now . . .' and he had another little stroke of the bonus, 'it wouldn't be the same at all.'

★   ★   ★

Monica smiled at the memory. No, nothing would ever be the same. There she was, looking only for a bit of holiday entertainment and now her old heart was being stirred and shaken by an entirely unexpected kind of hero. Because he was heroic in his own way, young Michael, dedicated to his learning and focused on his goal. Bloody Lucy bloody O'Donnell. Having dedicated a full hour to him and the two of them exhausted with education he'd smiled and said as he got out of the car, 'Thanks Monica, I can't wait till tomorrow's lesson . . . and till I get to show all this to Lucy.' Oh well, at least she got to taste the fruit at its freshest, that was one consolation, though it didn't quite shake off the despondency that was gnawing away at her softly rounded edges. Tea was an upbeat affair. Imelda felt a little better and joined them for a nibble, Michael ate ravenously and Bernadette was on another planet, sitting at the end of the table sucking the ham out of her sandwich and rolling it in her mouth as if it was the most delicious thing she had ever savoured. Monica couldn't conjure up an appetite at all. She looked at her food and sighed crossly. This wouldn't do. Pining and fretting was not her style, nor was giving in without a fight. She looked across at Michael. Of course he was too young for her but that was a temporary setback: he'd be growing older and she was quite prepared to age him. The few spots would clear too and he'd fill out with a bit of decent feeding. Nothing there that couldn't change. But this dedication to Lucy – that was the sticking point. He had his heart set on the girl and Monica had to face the fact that Lucy was the real obstacle.

She pushed back her chair and excused herself from the table.

'Right, folks,' she said, 'if you'll excuse me, I have a few jobs to do in the village. Can I get anyone anything?'

Bernadette's eyes narrowed. 'Where in the village? You're not going visiting, are you?'

'No,' Monica almost didn't notice the suspicion in her voice. 'I'm just popping to the super-market . . .' her eyes twinkled suddenly, 'for a battery. One of mine has inexplicably gone flat.' She smiled at Bernadette. 'Can I get you one?'

'Certainly not!' Bernadette stiffened. 'I don't require batteries.'

Monica shrugged. 'No j-cloths even?'

Bernadette looked as if the ham, so recently delicious, was sticking in her throat. 'I don't need j-cloths,' she growled.

'Right so. I'll get you some Lucozade, Mel and for you . . .' she cast an affectionate eye at Michael, 'I think a little cream.' She winked at him. 'Might that be nice?'

Michael's face glowed so brightly you could use him in an ad for back-up generators. He nodded.

With a wave to them all, Monica left the room and grabbing her coat was out the front door before another word was spoken. She buttoned up as she walked. There was no time to lose. Supasave had late opening on a Thursday and if she wanted to get a good look at Lucy she'd have to hurry. It was a cold evening and she smiled at the frost already forming on the windscreen of Bernadette's car. It would be well cold in the morning and serve her right, the old rip – sabotaging Father Barry's car just to annoy her. She tightened the collar of her coat up around her neck. She wouldn't mind him pulling up right this minute to give her a lift. She quickened her pace and let the memory of him accompany her. The ruddy cheeks, short nose and those pouting lips – always smiling at her. And his little sticky-out ears. No oil painting but who needs oil paintings when you can be cosy instead. Before she knew it, she was at the main road and the lights of Supasave glowed invitingly in the distance. The walk had restored her appetite but set her fingers and toes off aching again and she knew what she'd do. She'd go in and get herself a nice cup of coffee and a bun and she'd sit there and have a good look at this Lucy person. She had only a vague impression of her from after Mass last Sunday, young, sulky looking – just right for Michael really. Well, she'd have a better look at her now and then that'd be all she'd need to get things right in her head. No use pining over what's not for you, she learned that with Sean. All she had to do now was have a good blast of reality and then she'd shrug off her blues and get on with life.

The smell of coffee and fresh bread met her at the door, lifting her spirits immediately. She pulled a magazine from the rack to use for cover and slid a tray onto the bars. Ummm, great selection of cakes, maybe she'd get two. She poured out a large mug of coffee and edged her tray towards the pay desk as she fumbled in her cleavage for her ten-euro note. She had just hauled it out and was flattening it when a young girl's voice asked, 'Can I help you, madam?'

It was Lucy.

For a minute Monica said nothing at all. So this was the famous Lucy O'Donnell. Monica gave her a quick once over – nothing remarkable – just an ordinary girl. She stood there holding out the warm ten-euro note while the girl waited, one hip stuck out in that bored pose so beloved of teenagers. Monica handed over the money and turned to find a table. As she moved away she felt a thin line of hair springing upright the length of her spine. Ordinary but vaguely familiar. Monica's flesh was tingling and she couldn't work out what was happening. Maybe she had Imelda's bug. She put her tray onto the middle of the table and sat down facing the pay desk, and pulled a couple of sugar sachets out of the container.

'Oi! You forgot your change!' Lucy held up some coins.

'That's all right, dear, I'll come and get them in a minute.' Already there was a short queue of weary shoppers forming and Monica didn't relish the thought of standing up the way she was feeling, fingers and toes aflame. She twisted the tops off the sachets with difficulty and poured the sugar into her coffee. As she stirred she watched the girl, disappointed. There was nothing remarkable about her. What on earth did Michael find so alluring? As far as Monica could see she was the same as every other teenage girl in the country – except for those who go away to school and have violin lessons on a Saturday. She was average height, skinny with a flat backside and pimples for breasts. Her face was unremarkable, pink cheeks, pert nose and a plaster on her eyebrow to hide the piercing. Her top was tight, had 'Urban Babe' written on the front in blue sequins and fell short of an oversized belly button with two vicious open rings pierced through its edges. She had no belly. Monica smirked as she sipped her lukewarm coffee – washboard. Tight around the hips (or where the hips would be if she had any), her jeans billowed out around the ankles and had more pockets than her portable possessions could ever warrant. They trailed on the floor leaving two shiny dusted paths behind her as she moved from cash register to microwave. Her hair was scraped into a tight ponytail that made her forehead look high and her head as if she was thinning slightly in front. A Ballyfermot facelift. As she moved her head, her ears sparkled from the row of multicoloured earrings that lined her protruding lobes, and culminated in a pair of huge loops.

Monica took a bite of her chocolate muffin. Well, at least she had nice hair. Although it was scraped back and had some streaks of blue, when she turned away you could see that the natural colour was a kind of reddish blonde, and curly. Monica liked curly hair. Michael had curly hair. When he bent down it curled over the top of his collar and she liked the way it curled around her finger when she stroked his neck . . .

She shook her head crossly and took another bite of her muffin. Mustn't think about Michael, that wasn't what she was here for. She was here to see Lucy.

Over by the till Lucy was arguing with a man about change.

'I gave you a twenty,' the man said.

'I've only got a ten here, so you can't have.' Lucy's voice had the edge of a whine in it. It reminded Monica of someone but she couldn't think whom. The man was insistent but Lucy stood her ground, her voice becoming more and more whiney till the manager came and sorted it out. He pulled the five from the till and handed it over. Lucy glared.

'Maybe you put it in underneath?' the manager suggested.

'I didn't.' Lucy shook her head crossly and Monica watched as the huge loop earrings swung from side to side.

The manager's voice hardened. 'As there's no one else waiting, why don't you take your break now, Miss O'Donnell?'

169

Lucy shrugged. She grabbed a Mars Bar from the display and a can of Cherry Cola from the fridge. 'Fine.' As she rounded the corner of the counter Monica winked at her sympathetically and Lucy stopped. She took the little pile of coins she had left beside the till and came over. 'Here,' she said, 'your change.'

'Thank you, pet.' Monica gestured to the empty chair opposite her. 'Why don't you sit here with me?'

Lucy looked as if she was about to refuse but Monica pushed out the chair with her foot. 'Go on,' she said. 'Then he can't have a go at you for not being nice to the customers. I'll tell him what a pleasant girl you are and that'll put him in his place. Imagine not backing you up – disgraceful.'

Lucy smiled gratefully. She sat down and leaned towards Monica.

'He's an old fart,' she whispered.

Monica smiled. 'They often are.'

'Yea.' Lucy pouted. Monica watched her. The hair was standing on the back of her neck now and she was feeling increasingly disturbed. Lucy seemed like a perfectly ordinary moody teenager: what was it about her that was so unsettling? As she ripped the top off the Mars Bar with her teeth Monica noticed that she had pretty lips, plump and pink. That was good. Michael had nice lips. Stop it, Monica, focus.

'Are you one of the ladies staying at the Teegans'?' Lucy asked.

Monica nodded.

'Are you relations or what?'

'What.' Monica smiled. 'We're actually here to see Father Hegarty and Mr Hegarty.'

Lucy giggled again. 'The old pouf.' She leaned forwards and lowered her voice. 'He's so gay, isn't he?' She puffed out her breastbone, rested one hand on her hip and let the other hang limp in the air. 'Old teapot.'

Monica nodded. 'Is it that obvious?'

Lucy took a bite of her bar. 'Everybody knows. He has a pink office even. My mum used to do cleaning for him but she had to stop because he's so fussy. She said he even used to dust before she got there!'

'I saw your mum with you after Mass. So she doesn't clean for Cormac any more.'

Lucy shook her head. 'Gave it up. She just does the hospital now but she used to do the church and the school and the priest's house years ago. Can I borrow your knife a minute?'

As she handed her the knife, Monica smiled at the thought of anyone invading Bernadette's territory. She'd get short shrift. She was still smiling as she watched Lucy prise the knife under the ring-pull of her can. For such a thin creature she had surprisingly chubby fingers. They were square and fleshy and Monica suddenly realised what it was that had struck her when she first came face to face with the girl. She had seen those fingers before – twice.

The first time was twenty years ago, covered in wiry red hairs, wrapped around the steering wheel of the Volvo. She rubbed a shaking hand on her belly, now trembling with dread. No wonder she seemed to suit Michael so well. No wonder he kept coming into her head.

The first time she saw those fingers they had Father Barry attached to them.

The second time, they had Michael.

CHAPTER 9

There is something wonderfully soothing about kitchens in the evening, Bernadette thought as she sat at the table doing embroidery and flicking through her *Woman's Weekly*. Imelda was weary and had gone to bed and Michael, though he had finished painting at four o'clock, had declared himself exhausted and was now snoring his head off on the sofa in the sitting-room. Still full of energy from her little chat with Cormac, Bernadette hadn't a notion of sleeping. She sat at the table running the conversation over and over in her head till her hands shook with the thrill of it all. All that talk of unsuitable influences and Michael needing a man when all he really meant to say was, *Bernadette*, or even *darling*, or even *Bernadette darling, will you marry me*? And she would – she would! She, Bernadette Marguerite Cecilia Teegan, would hitch her skirt and perch victorious on the threshold of Holy Matrimony to Tullabeg's most eligible bachelor! Every woman in the parish would be spitting with envy and though Bernadette was not one to gloat, she did relish the thought of the way she'd rest her hand on the pew on the way into Mass on a Sunday so that the light from the window might sparkle on her diamonds.

Or maybe she wouldn't have diamonds. She frowned. Maybe diamonds are passé? Maybe emeralds would be better, bring out the colour of her eyes – or is that too obvious? She noticed the skein of embroidery thread on the table – that's it! Amethyst, the colour of violets, that'd definitely be the best. Although it wouldn't do for folk to think that they were poor or anything and couldn't afford diamonds, and there were good quality emeralds that cost even more. Maybe she should cut her losses and have one of each, in a row. She rested her hands on the table and took a long deep breath. It was so stressful when you stopped to think about it. Honestly, people don't realise how much there is to do when there's a wedding to be planned. And of course, not having anyone to help it'd all fall to her, as usual. She picked up her needlework and smiled. Of course after-wards there'd be someone. She raised her eyes towards the ceiling affectionately. Imelda, her soul sister.

No sooner had the happy thought come into her head than the back door opened and Monica came crashing into the kitchen.

'You're still up – thank God!'

Bernadette looked at her. What now? Was she planning another tirade of vulgarity and obscenity to mar the peaceful evening? She certainly looked odd, pale but with two high spots of colour on her cheeks. She was shifting from foot to foot, obviously very uncomfortable. Bernadette wanted to ignore her but as usual her good breeding came to the fore. She stood up.

'Good evening Mrs Moran, you look cold. Did you get everything you wanted in the supermarket?'

'Everything and more,' Monica replied, dropping a bag onto the table and kicking off her shoes. 'Oh, my poor feet! Everyone in bed?'

Bernadette nodded.

'So it's just the two of us,' Monica said. 'Good, I was hoping to have a chat with you, in private.'

Bernadette got up and filled the kettle. She couldn't think what could possibly be good about a private chat with Monica Moran unless . . . she snapped off the tap and turned, glaring. 'You want to talk to me about Cormac, I suppose. Well, I think you'll find you're too late.'

Monica sat wearily. 'It's actually Michael I need to talk to you about.'

Michael – of course! She was going to tell her that as the car wasn't working the lessons would have to stop. Bernadette tried to hide her smile. She'd play this one like a pro. She'd understand perfectly that it was impossible to continue and insist that Monica didn't feel bad and say that no, she really didn't mind at all and she'd be so forgiving. She turned the switch on the kettle and sat down. 'Yes, my dear, what is it?'

Monica fiddled with the bag in front of her for

a minute then looked Bernadette in the eye and said, 'I know Michael is your son.'

Bernadette tutted. How could she not have noticed before that one of the leaves on the embroidery was the wrong shade entirely? She picked it up and held it out. 'Look at that,' she said, 'it must be the light in here but I've used the wrong colour! Isn't that a nuisance, now I'll have to unpick the whole thing.' She bent over her work and started to pull at the threads.

'Michael is your son.'

Bernadette smiled. 'I've looked after him since he was a baby.'

'No, that's not what I meant.' Monica shook her head. 'Michael is your son.'

The kettle had started to steam so Bernadette stood up. 'The kettle's boiled. Would you like a cup of tea? You look as if you could do with one.'

Monica actually looked quite annoyed. 'Miss Teegan, you haven't time for games. This is really quite serious.'

Bernadette scooped two spoons of leaves into the pot and stirred it. Then she took two cups and saucers out of the cupboard and was about to put them on the table when she stopped and looked at Monica. 'This isn't right, is it?'

Before Monica had a chance to reply, she put the saucers back into the cupboard.

'Not tea, you need something stronger.' She reached down to the cupboard below the sink and pulled out a half-empty bottle of Rémy Martin.

'Here you are.' She put one cup in front of Monica and one at her place and filled both. 'There! That should warm you up. Now,' she arranged the pleats of her skirt neatly under her bottom and sat down again. 'What was it you wanted to talk about?'

Monica took a slug of the brandy and shook herself like a wet dog. 'Ah, that's better.' She looked at Bernadette sitting, smiling at her from the other end of the table. 'I can see there's no point coming at it from that angle so we'll try the other. Michael, your . . .' Bernadette was watching her closely, 'anyway, Michael is in danger of getting himself into a potentially very nasty situation.'

Goodness! Bernadette was surprised. As far as she was concerned, Michael couldn't get himself from one day into the next without twenty-four hour supervision. 'What sort of situation?'

'He's in love.'

Bernadette laughed that tinkling, youthful laugh of hers. 'Oh, my dear. Is that all it is? It must be something in the air. In love! Michael as well, how lovely!'

Monica slapped her hand on the table. 'It's not lovely. He's in love with Lucy O'Donnell.'

Bernadette stopped laughing and thought about that for a minute. Lucy O'Donnell? That half-dressed, sequinned hussy with spray-on tops who worked at Supasave? Sure she wouldn't even have a decent dowry to bring with her, living as she did with only her mother and not a father in sight. She took another sip of her brandy. Still, it might be handy with her working in the supermarket. Bernadette had every intention of baking her own wedding cake and dried fruits cost a fortune. Maybe Lucy would be able to get her a reduction. 'The young will grow up,' she told Monica sagely. 'We can't stop it.'

Monica threw her hands in the air. She really was a volatile woman, not much self-control. 'We have to stop it.' She placed a hand on either side of the table and loomed over Bernadette. 'You have to stop it.'

And a double wedding might actually be cheaper. You'd only need the one delivery of flowers and if Cormac was having his suit made, maybe they could order an extra bit and run up one for Michael as well. He wouldn't take much fabric. 'Oh, I don't know,' she said aloud, 'I think it might be quite convenient really.'

'Convenient! For the love of God!' Monica thumped on the table. 'Do I have to spell every-thing out for you? Lucy O'Donnell is Michael's sister!'

Bernadette sat silent for a minute then she took a gulp of her brandy and snorted. 'And I suppose I'm her mother as well?'

'No . . .'

Bernadette could see Monica was trying to calm down. As well she might. It must be a full moon outside or something because the poor woman had lost the run of herself. She was fantasising.

'You're not her mother . . .'

Bernadette gave a sigh of relief. There was some sanity left anyway.

'She's Father Barry's daughter.'

Suddenly the steam from the kettle turned to ice in the air and Bernadette felt it hit her forehead like a million tiny shards. She stood up, furious. How dare she? How dare that nasty woman come into her kitchen and drink brandy out of her good cup and say such an evil thing. As if Father Barry (she blessed herself) would ever be involved in an immodest way with the likes of Kathleen O'Donnell – a cleaner!

'Oooh!' she said, too angry to find words. 'Oooh!' She stamped her foot. 'I won't let you say such a nasty thing, I won't!'

Monica shrugged. 'It's the truth.'

'It is not the truth,' Bernadette's fists were so tightly clenched that her nails were digging into her palms. 'I'll make you take that back.' Monica shook her head and Bernadette could feel her fury like bile rising in her throat. How could her lovely evening have gone so wrong? Then she remembered. Of course. She straightened her back and announced proudly. 'And if I don't make you take it back my fiancé will.'

Now it was Monica's turn to look shocked. Bernadette smiled triumphantly. 'There, that's put you in your place. You thought you could come in here and say terrible things and there'd only be me to hear you but I'm not alone.'

Monica's tone was incredulous. 'Your fiancé?'

Bernadette nodded. 'It's not official yet but yes, my fiancé, Mr Cormac Hegarty.'

Monica's chins wobbled in merriment as she threw her head back and hooted with laughter. 'Cormac Hegarty! Your fiancé is Cormac Hegarty. Don't be ridiculous, he can't be!'

Only the memory of Cormac as he knelt in front of her, his hands and eyes warm with affection – that and the price of brandy – stopped Bernadette from grabbing the bottle and smashing it over her mocking head. 'And why not?' she asked calmly.

Monica waited till her laughter subsided before she could answer. 'Bernadette, he's gay.'

Bernadette shrugged. Since when was cheerfulness a hindrance to marriage?

'He's a pouf.'

Bernadette bristled. He was not a pouffe. He was perhaps a little well padded but that was only because he was a gourmet and relished fine foods. 'I can slim him down,' she said, tossing her head jauntily.

Monica raised her eyes to heaven. Then she stood and, sticking out her elbow she rested one hand on her hip and held the other arm out, limp-wristed. 'Bernadette, listen to me,' she said. 'He's a teapot.'

Now it was Bernadette's turn to laugh – in relief. Just as she had suspected; the bloody woman was a lunatic! 'A teapot?'

Monica nodded. 'With handles and a spout.'

As gently as she could, Bernadette moved to the

180

other end of the table and took Monica's hand in hers. 'Monica,' she said. 'I don't know if you'll be able to understand this but I'll try anyway. Cormac isn't a teapot. Or anything like a teapot.' She shook her head very emphatically. 'He's so much more than that.' She sat upright and stared proudly ahead. 'He's an estate agent.'

Poor Bernadette did not sleep well. All night she tossed and turned as scenes from the past played themselves out before her eyes: Father Barry's anguish as he had another of his little turns in the car, and on the hillside and even on the sofa in the presbytery parlour; his face when he first saw Michael and his promise that he would always pray for them, both; and then the pain of his leaving Tullabeg, exhausted.

She woke with the pillow stuck to her face and her curlers askew from all the tossing and turning. Without switching on the lights she sat up and rolled wisps of hair around the little sponge tubes, cursing as she nipped her fingers when she fastened them again. Bloody Monica Bloody Moran, she muttered as a couple of rogue tears slid over her cheeks, threatening to melt the Pond's cold cream. No wonder the poor man had a heart attack and died at only seventy – and he in the prime of his life. All that strain and worry. Dammit! The curler snapped and she leaned out to put it on the bedside table. She'd just have to get up that bit earlier and have a go with curling tongs. As she clicked on the light she noticed the list she had carefully written up – 'Things to do before the BIG DAY!' She picked up her pen and, in her neatest handwriting, inserted a line at the very top. It said, 'Secure Position – talk to Father Sean.'

Father Sean looked surprised when she knocked on his door the following morning and then waited for him to open it. 'Miss Teegan! You usually walk straight in. How good of you to knock first.'

Bernadette ignored the faintly peevish tone. 'Good morning, Father. I hope I'm not disturbing you.' She glanced at the pile of paperwork on his desk and the pen held aloft in his hand.

'Actually . . .' He pointed at the papers.

'Oh good, because I wanted to have a little word with you.' She took a seat by the desk and tossed her head in a businesslike way. 'Well, sit down, why don't you, and take the weight off your feet.'

Father Sean's mouth was opening and closing and his colour was quite high really for so early in the morning.

'You look a bit stressed actually.'

'Miss Teegan, I –'

'But don't worry about that now. We have something important to discuss and I think it's going to put your mind very much at rest.'

Sean sighed deeply and sank into his chair. Without looking where it might land, he tossed his pen onto the desk and, pressing his fingertips together, rested his head on them, eyes closed.

Bernadette picked up the pen. 'Tut, tut, you'll be looking for that later.' She popped it into a holder and smiled at him flirtatiously. 'You Hegarty men do need looking after, don't you?'

He said nothing.

'Actually, that's what I came to talk to you about. Looking after the Hegarty men. I think the time has come for a few changes.'

Sean lifted his head and let both hands fall onto the desk. There was a strange brightness in his eyes. 'You're leaving? You can't be my house-keeper any more?' Even his voice sounded a little high-pitched.

Bernadette tinkled gaily then reached over and laid her hands on his. 'Don't you dare go upsetting yourself. I will never abandon you.' Under her palms she could feel his fists clench. He was very tense all right. 'Unless . . .' She sat back in her chair and straightened her skirt. 'Unless of course my husband has an objection to me working. Some men do.'

Sean didn't look as if he understood her at all.

'It seems old-fashioned, I know, but then he's an old-fashioned sort of man.' She smiled dreamily as the picture of Cormac, down on one knee, struggling to find the right words, flashed before her. 'I can just imagine how he'll want to be ringing me at all hours of the day, checking where I am and what's for dinner.' A shiver ran down her spine at the thought of it and she shut her eyes and savoured the sensation.

Sean's voice cut through her reveries. 'Miss Teegan, would you mind telling me what you're talking about?'

Bernadette kept her eyes shut for another little minute. This was it then. She was no fool and not blind to the fact that it was all-important that Sean approve her – their – plans to get married. Monica Moran was a childhood neighbour of the Hegartys and who knows what influence she might have on them. Bernadette knew only too well how influential she could be, she and her pneumatic cleavage. It had already ruined one good man and lured another (she shook her head at the memory of what she had seen through Cormac's front window last Sunday). If Cormac was to be saved the same fate as poor Father Barry, then the sooner he was safely married to her the better. She took a deep breath.

'I think I should marry your brother Cormac.'

The expression on Sean's face was hard to define.

'It's for his own good.' She cast around for a stronger foothold on the argument but her mind was in a jumble. What swings it for priests – respectability, purity?

Suddenly it came to her. 'Mass!' she announced, 'He hasn't been going to Mass.'

Sean leaned over the desk and spoke quietly. 'You intend to marry my brother because he hasn't been going to Mass?'

184

Bernadette tutted impatiently. 'It's not as simple as that. It's not *that* he hasn't been going, it's *why*.' She too leaned forward so that their faces were only a few inches apart. 'Between yourself and myself, Father, and with the greatest respect and affection, I don't think . . .' she cast a quick glance around the room, 'that he's altogether in a state of grace.'

Now Father Sean did look surprised. 'What do you mean by that?'

Bernadette shook her head very sagely. 'Dear Cormac, so well intentioned but he's, how can I put it, prone to temptations from unsuitable sources.'

Father Sean had the slapped expression of a stunned mullet. 'Goodness, Miss Teegan, you realised that?'

Bernadette nodded. 'Oh yes, I realised it for a long time and,' she wiped a tear from the corner of her eye with the handkerchief she had brought especially for the purpose, 'I'm afraid to say I witnessed it as well.'

'Oh dear. Oh dear, that isn't good at all.'

Bernadette folded the handkerchief back into her pocket. 'It was most distressing.' Even the memory of Cormac gazing longingly at Monica's décolletage from the comfort of his own sofa, while poor Bernadette was ruining her good shoes in the flowerbed, caused her insides to curl. 'And practically public too!'

Sean was looking increasingly upset.

'I mean, if I saw it, anyone could have walked by!'

'Indeed.'

Bernadette lowered her voice so that it became soft and soothing. 'He's not a bad man, he's a wonderful man. It isn't his fault that he has these urges. I'm sure that left to his own devices he'd never do a thing out of place but,' she whipped the handkerchief out again, 'I think he's lonely.' A little dab on both sides. 'I think he needs a companion, a suitable companion, to keep him on the straight and narrow.'

Sean was nodding by now.

'And having him so . . . exposed to temptation, as it were, in his present single state is really not a good idea. I mean he's fifty years old, unmarried, got time on his hands and nothing to stop him falling prey to whatever unsuitable type happens to come his way. He's so vulnerable, poor man what with his fondness for inappropriate types of people – and he the Parish Priest's brother! People might begin to talk!'

By now Sean looked positively incensed. 'You're right, Miss Teegan!' he said, banging his hand down on the table. 'You're absolutely right! He can't be carrying out unsuitable –'

'Unsavoury even.'

'Unsavoury relationships in public view in a place like this. Tullabeg is not the big city.'

'It certainly isn't!' Bernadette was nodding so furiously that all her careful curls were coming unsprung but what the hell, it was all in a good cause. She stood upright and stared proudly ahead. 'We must save him, Father. It's our duty.'

'Oh, Miss Teegan, you're so absolutely right.' He looked as if he wanted to take her hand but Bernadette knew that she must keep a firm grip on the situation. Naked emotion and gratitude tend to weaken – sully the professionalism. She watched from the corner of her eye as he slumped back in the chair. 'But will he agree to marry? I have spoken to him about it before.'

Now Bernadette was surprised. 'You did? You spoke to him about marrying me? What did he say?'

Sean's high colour came back. 'Well, he didn't commit to anything one way or the other really.'

Bernadette laughed. 'Of course he didn't! He wouldn't.' She flicked the handkerchief open and began to fan herself with it. 'He's so old fashioned, he wanted to ask me himself!'

'I'm not sure that . . .'

Bernadette pushed her now straightened curls off her face and smiled confidently. 'There's a lot you don't know Father,' she said, 'but know this. You and I both realise what road Cormac could go down if left unsuper – unprotected, don't we?'

Sean nodded.

'And we both know the best thing for him is to be safely, happily married to a respectable woman?'

Another nod.

'And we are both agreed who that suitable woman is?'

'Absolutely.' The voice was weak but the tone firm.

Bernadette straightened up. The image of Monica Moran was fading from her memory with every second that passed. 'So it's agreed then. I'll make the arrangements and you'll do the honours?'

Father Sean stood up and took her hand. He was not as soft as Cormac but it was nice all the same. 'Thank you,' he said huskily. 'You've taken such a load off my mind.'

Bernadette allowed herself a little squeeze before she let go his hands. 'It's my pleasure, Father. I am honoured to be able to help.' She turned and headed for the door. 'And I think we can all look forward to a long and happy future, Father.' She gave a little giggle. 'Brother!'

And she was gone.

'There's a person downstairs looking for you,' Gerald Grealy announced languidly from the stairs outside Cormac's office later that afternoon. 'She says it's urgent and you're to come down right this minute.'

If he was trying to hide the sneer in his voice he was doing a very bad job of it. Cormac prised himself out of the chair and peeped out the window. Don't tell me that mad Teegan woman has come back to haunt me, he thought to himself, but there was no sign of her car in the street outside. 'What sort of a woman?' He opened the door fully and ushered Gerald inside.

Gerald smirked. 'A woman sort of a woman.'

Not twitchy Teegan then. 'Oh, all right, send her on up.'

Gerald shook his head. 'Unlikely I'm afraid. I shouldn't think this one *does* stairs.' He turned on his heel. 'But I'll tell her anyway.'

'How kind of you.' Cormac felt the usual wave of resentment he experienced nowadays when talking to any of his staff. They were becoming arrogant boys, snide and lazy. He clasped his hands together and took a deep breath of the lilies on his desk. Aah, what he wouldn't give for youthful guilelessness – or even a guileless youth. Life was becoming so tedious. He returned to his desk and picked up his pen. Twenty-seven acres of soggy bog land, how could he make that sound saleable? 'Own a strip of Heaven – fertile, picturesque . . .'

'Give me a – seat for the – love of God!' Monica fell through the door gasping. 'What d'you need to – be up two flights of – stairs for!' She fell into the nearest chair, glaring at him reproachfully.

Cormac smiled. 'Ah, it's you! I'm usually downstairs but as I'm poorly at the minute I thought it best to take refuge in the inner sanctum. And it's not two flights, it's only one with a bend.'

'Suits you then! Phew, that's better!' She kicked off her shoes and he shuddered as he watched her hot feet steam into the coolness of his deep pile carpet. 'Nice up here. Did you decorate it?'

He nodded.

'Quite the little house-husband, aren't we?' Her colour was returning to normal and her eyes were twinkling in amusement. 'Though I'd not have put you down as husband material myself.'

'You'd be right there.'

'So, what changed your mind?'

Cormac stared at her, confused. 'About what?'

'Becoming a husband. I heard all about it.'

'More than I did – what are you on about? Or is it just that the altitude and effort has addled your remaining brain cells?'

'Oooh, aren't we waspish today?' Monica pulled her damp blouse free of her chest and let the air circulate. Even from the far side of the desk Cormac could smell the perfume. 'I heard you were hitching yourself to a cosy little family wagon.'

Cormac ignored her. She was probably about to launch into a lurid description of her lesson with Michael – one clutch after another – he didn't think he could bear it. He heaved a great sigh and looked at her disdainfully. 'Was there anything else?'

'So it's not true then? You're not about to become the lawfully wedded husband of Tullabeg's most desirable spinster?' When he didn't answer, her voice rose an octave and she thrilled, 'Miss Bernadette Teegan?'

Cormac looked at her crossly. She was such a goad. He opened his mouth to reply then shut it again. Well, he wasn't going to rise to it. She was obviously bored and this was her idea of sport, to go around aggravating people. He stretched out his hands slowly in front and admired the soft, padded fingers and carefully manicured nails. Pretending to consider them, he leaned his head from side to side then murmured quietly, 'Might be.'

It was worth such a preposterous lie to see the shock on Monica's face. She spluttered on her own spit – vile woman – and shot forward. 'You're joking! Ah, Jaysus, Cormac, tell me you're joking!'

'Not at all.' He flicked an imaginary speck from the cuff of his jacket and raised his eyebrows at her. 'Why would I joke about something as sacred as the blessed union?'

Monica looked seriously worried. 'But why would you marry her?'

'Why not?'

'You have nothing in common. For God's sake, she's a dried up, frigid old prune and you're . . .'

Cormac's left eyebrow rose a fraction higher.

'You're not exactly husband material.'

Cormac smirked. 'I don't know. I think we'd get along just fine.'

Monica snorted. 'Huh. I can see the two of you, sitting side by side in the kitchen, eating fresh scones and doing your embroidery. *Watch you don't get a crumb on that leaf now, Cormac dear.*'

Cormac refused to rise. He leaned his chair onto its back legs and rocked slowly back and forth, watching her all the while. She had stopped panting but the beads of sweat on her upper lip were becoming more obvious by the minute. He narrowed his eyes and waited, almost bored. Poor Monica. Gone were the days when she was quite a worthy sparring partner. Now she looked agitated and distracted. Something was bothering her. He rested the chair back onto the floor and spoke quietly. 'What was it you really wanted to talk to me about, Monica?'

It did the trick. No sooner was the last word out of his mouth than her eyes filled with tears and she turned to him, imploring. 'Oh Cormac, I'm so worried about Michael.'

That delicious tickling in the belt region. 'Michael?'

Monica swiped her nose with the cuff of her blouse and sniffed. 'He might be about to get himself into the most terrible pickle . . .'

Michael in a pickle, Michael in a stew, Michael in a large bowl of smoothest fluffiest cream . . . Cormac shook his head. 'You were saying?'

'She refuses to listen. I tried to tell her but she simply refuses to listen.' Her voice broke and she gave a loud gulp. 'Oh Cormac, it wouldn't be right – it'd be incest!'

He was completely lost by now. 'What d'you mean *incest?*'

Monica pursed her lips crossly. 'You know what incest means, in a family.' She shut her eyes, looking disgusted.

Cormac could hardly breathe. 'Michael? Committing incest?'

Monica shook her head, 'No, of course he isn't. But he wants to.'

'He does?'

'But he doesn't understand how wrong it'd be and she won't listen to a word from me. All she can think of is you, the new man in the family.' She sniffed loudly and turned to face him. 'So if you are the new man, *you'll* have to tell him, *Uncle* Cormac. Explain to him it's not on.' Her voice softened slightly. 'But let him down lightly, he's just a boy.'

Cormac felt as if he was on a fast track to somewhere but he hadn't a clue where. The conversation was racing along and he hadn't been able to keep up since the manicured finger-nail stage. He took a deep breath. 'Hold on a minute. What exactly do I have to tell Michael?'

She looked at him as if he was stupid. Huh. As if. Throwing her eyes up to Heaven she said, very slowly, 'You have to explain to the poor besotted boy that it is wrong, that it is improper, that it is bloody criminal to have sex with a member of your own family! He's so determined.' She seemed incensed. 'I tried to explain to her last night how unsuitable this obsession of his was but she refused to listen. All she could talk about was how she was going to marry you. She wasn't the least bit concerned about poor Michael!' She leaned forward and banged her hand on the table; there was an edge of hysteria creeping into her voice. 'She even, can you believe it, she even seemed to think it might be convenient! What a lunatic! Convenient! One little family all cosy together!'

Cormac's trundle into the great unknown suddenly jerked to a halt as the light at the end of his tunnel hit him, full force. Well, I never. 'Do you mean to tell me,' he said slowly, 'That Bernadette Teegan actually approves of the idea of a bit of . . . you know?'

Monica nodded. 'Can you believe it? Not that she actually approves outright, of course. More like she just refuses to see that it's not on. She just sipped her bloody brandy out of her bloody cup and prepared to turn a blind eye to the whole thing!' She squeezed her face as tightly as she could and mimicked Bernadette, 'My Cormac, my fiancé . . .'

Cormac teetered on the threshold of ecstatic delirium. One little cosy family. And Bernadette Teegan, with a blind eye and a notion that it might actually be convenient? What a woman. What a simply marvellous woman.

'And you actually want to marry her?'

Cormac was about to say, *don't be ridiculous*, but somehow the words never came out. As the full implication of what she had just said trickled into his brain and filled it up, all sorts of lovely possibilities swished and swirled in his head. How could he have misjudged Bernadette so? He could still see her generous little face as it cast around his office in mock search of a man to take her Michael in hand, as it were, and be his guide.

'Well,' Monica's voice demanded, 'do you? Do you really intend to marry the lunatic?'

The boy needs a man in his life, where will I find one, the boy needs a man in his life, where . . .

'Well, do you?'

Cormac opened his eyes, and then his mouth and the words that came out surprised even himself.

'Actually', they said, 'I rather think I do.'

CHAPTER 10

As she sat at the kitchen table cutting heart shapes out of lavender tissue paper, Bernadette let her mind waft gently over the events of the past week. Even thinking about the speed with which things had happened caused her breath to quicken and her woman's heart to flutter. She paused a minute till she felt calm again and scanned the article in the magazine she had bought on the way home from Father Sean's: The Stress-Free Way to Your Big Day. Preparation, preparation, preparation, that was the key. And Bernadette was nothing if not keyed in to what lay ahead of her. The start of the rest of her life – it was going to be perfect. And the only way to ensure that was to do it herself. She would personally select (at Supasave, at a discount) the ingredients for the cake, and when it cooled she would ice it. Fresh violets around the edges would represent her and a few thinly sliced Turkish delights cut in the shape of hearts for Cormac – subtle. She wondered about the wisdom of having tiers: too many and it would look ostentatious; too few and it would look mean. Balance was what was needed. Six would be just fine.

Then there were the flowers. She had considered the possibility of growing them herself but that small voice at the back of her head counselled against such a project. What if they had a spell of bad weather? Or a spell of unseasonably good weather that brought a drought? Would poor Cormac maybe see it as an omen and become stressed? She smiled to herself – such a sensitive man. No point in delaying things when he was obviously desperate to be the man in her life. 'I mean,' she said aloud to the empty kitchen, 'hasn't he been down on his knees to me that many times he'll do himself an injury?' The thought of it, poor Cormac, temporarily crippled and having to take to his bed, her bed, their bed, while she, Florence Nightingale herself, nursed him back to health. He'd probably even start calling her Florence as a pet name – not in front of other people mind, just between themselves. Or even Flo so that if anyone did overhear they might think it was short for flower. And only the two of them would know the truth and it'd be another little secret between them, another confidence. Bernadette shivered in delight, all those confidences, whispered in the dark of night between a married estate agent and his loving wife. The very thought of it warmed her heart so much that the tissue hearts stuck to her hands and she had to abandon the task for the moment. She could practise getting the shape perfect later.

She stood up and straightened her apron. That'd have to go too. No decent wife ever needed a full apron, that was for careless women prone to making messes. Bernadette opened the bottom drawer on her tall unit and took out material. As soon as she felt cool again she'd maybe run up a few pinnys, just short ones that she could tie around her waist area with a single pocket for things like secateurs which she might have occasion to carry in from the garden if she happened to cut a few roses to have on the table at tea-time – assuming Cormac was a rose man, of course – he might prefer sweet pea. Oh dear, so much to learn.

She was about to pour herself a fortifying glass of lemon barley water when she heard the front door open and voices in the hallway. By the sound of things Monica was holding forth about something and very irate. Bernadette smiled. Irate indeed, and well she might be. Consumed with jealousy more like! Bernadette was about to open the door and catch her in full flow when she had a better idea. Why spoil things when Monica obviously needed to get them off her chest – if you could call that vulgar expanse of unnecessary flesh a chest. No, it would be far better if she were left undisturbed. As quietly as she could, Bernadette opened the table drawer and swept her cuttings into it. Then she tiptoed to the large cupboard where she kept her brooms and ironing board and squeezed herself in neatly. She pulled the door behind her. And waited.

'Ah Mel, for the love of God, it's insanity.' A slice of Monica's voice slid in under the cupboard door. 'What would he be marrying her for? Sure they have nothing at all in common!'

'I'll admit it's a surprise,' Imelda's voice said, more softly, 'but isn't it wonderful! I mean all those years worrying about his . . .' her voice softened even more, and with one ear wedged against the ironing board Bernadette couldn't quite make out what she was saying, 'And now we don't have to worry any more!'

'Don't worry? Don't worry? Are you mad? If you were worried before you ought to be bloody frantic by now. She'll drive him crazy.'

'Now Monica, you're very hard. You know Bernadette is the loveliest person. She's kind and she's generous and she's just what Cormac needs. Someone to give him a bit of . . . well, let's be honest, respectability.'

Inside the cupboard Bernadette's eyebrows shot up as far as her confinement would allow. Respectability? Cormac? He was the most respectable man she knew.

'Respectability my arse!' Monica spat. 'Never mind the respectability. She'll have him in his grave before you could spell the word. I'm telling you, he'll wake up one morning soon when this temporary insanity has worn off and he'll realise what he's after doing and you know what'll happen then?'

There was a pause as Bernadette strained and fought the urge to burst out of the cupboard and sink her neatly clipped nails into the folds of that one's face. But she wouldn't. She would be a model of restraint. She tensed and waited.

'He'll have a bloody heart attack, that's what'll happen. A quick rush of blood to the head and he'll have a heart attack! She wouldn't know where to begin.' Monica's voice faded as the two women outside left the kitchen.

Inside the cupboard, Bernadette's knees turned to jelly and she clutched the ironing board to stop herself from fainting with the excitement of it all. Cormac, with a rush of blood to the head. What a notion! And maybe a flutter of the heart. And then his face would go all red and his breath would quicken and she, his devoted wife beside him having to scrabble and fouster around for his tablets and him saying, oh hurry, that's it, right there, good girl yourself . . . And that one thinking Bernadette wouldn't know where to begin?

She couldn't be more wrong.

Bernadette did not rush out of the cupboard as soon as Monica and Imelda left the room. Instead she stayed there, wedged quite comfortably against the ironing board till her heart slowed and her breathing relaxed and she felt it appropriate to

200

come out and make a nice cup of tea. She opened the door quietly and sliding one stiff leg forward, was just prising herself out when –

'Aunty Bernadette! What are you doing?' Michael was standing at the table.

'Oh Michael dear, I didn't see you there!' She flattened her creased apron and ruffled her curls.

He looked worried. 'Your face is very red . . .'

She put her hands to her cheeks. 'I'm fine, dear, really.'

'On one side only.'

Bernadette could feel the heat where her face had been pressed up to the ironing board. 'Honestly, Michael, have you not more important things to worry about. Why are you home so early?'

Michael pointed to the clock. 'It's past six. It's teatime. There's no food and you were hiding in the cupboard.'

Bernadette thought quickly. Time for her to apply some of her psychology – don't defend, distract. She picked up the tea towel from beside the sink and flicked it at him playfully. 'Honestly, you men, so impatient! How am I ever going to be able to keep up with two of you?'

Michael looked around him and his generally confused expression intensified. 'Aunty Bernadette, there's only me.'

Bernadette's smile was feminine and mysterious. She sidled to the table and opened the drawer. 'Look in here, Michael and tell me what you see.'

He didn't come forward but merely leaned nervously. 'There's em, some material with flowers and a lot of scraps of tissue paper.'

Bernadette brushed the material aside and took some of the tissue out. 'Here,' she said, 'look closer. It's not scraps, it's shapes.' She held one up close to his face. 'Heart shapes.' When he didn't appear any the wiser she laid the heart on her palm and stroked it gently. 'And you know what hearts are for – someone in this house is in love.'

Michael went from pink to puce.

'That's right, Michael, madly in love, passionately in love.' She reached over and stuck the heart onto his jumper. 'And when you're in love there's no point in sitting on your laurels, you have to go out and do something about it.'

Michael gulped furiously so that his goitre appeared to have a life of its own. 'How did you know?'

'Michael, Michael, Michael, how often do I have to tell you?' She grabbed a handful of the tissue hearts and threw them into the air. 'I'm a woman!' She twirled around so that her pleats all flattened and her curls bounced. 'A woman in love.'

The goitre paused, mid-gulp. 'You, Aunty Bernadette?'

She sat down and gestured him to sit beside her. 'I have something to tell you, dear, that affects us all.' Her expression changed and her face took on that look it had when she was praying or contemplating the burden that had been cast upon her in this life. 'It hasn't been easy, you know, just you and me, an orphan and a spi – single lady, cast together, all alone. But we've managed. Never asked for a thing from anyone. But,' her face brightened, 'virtue may be its own reward but that's not enough for us! We deserve more – much more. We deserve a family. You deserve a family.' She smiled at him sweetly. 'I mean, think of all that hard work you've been doing recently, painting at the presbytery all day and driving lessons all evening. Sure, you're exhausted you poor thing and you haven't even the comfort of your own bedroom to go to at night.'

Michael's face was awash with confusion. He didn't appear to be getting the point, 'I don't mind really, Aunty Bernadette. The sofa's fine.'

But Bernadette was adamant. 'No, it's not good enough.' She stood up. 'As soon as the tea is over, I'm going to tell Mrs Moran that she'll have to leave.'

Michael's face fell. 'Leave? But she can't!'

If she was surprised by the wail in his voice, Bernadette showed no sign of it. 'Oh, yes she can. There's no room for an extra body.'

'She's not an extra body! She's a great bo – person, em . . . who . . . em teaches driving. That's it – driving.' The boy looked positively hysterical. 'I need her here to teach me driving. How will I learn it if she's not here?'

Bernadette's smile was now triumphant. 'You'll still get your lessons, my dear.' She puffed out her rib cage. 'My husband will teach you. My husband, Cormac Hegarty.'

For a minute Michael said nothing. He just sat there looking at her as if he was trying to figure something out. He leaned his head from side to side but it didn't look as if the picture was becoming any clearer. Bernadette tucked a stray red curl behind his ear. 'We'll be a family, the three of us.' Out of the corner of her eye she caught sight of a Supasave flyer advertising late-night opening on Thursdays and remembered that Monica had wittered something about Michael fancying that assistant there. 'For the minute at least. You're growing up and no doubt you'll be finding a nice girl of your own soon and you'll want to move out and get your own place.' She straightened up and her tone became businesslike. 'Well, you won't have to be worrying about me then, will you? I mean, about leaving me all alone. Because I won't be. We'll be here together, Cormac and me. Just us and,' she reddened slightly, 'two spare bedrooms. You can always come and visit.'

Before Michael had a chance to say another word, there were voices on the stairs, and Imelda and Monica came into the kitchen. On seeing Bernadette, Imelda's arms flew out and she rushed to congratulate her. Michael sat at the table looking numb and Bernadette sneaked a glance over his shoulder at Monica in the doorway. She looked numb too. She looked smaller. Bernadette's smile widened. Monica was smaller, infinitely smaller and sadder. Just like Father Barry had looked after that rip spent the summer taunting and exhausting him all those years ago. And now he was avenged. And Bernadette had won.

Game, set and match to Miss Bernadette Teegan.

Or rather Mrs Bernadette Hegarty.

Michael didn't stay for the tea. For some reason Aunty Bernadette's news made him feel very strange. Obviously it was great and all. Mr Hegarty would be coming to live with them and would teach him to drive properly and maybe even give him a loan of his fancy car and he could drive around to Lucy's and pick her up in that and it would be great and he should be delighted – but he wasn't. Something inside of him had gone flat and where there should have been a load of looking forward there was nothing, nothing at all. He excused himself from the kitchen even though nobody noticed because Aunty Bernadette and Imelda were twittering and giggling like two girls in a bus queue on a Saturday night and Monica was still standing at the door. He didn't look at her. He couldn't. It didn't seem right somehow. He needed to be somewhere else, away from people, and her especially. Without him having to think about it at all, his legs took him out the front door, over to the garage and before he knew where he was, he was sitting in the driver's seat of Father Barry's old car, his hands wrapped around the steering wheel and the smooth leather cool beneath him. He shut his eyes and listened to his breathing, waiting to feel something that might let him know what he thought about all this.

A soft click of the passenger door told him that someone was getting into the car beside him but he didn't open his eyes. He didn't have to. There was a warmth and a smell that felt more like home than anything he could ever remember feeling before.

'Are you all right, pet?' Monica's voice was soft.

'I don't know.'

'She told you then?'

Michael opened his eyes but he didn't look at her. 'Aunty Bernadette's getting married.' He hoped he sounded pleased. You're supposed to be pleased about news like that. 'She says we'll be a family.'

'That you will, I suppose.' She took a deep breath. 'Mich . . .' she looked uncomfortable with what she was about to say.

'What?' To his surprise he did feel something. He felt angry, angry with her. He turned his face to her and glared. 'Go on, what is it?'

'About Lucy . . .'

Lucy? For a minute his brain wouldn't let him think who Lucy was. All he could see in his head was Miss April, perched on her cliff-face with a hard hat, huge boots and a rock hammer, calling to him. But he couldn't hear her. In his ears the only sound was Monica's laughter muffled by the folds of her warm flesh. He thought he might start to cry.

'I don't want to talk about Lucy.'

'I think we need to, pet. There's things I have to tell you.' She looked lost, vulnerable.

Michael took his hands off the steering wheel and tried to put his arm around her. Across the beautiful expanse of her flesh he could only reach to the back of her neck but what the hell, it felt nice anyway. 'Don't tell me anything. I don't want to think about Lucy or Miss April or Aunty Bernadette or anyone else now.' He took a deep breath. 'You have to go.'

She smiled sadly. 'I know.'

'I'll miss you.'

She leaned forward so that his hand reached further around and he could fondle one of her great dangly earrings as they spoke.

'And I'll miss you.'

Now he really was crying. Huge tears welled up and slid down his cheeks and he had an overwhelming urge to roll his bottom lip over and howl like a baby. He nearly did too, only Monica leaned the rest of the way and took his lip between her teeth and held it there.

'Doncryswdhart.' She mumbled.

'Budillmssyuu.' He tried to mumble back but all of a sudden the numbness had disappeared and all the confusion about what he was feeling disappeared with it. The hitherto cool leather seat of the car was aflame and his backside glowed with the heat of it. Miss April with her washboard ribs was tumbled off her mountain perch as Michael tumbled after her – right into the delicious mountain of woman that was Monica Moran. Fuelled by his ardour all the lessons she had taught him, all the little tips and techniques, slid into place and he slid along with them, up and over the peaks of her glorious breasts and into every nook and cranny of her flesh. The windows were steaming up and he didn't know if the car was sweating or he was. All he knew was that every bit of him felt wonderful and Monica was everywhere. The air was full of straining and rustling as she tried to wedge out of her skirt and prise him free of the steering wheel, clear of the horn that was blipping and hooting in time to their celebration.

'Up the airy mountain, down the rushy glen, We dare not go a-hunting for fear of little men . . .' she sang as she swung him aloft. 'Come here to me pet and let me get a hold of those ears.'

And Michael, who all his life was considered a bit slow on the uptake, discovered that he wasn't actually slow at all. He was great. He'd failed every Geography test he ever did, and earned snotty remarks for lack of stamina in PE but things had surely changed. The geographical features he had hold of now turned to putty in his hands and he had no trouble at all keeping going. Every lesson she had taught him had sunk in and now it was pouring out and he was getting everything right. And he wasn't going to worry that she was going away and he'd still have things to learn. The condensation on the windows had built up and was now flowing down the sides, gathering in excited little rivulets on the black rubber. Thicker and thicker the condensation gathered and faster and faster the little rivulets flowed. Any minute now they would all burst their banks and the car would be saturated.

They did. And it was.

The church in Tullabeg was large, gloomy and looking a little in need of some TLC, decoratively speaking. Monica felt it suited her exactly. Usually a bit of physical exertion left her feeling aglow with life and energy but this time it had the opposite effect. Where Michael, once he'd got his breath back last night, had leapt out of the car and insisted on a walk in the moonlight, Monica hadn't wanted to do anything at all. She went to the gate with him and watched as he ran whooping and hollering down the road and she felt empty. She went back into the house, got onto the bed and lay there, sleepless, till it was morning again. At seven she got up, slid her feet into her most comfortable kitten heels, a quick slug of mouthwash and was out the door, heading for the High Street. As she walked she began to notice a small crowd walking with her, mostly elderly with intense looks or younger with guilty ones and it wasn't until they turned in the gate of the church that she realised where they were headed – early Mass. She gave a quick shrug, well, why not.

Father Sean looked surprised to see her there, watching her nervously for the first half of the Mass and then with a concerned expression as it wore on and she just sat staring ahead. When it was finished the small crowd dispersed and there was quiet again save the sound of clicking and whispering as a few of the ladies got in a quick Rosary before breakfast. Monica sat and waited.

Eventually the sacristy door opened and Sean edged his way out and stood at the end of her pew.

'Ahem?'

She gave him the faintest smile. 'Morning, Father.'

'I don't often see you here.'

'No,' she said, 'not one of my usual haunts.'

He waited as if he expected her to say more then turned to leave. 'Well, good morning then.'

He was halfway down the aisle when she suddenly had the idea. She leapt up and followed him, cursing the loud tap-tapping that announced her movement and the way the sound of it seemed to be making him speed up. You'd think he was trying to get away or something.

'Hold up there!' she panted, catching his sleeve and doubling over to get her breath. 'I need – talk to you.'

Sean prised his shirt free of her grasp. 'Confessions are at eleven. Why don't we talk then?'

Monica straightened up, her eyes flashing with tears and temper. 'Sean Hegarty, the bloody nerve!' She poked him hard on the shoulder. 'And what makes you think I'd only talk to you if it was confession I needed?'

'I just assumed . . .'

'Well, you assumed wrong, you jumped up son of a county council bin man!'

'You leave my family out of it.'

Monica took a couple of deep breaths. 'That's precisely what I want to talk to you about, your family.' When his expression didn't change, she lowered her voice. 'Look, our families have been neighbours, and friends, for years . . .' She ignored the way his right eyebrow raised slightly as his lip curled. 'And I want to help now.'

Sean shrugged. 'I have no idea what you're talking about.'

Monica linked her arm through his. 'Right, back to your place. You can cook me a bite of breakfast and I'll tell you all about it.'

She couldn't help herself, she really couldn't. If Sean's house had been any nearer to the town they could have walked and she would have been able to tell him the whole story and he would have understood her dilemma and talked to Cormac and Michael and that would have been it. But it wasn't. A mile and a half was too long a walk at eight-thirty in the morning for a busy priest and a woman with shoes designed for looking at. Either because he was embarrassed to be seen linking her up the main street or – more likely she considered, because it brought back memories of days long gone that were bringing uncomfortable stirrings – Sean bustled her into his car. He muttered something about having a few last-minute jobs to do and told her to wait. Monica didn't mind. She felt relaxed. All the anxiety was easing away with the knowledge that as soon as she told Sean about Michael and Lucy, he would take control and everything would be okay. Sean would take control. She slipped her shoes off, lay back and shut her eyes. That was a nice thought. Sean taking control. From the comfortable fabric seats a warmth spread around her. Sean in control. She gave a great sigh. How she used to dream about that when she was a girl. Of all the Hegarty brothers he was the strong silent one, the one she most had her eye on. When he didn't seem willing she'd gone through the others. Fergus was fine but then his father had forbidden her from cheering him on in football matches because her appearance on the sideline was a distraction, old crab – just because she didn't feel the cold! Dermot was keen but with a face more prone to eruption than Mount Vesuvius, he wasn't worth the risk in the dark. And Cormac? She'd had her suspicions about him all along. There they were, in the back row of the pictures and the film nearly over and still he hadn't made his move. In frustration she took the last Rowntrees éclair out of the packet and slowly and sensually sucked the chocolate out of it. Then she leaned over and before he knew what she was up to, slid the warm toffee into his mouth. *Do you want to know*, she whispered silkily, *where the rest of it has gone?*

'I do not,' he declared, rising huffily out of the seat. 'You're after eating the best bit and now I'll have to buy another packet!'

And then there was only Sean left. She made a point of bumping into him on every possible occasion, standing beside him, leaning against him, falling on top of him but he never gave in. He'd go red, mutter about remembering something he had to do and fly off leaving her destitute. She was feeling a little destitute now really. Cormac, for all that he thought sofas were only for sitting on, was getting married; Michael was rhymed and primed and ready for action – with Lucy washboard O'Donnell; and she was all alone, destined for eviction. She felt a little lonely. It wasn't nice being a hungry widow. She shut her eyes to stop the tears. Nothing more she could do. When Sean got back she'd tell him everything and he would sort it all out. Good old Sean, Mr Fix-it – Mr Capable – a sort of a hero, her hero, and as she sank deeper and deeper into her reveries the image of Sean as hero transformed in her mind along all sorts of wondrous paths. By the time the car door opened and he climbed into his seat she was deep in sleep and the kind of dreams you'd be confessing for a month if you felt guilty enough. Monica didn't feel guilty at all. As the car pulled up to the junction at the main road she opened her eyes lazily and peeped through her lashes. All she could see were strong hands on the steering wheel and black serge trousers. She reached out and laid her hand on the knee.

'Heroes,' she mumbled sleepily, 'wear their underpants on the outside.'

The car ground to a halt and, unbelted, Monica nearly shot through the windscreen.

'Get out.'

She was suddenly awake. She held onto the dashboard for support and looked around. 'Wha –?'

'I said, get out.'

'But,' events of the last few seconds flashed in her mind and she realised what had happened. She smiled. 'Oh sorry, pet, I must have fallen asleep, I was dreaming.'

His voice was cold. 'And I was having a nightmare. Please get out.'

Monica gestured helplessly. 'But it was a mistake. I really need to talk to you. It's important. It won't take a minute.'

He has started to drum his fingers on the steering wheel. 'Summarise.' The drumming intensified.

Monica's mind was in a whirl. Where should she start? Cormac was only marrying Bernadette to get close to Michael who was in love with

Lucy O'Donnell who was really his sister . . . Father Barry! Of course! That's where it all started, Father Barry. She took a deep breath. 'Well, you see, Father Barry had two children by two different mothers and now –'

'GET OUT!'

The passenger door was open and Monica was unceremoniously being pushed out onto the pavement. Drivers in the cars behind who had started to hoot at the delay looked on in amazement as a large, blonde woman, her mascara streaked, flew out of Father Sean's car onto the roadside. A pair of pink kitten heels with silver buckles on the front followed and then the car drove off, smoke billowing from the exhaust.

Rolling onto her side and easing herself upright slowly, Monica got to her feet. 'Damn, damn, damn!' Why could he not have had the patience to listen to the whole story? Typical bloody man – react straightaway and then it's over before you've got to the best bit – well! As she brushed herself down she noticed the amazed stares from the queue of cars that had formed. They looked as if they didn't know what to think. For a split second Monica's eyes twinkled. Maybe she should remedy that. Pretending she hadn't noticed them she peeled her skirt up to her waist, and with great precision hauled her knickers comfortably over her stomachs. Then she rolled her skirt down again, slipped her feet into her shoes and stepping out into the middle of the road, started to walk back towards the town. As she walked she whistled to herself. She hadn't managed to tell Sean what was really important and she wasn't going to be able to save the day but what the heck, she'd done her best.

It was time to go home.

CHAPTER 11

All the way back to Teegan's, Monica was in agony. Her head was throbbing, her knees were aching and below them, she had lost all feeling. But she didn't stop walking. It wasn't till she reached Bernadette's front door that she gave in. Clutching the handle for support, she raised a swollen foot and tried to prise her shoes off. It took a while. They were wedged firmly and when they finally came away the pain was excruciating. What had once been five toes was now a single growth – mangled, livid and steaming. Gritting her teeth, she eased the foot back onto the cool concrete of the step and released the other one. It was no better. In disgust, she dropped the shoes and prodded the doorbell. Imelda answered.

'Mon! Where have you been? We were worried about you!'

From the kitchen Bernadette's voice trilled. 'Is that the doorbell? Who is it, dear?'

Imelda slid her hand under Monica's elbow and, struggling under the weight, helped her into the house. Monica could only make it to the bottom of the stairs where she collapsed, panting. The pain in her head was worse and she was so hot. She felt Imelda's hand on her forehead.

'Oh goodness, she's boiling up!'

Bernadette came out of the kitchen. She peered into Monica's face.

'What should we do?' Imelda's voice was full of concern. 'I do hope she hasn't picked up what I had.'

Bernadette shook her head, 'I shouldn't think so.'

'Because that had me laid up for a full week.'

Bernadette bolted upright. 'A week? She might have to go to bed for a week?' She looked up the stairs and then at Imelda. 'Oh dear – here? That wouldn't do at all.' Then she reddened slightly, 'I mean, with all the activity here and her not feeling well and needing quiet. It wouldn't be fair.'

'Don't worry yourself,' Monica's voice was weak. 'You just check the bus times for me. I think the best thing is if I go home.'

Imelda nodded. 'Yes, maybe you're right. Bernadette has been so kind putting us up and she has so much to do now what with the wedding and all.' She smiled fondly at Bernadette. 'We'll pack up and let you get on with it in peace.' She reached over to Monica to help her up. 'Come on dear, you go in the sitting-room and I'll get you a basin of water for your poor sore toes. Honestly, the state of them – what were you thinking of?'

'But, I didn't mean –' Bernadette started to say something but then pursed her lips.

Through her pain Monica could feel all sorts of under-currents but she hadn't the energy to pursue them. All she wanted was cool water, two aspirin and sleep, blissful sleep.

When Michael woke later he didn't know what was happening. The sofa made an uncomfortable bed and usually he was awake early but what with the lovely time he'd had last night, in the garage and then out in the fields, leaping hurdles over fences till he was exhausted, he had fallen into the deepest sleep. He was sure he'd shut the curtains when he got in but now they were open and the light was shining strongly on the coffee table. It must be late. Who cares? That was a lovely dream and he wasn't finished with it yet. He pulled the duvet over his face and as he did, a strange smell filtered across from the other side of the room and slid under the sheet with him. It was like cheese, strong cheese and salt. And there was a noise, a rhythmic noise. One minute it was quiet and then a smooth rushing of air that built up till his ears were full of it. As soon as it reached a crescendo it broke into sound-bites that plopped and softened till it was quiet again. He sat up and turned to its source.

The sight that greeted him made the sleep fall from his eyes and his heart lift. In the armchair by the fire Monica was fast asleep, her head thrown back and her feet slopping gently in a basin of water. Her hair was ruffled and beneath her eyelashes last night's mascara swept down to almost the top of her cheeks. She had lost one earring. Michael smiled as the vibration of her snoring made all the little beads on the other earring quiver as she exhaled. A thrill fluttered along his spine in response. Even in slumber she was bloody magnificent! He nestled back into the duvet and propping his chin on the armrest, lay watching her. He was so engrossed he didn't notice the door open.

'Psst! Michael! Are you awake? Get up now!' Aunty Bernadette's face peeped around. She looked agitated. 'C'mon. Get out of there now.'

He hauled himself out and grabbed his sweat-shirt off the floor. Bernadette glared at him. 'You don't mean to tell me you slept with your clothes on – that's disgusting. What on earth have you been up to?'

Michael glanced over to Monica's sleeping face and back to Bernadette's angry one. He was about to say, 'nothing' sheepishly as he usually did but when he opened his mouth to answer, the breathy rumble of her snore stopped him. He drew himself up to his full height and smiled. 'Aunty Bernadette, I couldn't possibly say.'

Bernadette started at his tone. What had got into the boy? A couple of weeks ago he was a gorm-less, apologetic loon and now he was acting as if he wasn't scared of anyone. He had a cocky atti-tude and a smirk that she didn't like – she didn't like it at all. She stepped further into the room to give him a rectifying clip on the ear, but as she raised her hand, she stopped and wrinkled her nose. What was that smell? As if in answer, Monica gave a loud snort and opened her eyes. They were bloodshot.

'Ow!' she said.

Michael and Bernadette turned to her.

'What happened? Was I run over?' She laid her hand on her knee and winced. 'Ouch!'

At the sound, Imelda came running in. She felt Monica's brow again and gasped. 'She's still roasting. And I gave her two aspirin.' She leaned in close to Monica. 'Is it your feet, Mon? Is that what's sore?'

'Nooo!' Monica's face was contorted. 'It's everything. It's my joints everywhere – elbows, knees and my toes! And my big toe especially. Ouch!'

While Michael and Imelda looked from one to the other in panic, Bernadette said nothing. She was listening and remembering. She'd heard those complaints before. Sore joints, big toes – she knew all about that. Poor Father Barry had suffered from those on occasion, usually after Christmas, or Easter, or his birthday, or anyone else's birthday when he'd joined them for the celebration and had too much spicy food washed down with good port. She threw a quick glance at the empty decanter on the sideboard and nodded to herself. And the temperature. And the aspirin making it worse, not better. Bernadette knew exactly what was wrong – the bloody woman had gout! This was not turning out well at all.

'Ow – don't just stand there, will you? I'm dying for God's sake! Do something.'

Don't tempt me, Bernadette thought.

Imelda wrung her hands. 'What do you think, Bernadette dear, should we call the doctor?' Another moan from Monica. 'Or should we call for an ambulance?'

A light went on in Bernadette's head. Of course! She shook her head. 'No, not the doctor.' He might guess straightaway, give her medication and leave her here to recover. 'Nor the ambulance.' Same thing. Bernadette needed to be rid of her; she needed to play for time. 'I think,' she said, looking from one to the other, 'I think she is too ill for any of that.' She leaned her head to one side in sympathy at the others' shocked faces. 'What we need to do is to get her into the car and take her straight to the hospital ourselves. In fact,' she smiled her sweetest, most beatific smile, 'why don't you two find some clothes and a nice pair of slippers for her and open the car door? I'll take her myself.'

'We'll come with you.' Imelda said. Michael nodded furiously but Bernadette held up her hand.

'No, she said, 'there won't be room. We'll need to have the seats right back to give the poor dear space.' She turned the smile on Monica, 'we wouldn't want her squashed and uncomfortable, would we?'

The nodding turned to head shaking and after

a last, concerned look at the patient, the pair left the room. Bernadette knelt at Monica's feet. 'Oh dear,' she said, her nose curling, 'it looks painful.' She got up and went over to the sideboard. 'What about a nice glass of port to give you strength?' She took out a fresh bottle and poured a generous helping into a tumbler. 'Here, drink that straight up and we'll be off. Imelda can put a few of your things together while Michael gets you to the car. I'll bring it round.' She handed the glass over. 'Should I drop another aspirin in it as well?'

When Monica nodded, Bernadette smiled and headed for the kitchen. In the hallway Imelda was dragging a case downstairs and she stopped when she saw Bernadette.

'Bernadette Teegan, you are an absolute Florence Nightingale, that's what you are. You know exactly what to do.'

Bernadette lowered her eyes humbly. 'I wouldn't be able to cope without you here to help me though.' And then went into the kitchen.

And as she popped the aspirin out of the packet, Bernadette bit her lips to keep from laughing out loud. Imelda was so right. Bernadette did know what to do. And she knew what not to do. Like giving port and aspirin to someone with gout – if you wanted to make them better. But of course if you wanted to make them worse, maybe bad enough to have to stay in the hospital, they were just the thing.

★　　★　　★

Poor Michael didn't think he had ever felt so confused in all his life. He knew he was madly in love with Lucy O'Donnell. He had been in love with her since she and her mother sat in front of them at the pantomime five years ago and when she sat down, he could see the top of her Pocahontas knickers poking out over the low waist-band of her jeans. And then when she started to wear a bra and tight tops and you could see the bulges in it – where the adjustable bits were on the straps and the little fastener bits at the back – it was as much as he could do to keep his eyes on the stage.

That was when he decided to grow his fringe. He could look out from under it if he kept his head down and nobody would know. Unfortunately, his forehead was high and when the hair came to halfway down it just swept into a big curl that stuck out in the front and looked more like a sun visor than a fashion statement. Aunty Bernadette nagged and nagged and when he refused to get it cut, preferring to gel it down, she waited till he was asleep and cut it off anyway. He woke up and there it was on his bedside table, tied with an elastic band and a note on lavender paper saying, 'I told you so.' After that it wasn't worth the risk trying again.

Then Lucy got a part-time job in Supasave. Suddenly he was Aunty Bernadette's best boy, offering to do messages every day, though she got mad when he was always forgetting things and having to go back, sometimes two or three times. But Lucy was there and when she put the change into his hands and his fingers involuntarily closed around hers and he forgot to let go for a minute, she didn't look at him as if he was a weirdo. She just kept on fiddling with the till roll and didn't even seem to notice. She was so cool. She moved into his head and lived there, even when he was asleep – especially when he was asleep really. And when he couldn't sleep and he had to look at his magazines for a while it was her face he could see on all those women . . .

So what was wrong with him now? With Aunty Bernadette and Imelda out of the house he was lying comfortably on his own bed, with his own magazines for company, scanning page after page to see if he could see Lucy – but he couldn't. All the old favourites failed him. When he looked at the girl with the French maid's uniform leaning over the table, all he could think of was that there was probably a plate of Battenberg cake on the far side and she was reaching for it. The model wearing only a smile and impossibly high heels did nothing for him either. He wanted to ring the magazine and get them to warn her not to walk too far in them. The mess pointy toes can make of your feet . . . and as for Miss April? The more he peered under her hard hat to conjure up Lucy's face, the more the picture seemed to take on a life of its own. Miss April seemed to be clinging to the rock face for

225

dear life and as he stared, her usual confident expression hardened.

'Michael,' she said, 'what's the matter with you? Don't you love me any more?' Of course he did.

'*Then why aren't you pleased to see me?*' She edged forward on the rock face and thrust her chest towards him. He could see her ribs.

'I am always pleased to see you!' She had really sticky-out ribs. 'I'm always . . .' But he couldn't continue. From the corner of his eye he could see hordes of washerwomen come trooping round the side of the mountain, soapy buckets at the ready to do a great pile of laundry.

Michael sighed and stuffed the magazines into the pocket of his jacket – what was the point? Lucy wasn't in any of them. She wasn't anywhere. The only thing that was firm in his head was the warmth of his bed that had been Monica's for the last week and the smell of her perfume that was on the pillow. He turned and buried his face in the comfort of it. Oh, Monica, Monica, where are you now?

Actually, he knew exactly where she was. She'd been quite lucid at first but after Aunty Bernadette administered her medication, she seemed to get very confused. It was impossible to lift her out of the chair and anyway, the pain in her legs meant that she couldn't stand. They'd had to shift her quickly onto a kitchen chair and then carry her in it out to Bernadette's car. All the time she was very brave. Even when they dropped her twice, she laughed and sang songs and waved her arms from side to side. Imelda said that the poor thing must be delirious. Then they slid her into the passenger seat and she looked like she might fall asleep but when Imelda ran inside to get the bags, Aunty Bernadette accidentally shut the car door on her toe and that woke her up. What a noise! Imelda ran out and insisted on going too, for support, and popped in behind Bernadette and then they set off – Monica howling in pain, Imelda looking concerned and Aunty Bernadette remarkably calm. She was good in emergencies. But not as good as Monica. Michael settled more comfortably into the pillow. The smell of her hairspray was hypnotic. He yawned. Monica was great. Monica was lovely. He felt ever so sleepy. Monica was dreamily, gorgeously . . .

The sound of a car on the gravel woke him up and Michael leapt off the bed. He was halfway down the stairs when the front door opened.

'Michael! Why are you still here? Why aren't you over at Father Sean's, painting?'

'I was worried' he said.

Bernadette scowled.

'I mean, I just wanted to know how Mo-Mrs Moran is.'

Bernadette paused before speaking. There was a mixture of expressions jostling for position on her face. She turned to Imelda. 'He wants to know how dear Monica is, Imelda.'

Imelda lowered her head. 'It's not good news I'm afraid. Her poor toes are in a terrible state, squashed, bruised and one of them is even broken! The doctor was convinced there was more as well, even insisted she had been drinking. At eleven o'clock in the morning, I ask you!'

Bernadette shook her head sympathetically. 'Terrible, really terrible. They've decided to keep her in for investigation. She could be there for days.'

Michael brightened. 'Then she'll be staying in Tullabeg? And coming back here to convalesce?'

Bernadette's expression hardened. 'I don't think that will be necessary but of course,' she cast a quick glance at Imelda, 'we'll do all we can to make her comfortable. Cup of tea?'

Imelda smiled. 'Thank you, dear.'

Michael looked from one to the other. What were they thinking of? Poor Monica was ill in the hospital and they were having cups of tea. He jumped off the bottom step and blocked Bernadette's way to the kitchen. 'But what about Monica? Who's going to make *her* a cup of tea?'

Bernadette tutted crossly and pushed him aside. 'For goodness sake, Michael, she's in the local hospital and she's perfectly fine. She has sore feet from walking too far in silly shoes; indigestion from dri – from following a poor diet; and that's it.'

'And a broken toe.' Imelda offered. 'Can't think how she got that.'

Bernadette's face looked pink in the dim light

228

of the hallway. She fumbled and fiddled with the knot of her headscarf and muttered something about it being a mystery all right.

'Maybe that was when you shu –'

'Michael! Have you no work to do? Get to it now before I clip your ear!'

Michael glared before shifting aside. He was fed up with the way she spoke to him. He wasn't a child any more. He was a man and he wasn't going to put up with it for much longer. He pulled his jacket off the hook and picked up his overalls where she had left them neatly ironed and folded by the front door, which he opened with a dramatic flourish. 'I'm going, I'm going.' Then he turned. 'But I'll be back.' He slammed the front door behind him and was halfway down the path before he remembered. The two ladies were still standing in the hallway when he pushed the door open. 'Em, Aunty Bernadette? Could I have a lift, please?'

Oh for goodness sake! Cormac picked up the carton and read the description on the side. Cream of mushroom soup. Cream that is soft on the tongue and smooth all the way down. It certainly claimed to be cream of mushroom but – he gave another swirl of the spoon – there were definitely lumps in this. Leaning over the saucepan, he trapped the suspect particles against the back of his wooden spoon and tried to press them flat.

Suddenly the doorbell rang and, keen to get

back to his particle pressing before the temperature rose too high and the delicate flavour was
ruined, he rushed to open it without turning on
the outside light first. Mistake. On his doorstep,
silhouetted against the street lamp, her hair a halo
of impossible curls, Bernadette Teegan stood
poised for flight.

'Oh Cormac, is that you?' she said, sounding
mildly surprised to see him there.

Cormac could smell the soup. It smelt hotter.
With one hand he pointed to the kitchen and with
the other, ushered her into the hallway. 'Why don't
you come in?'

Bernadette cast a quick glance up the street.
'You're quite right. Whatever would people think,
me turning up on your doorstep after dark!' She
gave a little giggle and jumped onto the doormat.
'Shall I shut it straight away?'

Cormac was already in the kitchen. The lumps
were still there, taunting him from the surface of
his soup. The Teegan woman had followed him
and was standing at the door, sighing expectantly.
He toyed with the idea of asking her to leave and
come back later but then maybe she would, so he
gave a last exasperated look at his supper and
turned the dial. The gas flame rose and died.

'Is that your tea?'

'It was.' He knew he sounded petulant but mushroom was his favourite and Supasave didn't always
have it. He'd been looking forward to that.

Bernadette flung her bag on a chair and pulled

her coat off. 'Cormac Hegarty, I simply won't stand for it! Do you mean to say that you're going to delay sitting down to your tea just because you have a vi . . . because I'm here?' She rested her hands where her hips ought to be and stared at him challengingly. Then she went over to the cooker and peeped in at the soup. She picked up the carton, examined the back of the wooden spoon and turned to look at him. 'And it was lumpy.' She pulled open a drawer and took out a sieve. 'Do you have another saucepan?'

Without a word, Cormac took a saucepan out of the press and handed it to her. Then he marvelled. With painstaking patience, she dribbled the soup from one pan to the other, all the while trapping and smoothing the lumps in the sieve. When it was all through, she poured it into a large bowl and set it on the table.

'There you are,' she said, her voice as smooth and soothing as the carton had promised, 'eat it all up while it's nice and hot. I'll wait in the front room for you.' She pulled a *Woman's Weekly* out of her bag. 'I'll just be reading this, it has lovely recipes.' She had a quick glance through the pages. 'You don't happen to like cheesy muffins, do you?'

'I love cheesy muffins!'

She winked, 'They're in here.' And with her bag and coat still hanging on the back of the chair, she left him to eat his soup in peace.

Well! As he ate, Cormac marvelled at this turn of

events. Whoever would have thought it? Neurotic, fidgety, giggly Bernadette Teegan turning up like that and sorting out his supper? And she had done a great job of the soup. Still, he shifted uncomfortably on the chair; he'd have to have a serious talk with her. This marriage thing had gone too far. And through no fault of his really, he'd only been in the same room when she proposed to herself and wasn't even fully aware of the point at which she'd accepted! Still, he'd had some fun out of it. He smiled at the memory of Monica's face when he said he was actually getting married. What a shock! What a hoot!

'What are you smiling at?' cream of Bernadette's voice slid across the kitchen floor towards him. She was leaning against the door frame, gazing.

Cormac put down his spoon. 'Actually,' he said, wiping the corners of his mouth with his hand-kerchief, 'I was just thinking about Monica Moran.'

The temperature in the kitchen dropped at least ten degrees. 'And would you mind telling me why you'd be doing a thing like that?' Her tone was gentle but her look could slice fresh bread.

The scene with Monica flashed before Cormac's eyes and he tried to think of a way to relate it to Bernadette. It wasn't going to be easy. He decided to play for time. 'She came to see me,' he said simply.

'Did she now.'

'Em . . . yes.' There was something in Bernadette's

demeanour that was more than a little worrying. The curls on her head seemed to have tightened and were coiled about her ears ready to spring at the first opportunity. He had the craziest notion that they might be armed. 'She called in to my office . . . yesterday . . . just a social call.'

'Um.' She had started to twist one of the pleats in her skirt and even as he watched, it was riding up her leg, threatening to reveal more than he needed to see when he was still at supper. He was beginning to feel very uneasy. 'She wanted . . . I think she wanted to . . . em,' inspiration dawned, 'to congratulate me – I mean us.' The twisting stopped and the side of her skirt slowly lowered to knee length. 'She wanted to congratulate me on my, our engagement.'

Bernadette's whole body uncoiled as a strange expression washed over her face. 'And did she say she was pleased?'

'Delighted!' Cormac tried to smile but it froze on his lips – Bernadette didn't look convinced at all. He waited to see if her expression might change but when it didn't he shook his head. 'No, that's not true. Actually she was very put out.' He beckoned Bernadette to sit. 'She was quite agitated and keen for me to talk to you about Michael.'

Bernadette reddened and started to fidget.

'He's my nephew.'

Cormac nodded – did she think he was an eejit or what? 'I know who he is. I know plenty about

233

him. Monica just wanted to say that when we, I mean after the . . . afterwards, I'll be his, well, you know, related to him . . .'

Bernadette nodded.

'I couldn't make sense of it really. Apparently she doesn't think it's appropriate for me and him to have a rela . . . em, be too close.' He stopped. How could he ever explain? Monica was certain that Bernadette approved of his ambitions towards Michael but Monica didn't know everything.

'Monica Moran doesn't know everything.' Bernadette's lips were tight.

He was right. Dammit.

'But as ever, she's completely misguided.' Bernadette leaned over the table. 'Michael's been far too much under her influence lately. Really, he's become quite above himself. But all he needs, all Michael ever needs is a strong guiding hand.' She rested her hand on his. 'A strong *man's* guiding hand.'

Oh sweet merciful heavens above! Cormac's heart did a double somersault and dived straight into the soup bowl. So it was true! Could she really mean it?

'A man like you.'

She did! She did! It was almost too much to hope for. He could hardly force the words out. 'But she said it wasn't right, within the family and all.'

Bernadette's expression was stony. 'Nothing that happens within the confines of our family concerns that awful woman, nothing at all.' Her eyes filled with the sweetest tears. 'Because we will be a family, you, me and Michael, won't we Cormac?'

In a rush of gratitude, anticipation and even the smallest hint of affection, Cormac covered her hand. 'Oh yes, Bernadette.' All his doubts from before faded to nothing. 'We'll be a family like no other – a special family. A very special family indeed.'

CHAPTER 12

When Michael returned to the house in time for his tea, there was nobody there. A note on the kitchen table informed him that Imelda was eating out with Father Sean and Bernadette had business to do in the town. He was to have a banana to tide him over and then let his appetite build up again for when Bernadette got home. Oh for goodness sake! Did she think he was a child? In a temper he took two bananas and stormed out of the house. He had pulled the door behind him before he realised that his key was on the kitchen table. What to do now? He scanned the darkening garden for inspiration till his eye caught that of a malicious looking gnome, fishing in the pond. Of course! The spare key to the garage! He lifted the gnome's laden bucket of fish and prised a foil-wrapped packet from beneath it. He unwrapped the key and smiled, that'd be the very thing to cheer him up! He would go into the garage and look at his magazines in peace in the one place where he had recently created, with Monica's generous help, some very happy memories. Checking that no one was watching, he opened the garage door and went inside.

When she left Cormac's Bernadette was surprised to find how dark and cold it was. The chill cooled her cheeks and the chilly rub of tweedy pleats between her knees was a sharp contrast to all the warm ripples that had assaulted her in his kitchen as she sat holding his hand. They were so right together she realised, as he ate his soup one-handed while every so often smiling at her incredulously.

'I can't believe you really feel like that,' he'd said at least three times, 'I really can't believe you feel like that.'

But she had.

She closed the front door behind her and almost skipped down the path. Cormac Hegarty loved her. Cormac Hegarty loved her. And it wasn't that silly teenagey sort of love that you'd read about in magazines – if you were the sort of person who read that type of magazine – this was real, grown up love. She was a woman in her prime and Cormac . . . Cormac was a man. A real man. Her man.

By the time she reached her car, the strains of *Stand by your man* were so loud in her head she wondered the neighbours couldn't hear them bursting out of her ears. She slid onto the seat and pulled the door. What the hell. She threw back her head and with the sort of joyful abandon typical of a woman in love, she let rip. Tammy Wynette, eat your heart out.

Her own house looked abandoned when she reached home. Michael should be back by now but she knew that Imelda was going to tea with Sean. Still singing and oblivious to the speed she was going, she swept up her drive and with a yank of the handbrake at the last minute, executed a perfect handbrake turn which brought the car skidding to a halt alongside the garage door. She got out and checked it. The passenger side was perfectly parallel to the garage door with not a millimetre to spare – what a woman! She was about to get back in and move the car away when lights at the gate heralded Imelda's return. Bernadette expected her to be in fine form after tea with her brother but it was a very sober Imelda who got out.

'Good evening, dear!' Bernadette called cheerily. 'Evening, Father!'

Imelda nodded to her, eyes lowered. Father Sean waved but didn't stop. He muttered a last few words to Imelda and then drove off. The two women stood and watched his tail lights as they disappeared out the gate then Bernadette shivered. 'Dear me, what a chill there is suddenly. Did you have a lovely evening? I did. Come inside and let's hear all about yours.' She linked her arm through Imelda's and guided her towards the door. As they went in and took their jackets off, Imelda was still silent. What could be wrong? They were all beans when they set off and Imelda had promised to go through some of the wedding plans with him. Oh dear, what if that was the problem? Bernadette was beginning to feel worried. What if she and Sean had decided not to give their blessing to the wedding? What if they thought it might be too much for a sensitive single man like Cormac to take on an instant family? What if they had secretly planned all along that they really wanted Cormac to marry Monica Moran? Oh no! Maybe that was in their idea all along for her to come to Tullabeg! Bernadette's blood froze.

'Imelda,' she said, trying to keep her voice calm. 'You're very quiet. Something's the matter, isn't it?'

Imelda nodded.

'Is it to do with Monica Moran?'

Imelda's face was growing pinker by the minute. She looked at Bernadette sadly. 'Yes. Oh, Bernadette. I don't know how to tell you.'

Bernadette felt the frozen blood chip off into little shards and leave her drained. So it was true. Monica and Cormac. And only an hour ago she had mashed his soup and he had looked into her eyes. And all the while the family plotted to betray her! After all she had done for those Hegartys, all that cooking and cleaning and never a rasher grilled after its use by date – how could they!

'I think we ought to go inside and talk about this, don't you?' She gestured towards the kitchen door.

Imelda nodded.

Bernadette stood back to let her pass. If they were going to gazump her, they jolly well owed her an explanation. And she wasn't going to make it easy. She would sit Imelda down and make her come clean without even a drop of tea to ease her treacherous throat. With a last glance at the car and a fleeting intention that she would come and move it later, she popped her keys into her pocket and followed the traitor inside.

With the garage door shut, Michael had settled comfortably into the big leather seats and in the intimate glow of a single orange interior light, spent a blissful couple of hours recalling all he had learned. By the time he exhausted himself with all the revision it was quite late and he realised that it was probably dark outside and Aunty Bernadette would be home soon. He stuffed his magazines into the glove box, checked it was locked and sidled along the garage wall to the door.

That's where his problem started. The handle turned easily enough but the door wouldn't open. Something seemed to be wedged firmly up against it on the other side. Leaning with all his weight he pushed and pushed – no good. Whatever it was, was not budging. Eventually, frustration turned to despair and he groped around in the dark for something to use to attract attention. True to form, Aunty Bernadette had the garage tidied to military standards. With the bulk of Father Barry's car taking up the space he couldn't reach the shelves at the back where everything was stored so he peered into the car to see if there was anything there. The horn didn't work and there was no point turning on the headlights. Since they had taken possession of the car, Aunty Bernadette insisted on heavy blackout curtains on the garage window, so nobody would know there was anything in there. So nobody would know there was anyone in there. So nobody would know *he* was in there, in the dark. Alone.

Help!

In a flash he was back at the garage door, nose pressed to the opening, tapping with his belt buckle for all he was worth. Tap, tap, tap, help me, Aunty Bernadette! Is there anybody there? Tap, tap, tap . . .

In the kitchen, Imelda and Bernadette sat at the kitchen table. Imelda kept her head bowed while Bernadette's cold stare bored right into her brain. She didn't move a muscle while opposite her Imelda fidgeted uncomfortably.

'Oh dear,' Imelda said, in that tinny voice of hers that up to ten minutes ago Bernadette had found fragile and endearing. 'I really don't know where to start.'

Don't know where to start, nah, nah, nah. Bernadette was sorely tempted to say aloud. Instead she said, 'Try the beginning.'

'Yes, of course, the beginning.' Then there was a silence.

'Well?' Bernadette leaned forward.

Imelda took a deep breath and lifted her head. Her eyes were swimming with tears and there were bright spots of colour in her cheeks. Shame probably, and quite right too.

'I'm so ashamed . . .' Imelda began.

Hah! Bernadette nodded. As she waited for the next bit she became conscious of a faint tapping noise. This tension was going to give her a headache. 'Get on with it then,' she commanded. 'Let's hear the whole sorry tale.'

Imelda perked up. 'You're absolutely right, Bernadette, as usual. A sorry tale, that's what it is.' And in time to the persistent tapping in Bernadette's head, she began to talk.

'I brought Monica to Tullabeg, as you know, to cheer her up after her husband's death,' Imelda began, 'she really wasn't herself and we thought it might be a good idea.'

I bet you did. Bernadette waited. In her aching brain Tammy was silent but Dolly Parton had taken up the drumming and was giving a very staccato version of *Jolene*.

'It's my fault,' Imelda continued. 'Monica's always been a bit, well, naughty with men . . .'

242

As the nasal strains of *Jolene* sliced through Bernadette's head, she wondered how she could ever have considered this woman to be her friend. She stifled a sob. She had no friends. Even Dolly, who knew exactly how she felt couldn't be trusted. You only had to look at her – a Barbified version of Monica Moran, that's what she was.

'She was never meant to be on her own, you know. So that's why I brought her here . . .'

Where was Tammy when you needed her? Bernadette didn't think she could take it a minute longer.

'And this is how she repays us – utter betrayal.'

Dolly stopped singing.

'Betrayal?'

'To think we were so worried about her!' Imelda sounded angry. 'How could she have behaved like that? Poor Sean, how will he ever live this down?'

In an instant the little blood shards melted and Bernadette could feel them sneaking warmly back into her veins. 'Sean?' she said, her voice an octave higher than when she last spoke. Imelda was talking about Sean and she wasn't sounding fond and sisterly towards Monica either.

Imelda's tears brimmed over and Bernadette's heart melted. Poor, poor Imelda. Something awful must have happened. Bernadette got up and went over to her friend and laid a gentle hand on her shoulder. 'Oh my dear, this is so awful for you. Why don't I make the two of us a lovely cup of cocoa and you can tell me the whole story, about Monica Moran, and Sean.'

While they sat there sipping the cocoa, Imelda told Bernadette everything that Sean had told her earlier. With every sentence Bernadette felt her strength return. Dolly Parton packed her bags and Tammy took centre stage again in Bernadette's head. Only now she was standing not only by her man but also by his sister, the betrayed friend; and by his brother, the disgraced Parish Priest, out of whose car, by all accounts, a semi-naked Monica Moran had tumbled only minutes after morning Mass, still hitching up her knickers! Bernadette's whole body glowed with delight. *I believe! I believe! I'm on my feet again!* Tammy screamed in her head, keeping time with the tapping that now seemed to be coming from somewhere outside. Every time Imelda paused for breath Bernadette nodded, 'uumed' and 'aahed' encouragingly. Eventually, the story came to an end and Imelda sat silent.

For a minute Bernadette said nothing.

Imelda looked at her. 'I can't believe she'd do a thing like that. Poor Sean. I knew she had an eye for him but I thought she'd gotten over it years ago.'

Bernadette patted her hand. 'There there dear, you mustn't take the blame.'

Imelda fished for a handkerchief in her sleeve. 'But I do! I thought it would be a good idea to bring her here to cheer her up after her husband died, might settle her down. I even thought that maybe she and Cor –' She stopped suddenly and looked at Bernadette. 'I had no idea that he was already, you know, spoken for.'

Bernadette didn't know what to say. The tapping noise grew louder and more insistent. So there *was* a plot to send poor Cormac into the arms, if he could reach them, of that awful woman. At the memory of how nearly it had succeeded – the two of them lying back on that sofa and the slut with her surplus flesh exposed to the world – her blood boiled. She gritted her teeth. 'Well, he *is* spoken for,' she snapped.

Imelda smiled. 'And thank God for that. That's another thing Sean and I talked about tonight, our one chink of light in all this. Whatever happens with Sean when the bishop gets to hear of things, at least we know that Cormac will be well looked after.'

Bernadette glowed. She could just imagine the scene. Sean and Imelda sitting in the priest's front parlour, his reputation in ashes on the floor and from the centre of it, rising like a phoenix, the ghostly image of Bernadette and Cormac giving hope for the future. She could see the whole thing, 'Hegarty Family's Reputation Restored' embroidered in gold on a banner floating above their heads and all around them little cherubs with bowls of rose petals . . .

'Do you hear something?'

Bernadette opened her eyes.

'A noise. I think it's coming from outside. Can't you hear it?'

Bernadette shook the petals out of her ears. Imelda was right, there was a tapping noise. She'd noticed it earlier but thought it was just Dolly on the drums. She got up and went to the window.

'I think it's coming from the garage.'

The garage! Father Barry's car! Someone was trying to steal it. Bernadette opened the cupboard door and pulled out a sweeping brush.

'Shouldn't you call the police or something?'

Bernadette paused. A car packed with tall gardai rushing up her drive in the dead of night to protect little defenceless her – that might be . . . 'No,' she said firmly, surprised to find that she didn't feel defenceless at all. 'I'm practically a married woman. I'll soon have a man to look after. I can't be rushing off begging for help every time there's a problem. You stay here and if I'm not back in five minutes, call them then.' And with a toss of her curls and a swish of tweed, she swept out into the night.

She had taken on bigger challenges (a vision of Monica's straining viscose flashed before her) and won. Whatever was out there, she was ready for it.

The indignity of it! Not only had Michael to endure the third degree to ascertain it was really him and not some malevolent impostor who had decided, for reasons known only to himself, that it would be a good idea to impersonate Michael while trapped in the garage, but when Aunty Bernadette finally moved her car he was made to emerge slowly, hands in the air, a sweeping brush aimed menacingly at his neck.

'Look at the state of you! You're a disgrace!'

Michael opened his mouth to protest.

'What were you doing in there anyway, with the light off?'

Michael's mouth shut of its own accord.

'Well?' She lowered the brush to half-mast.

From the kitchen door Imelda's concerned voice called out, 'Is everything all right there, dear?'

'Everything under control.' She sounded so smug.

Michael took a quick glance at the driveway in front of the garage. Now that she had moved her car back you could see tyre marks sweeping round from the front of the house to the garage door. It looked like a handbrake turn. He followed the marks to where they stopped alongside the garage door. It looked like a very near miss.

'What's all that?' he demanded, hoping his voice sounded deeper to her ears than it did to his.

'It's parking.'

'But,' he pointed to the skid marks, 'I could have been trapped in there all night. What did you have to park so close for?'

Bernadette followed his gaze. 'It's not easy to do that,' she said, sounding as if she thought it was actually very clever. She turned to walk back into the house, smoothing over the ridges as she passed. 'Some day you'll be able to do that.'

'I will when Monica comes home and finishes teaching me,' he said, suddenly feeling over-whelmingly lonely.

Imelda came forward and she and Bernadette exchanged a meaningful look. Bernadette thumped the ground crossly with the sweeping brush. 'That woman will not be coming back into this house. Ever. She has disgraced herself. We'll be having nothing to do with her, ever again.' Michael opened his mouth but she silenced him. 'And please don't ask me to say another word about it. Imelda and I are far too upset.'

The women exchanged glances then Bernadette held the brush out to him. 'Here,' she said. 'Tidy up that mess you caused then you'd better hear the whole story. The whole sorry story.'

For the next hour Michael's ears were burned and his heart raged. How dare they say such things! Despite the fact that he was desperately hungry he couldn't swallow a thing. He'd had to sit there, chewing the same piece of stringy chicken while the two women alternated between declaring that they didn't want to hear another thing about it and regaling each other with increasingly vivid detail. As he chewed they gave lurid accounts of how, if you were intelligent enough to read between the lines, Father Sean had apparently tried to murder poor Monica by pushing her out of a car!

'How she could behave like that! God knows what she tried to do to the poor fellow!'

'Oh my dear, I don't even want to talk about it! He told me –'

'Oh I know, it doesn't bear thinking about. I mean imagine . . .'

And on and on. They made it sound as if Monica had done something wrong. As if she had somehow lost her mind. But Michael knew better. He had experience of how nice it was to be in a car with Monica and he knew that no man in his right mind would ever want to hoist her out of it. She was obviously trying to protect herself. And Father Sean a priest and all – you hear about that sort of thing. Poor Monica, she must have run all the way home to get away! No wonder her feet were such a mess and she was delirious when they took her to the hospital.

He tried to explain all this to Bernadette but she wouldn't listen. By the time they had exhausted every detail and realised that it was nearly time for *Eastenders*, Michael's ears were burning. He swallowed the chewed chicken, wincing as it squeezed past his goitre. 'I don't think you're being very fair,' he croaked.

'Fair!' The witches screeched.

'On Monica. You're acting as if she is some kind of criminal and you haven't even stopped to consider what Father Sean was –'

249

'Michael! I will not have another word said about it in this house! That woman has brought disgrace on –' she smiled lovingly at Imelda and her voice softened, '*our* family.'

'*But* –'

She held her hand up, palm towards him. 'Not another word!'

Michael stood up crossly. 'Why won't you listen to me! Mon –'

Bernadette stood up also and leaned her face close to his. 'I said, not another word. What has gotten into you this evening?' With one hand she pointed at the rest of his chicken breast and with the other at the door. 'If you're not going to behave yourself and eat your dinner nicely, you can go to your room. This minute!'

Michael seethed. Who did she think she was talking to? He glared from one to the other of them, all smug and triumphant. They couldn't tell him what to do. Without another word he pulled the napkin she insisted he wear when the chicken had gravy on it from his neck and threw it on the table. Let them have their nasty thoughts if they wanted to, he'd have no part of it. He yanked open the kitchen door and banged it shut behind him. Then he stomped up the stairs and made a great noise about going to bed.

For nearly an hour he lay on his bed listening to them wittering below, first in the kitchen and then in the sitting-room but soon the strains of the evening's soap operas filtered up the stairs and they were quiet. By then he'd made his mind up. Obviously this was all a plot. Ever since Aunty Bernadette had become engaged to Mr Hegarty she was determined to be Imelda's best friend and that meant ousting Monica. She must have managed to turn Father Sean against her too. Poor Monica – had she only one real friend left in the world? Only one man prepared to take up arms and defend her?

Suddenly the last traces of shock from finding himself locked in the garage faded and Michael felt a surge of power. Monica wasn't alone in the world – Monica had him. He'd be her friend, her protector. Wave after wave of affectionate warmth followed his power surge as he recalled how she had helped him. Now he'd help her. With or without Aunty Bernadette's knowledge.

He got off the bed and sneaked down the stairs. Through a chink in the sitting-room door he could see the two of them, sitting side by side on the settee, quietly sucking the jam off their cream crackers lest the crunching noise should disturb the other's viewing. All peaceful and serene – as if they hadn't spent the earlier part of the evening massacring an innocent woman's reputation and trying to poison him against her. Well, it hadn't worked. He boiled with rage. He knew what he must do. If they were prepared to forsake her, he wasn't.

In the kitchen everything was neat as usual. Michael looked around for something he could

251

bring to the hospital. Nothing. He opened the larder. On one side tins were neatly stacked according to date, and on the other a range of Tupperware containers stacked according to size. Each one was labelled: date opened/baked, approximate expiry and most importantly, how many slices/pieces were left. He couldn't touch any of those without risking the inquisition. It was hopeless. And he couldn't bring her a half-eaten chicken breast either. Increasingly annoyed, he pushed the ironing board aside to see if there was anything at all and hey! Bingo! Stuffed at the back of the shelves were the Battenberg cakes that Monica had brought. Bernadette was very ungracious in accepting them and had obviously shoved them to the back hoping they would be forgotten. Like Monica, abandoned. He grabbed a cake and stuffed it into his pocket.

Without even bothering to get his coat he sneaked out the back door and keeping close to the flowerbed so that he didn't make a noise on the shingles, he made his way down the path to the end of the drive. Then he picked up speed. It was very dark and an icy dampness clung onto his sweatshirt. Like ghostly hands – very spooky really. Behind him, the lights of Aunty Bernadette's cosy house faded and for a split second he was tempted to turn back but only for a split second.

With his fingers wrapped protectively around the cake he marched up the road towards the hospital.

Hold on, Monica, I'm coming, he sang aloud, for comfort at first but then as his resolution strengthened, for the sheer joy of it.

Hold on, Monica, hold on!

CHAPTER 13

Slap, swish, slap, swish. Monica woke from fitful sleep to the sound of a giant tongue licking the world around her. She ran her own tongue over her teeth and found only grit. Dry, sour grit.

Slap, swish. The wet licking was coming nearer so she opened one eye just a slit – mistake. Blinding, unearthly light. She shut it again and sighed. She was dead obviously but someone had made a terrible mistake. Death was supposed to be oblivion, an end to all corporeal sensation, but Monica's body was wracked with sensations, all of them painful. From the top of her head where the light forced vicious shards through her closed eyelids, down to her big toe which was throbbing, Monica was in agony.

Slap, swish.

Oh, for God's sake – or whoever's place this was! What sort of torture was this? She was slaked with thirst and all she could hear was great wet licks. What she wouldn't do for a great wet lick, of anything, to ease her thirst.

'Awake, are you?' The voice was close to her ear

and though she really couldn't claim to have first hand knowledge, it didn't sound like an angel's. It sounded rasping, like a smoker's, or someone used to breathing smoke. Monica groaned at the implications.

'What do you want with me?' she asked.

'Well,' said the voice, 'if you could just yank those blankets up a bit I could get in under there. The dust is desperate.'

Dust, in the afterlife? It stood to reason.

'You don't see it when it's dull but when it's bright like this, it's everywhere. And I need to shift it, Sister's on the warpath.'

Monica rubbed her eyes. Something definitely wasn't right. She squinted in the voice's direction. At first there was nothing there, only bright sunlight, but suddenly a figure appeared at the side of the bed. It was a woman in her late forties, short, skinny and familiar. She was dressed in a blue housecoat and looked like a cleaner.

'Good morning,' she said, wiping her hand on her hip and offering it to Monica.

Monica shook the hand cautiously. Even if her knuckles hadn't been sore she wasn't taking any chances. Wherever this place was, it certainly wasn't where she expected to find herself. She pulled the blankets tighter around her.

'Have a good sleep, did you?' The woman was grinning. She looked vaguely familiar.

'I don't know.' Monica would have shook her head but it was stuffed with hot cannon balls.

Now the woman laughed out loud. 'You should have, after the day you had yesterday. The whole town is talking about it.'

This might possibly be the oddest version of hell – it certainly wasn't heaven. Monica was beginning to suspect that she wasn't dead at all. 'Where am I?'

'St Teresa's Ward. They were going to put you into St Bernadette's but they changed it after what you said.' She chucked. 'What a hullabaloo!'

Monica felt as if she was going to cry. She hadn't a clue where she was, why she was here or how she arrived. The pain in her head was more acute and her toes were now on fire. She tried to shift so that she could sit up a bit but her body was lead, hot throbbing lead. 'Was I in a car accident?'

'Oh now,' the woman looked at her and winked. 'You were in a car all right but whether or not it was an accident, we're all dying to find out!' When Monica didn't respond, she continued, 'Don't you remember anything?'

Monica closed her eyes and tried to recall her most recent memories. With a rush of annoyance, she remembered being in the car with Sean and he on his high horse being totally obtuse in her distress. And she trying to do the family a favour! She remembered the walk home and the agony of peeling her poor toes out of ruined stilettos. She remembered that she was very tired and Imelda and Michael and Bernadette were there and Bernadette was being very kind, gave her a lovely glass of – oh! She put a hand to her forehead. The rip! She wasn't dead and suffering the torments of Hell at all! She had a bloody hangover! Although things got hazy after that she could remember Bernadette refilling her glass and urging her to drink it all up, it'd make her feel better. She opened her eyes again. The woman was smiling at her encouragingly, waiting for more information. 'Do I know you?'

'Not really,' the woman said, 'though you'll have seen me last week, with my daughter Lucy? I'm Kathleen O'Donnell.' There was a sound of voices entering the ward. 'And I'll be a sacked Kathleen O'Donnell if I don't get on with this.' She slopped the mop into her bucket and started wiping the floor again. Slap, swish.

Monica's brain raced. Lucy O'Donnell's mother! She hadn't thought of that! She looked at the group of nurses who had just arrived. They were stopped by the first bed. 'Don't go,' she whispered to Kathleen. 'It'd be nice to have a chat. I don't know many people in here.'

Kathleen glanced at the nurses. 'I can't stop but . . .' her eyes twinkled and Monica knew she was relishing the prospect of getting all the gossip first hand. She obviously knew about Monica in Sean's car, and would be very disappointed to hear that nothing happened. That's if someone were to tell her nothing happened, of course. And who could tell her anything like that as there wasn't anyone else there except Sean and he wouldn't want to talk about it at all. Monica smiled at her.

'It'd be lovely if you could come back and visit me later,' she said, keeping her voice low and sad. 'I haven't a soul here that I can – you know – confide in.'

Kathleen nodded. 'You poor thing.' She was having difficulty keeping the enthusiasm out of her voice. 'I finish at four. I could pop back then for a chat – if you're not expecting any other visitors, that is.'

'No,' Monica said, 'I don't think so.' She wondered for a minute if Imelda might come, but if Kathleen had heard about the car incident there was little chance nosy Bernadette hadn't. And she wouldn't miss an opportunity to do Monica down.

'Right so,' Kathleen winked at her. 'Four o'clock it is. See you then.'

'Bye.' Monica managed a weak smile. She watched Kathleen slapping and swishing her way down the ward and she felt miserable. What a situation to find herself in. She was thirsty, in agony and apparently abandoned. Did anyone care that she was here? Would anyone come to see if she was feeling better? She glanced at the bedside table to check if there was maybe a bunch of flowers, a 'Get Well' card, and a bag of lovely juicy grapes . . . nothing. Her eyes filled with tears and she was going to bury herself in the blanket and refuse to come out when she heard a rustle by her ear. She reached up and felt a package stuffed in at the edge of her pillow. Pulling it under the blanket she examined it. A Battenberg cake, warm and squashed but still in one piece. It had been opened and someone had carved a heart on the marzipan. A crooked heart with an 'M' in the centre. The cake itself was misshapen, squeezed in the middle with the imprint of fingers on one side and a thumb on the other. Someone had carried it tight for quite some time. Her heart warmed – Michael.

As she looked at the cake Monica's heart tightened in the middle too. He must have come over in the evening when she was asleep and left it here for her. The little pet. She could just imagine his fingers, with their short ginger hairs, wrapped around the cake. She stifled a sob. He was loyal. Out of the corner of her eye she saw Kathleen pick up her bucket and wave. Lovely loyal Michael and now she was going to break his heart. She waved back. She'd have to talk to Kathleen about Lucy. Oh Hell! How did she ever get herself into this situation? She peeled a bit of marzipan off the end of the cake.

Life couldn't get any worse.

When Cormac opened the door of Hegartys' Estate Agents the conversation stopped. Gerald Grealy and the other two were huddled together like Macbeth's witches.

'Morning, Mr Hegarty,' Gerald called out in his smarmiest voice while the others smirked as if he had just said something very clever.

Cormac was tempted to ignore him. That boy was no more than an irritant these days. He glared at the others. 'Have you no work to do?' They scuttled to their desks. 'Where are those photographs of the new houses on Collins Close I ordered? Haven't you done them yet?'

Gerald raised his eyes to Heaven. He picked a pile of schedules off the desk and held them out. 'They're here. They came in on Tuesday. They've been done for ages. And the artist's impressions for the new estate, they were done ages ago too.' He smirked. 'We're completely up-to-date with everything. On the ball, as it were.' One of the others stifled a snigger.

Cormac glared. Any minute now that fellow would find himself on his ear en route to the employment office – and he wouldn't be getting a good reference either. He looked at the other two. They were sitting, stupid grins on their faces waiting to see what would happen next. Right, we'll see about them. 'And have you two nothing to do?'

They held up their hands. 'Nothing, Mr Hegarty, we're on the ball too! We're just sitting here awaiting your instruction.'

Gerald was beside himself with mirth but Cormac had regained his composure and was ready for him. 'You mean you're idle. All three of you are idle. There is nothing to do and you are being paid to sit here doing nothing. Dear me, now what does that suggest to you?' He raised one eyebrow and regarded them in turn from beneath it. 'Shall I tell you what it suggests to me?' The smirks were slowly disappearing and a far more pleasing expression was creeping over their faces. Fear. 'It suggests that I have too big a staff, that's what it suggests to me. It suggests that perhaps it would make sense, good business sense, to reduce the size of my staff so that I wouldn't be paying people to sit around idle. I'd be paying people to work.'

Gerald immediately remembered some paperwork outstanding and some calls he needed to make and Cormac smiled. 'Oh good,' he said. 'How reassuring.' He slid his overcoat from his shoulders and held it out. 'If one of you could see to that, as you're not busy, and then perhaps I might have a cup of tea.' The coat was taken and the kettle filled. 'I'll just go upstairs and have a good look at my staffing situation. Always good to stay on top, don't you think?' He smiled sweetly and patted his stomach.

Nice one, Cormac old chap.

Half an hour later, Cormac wasn't feeling half so smug. With all his accounts spread on the desk he was beginning to see that the joke was on him. He really didn't need a staff of three at all. One upstart around the place, with another, possible

261

part-time for good measure, was more than enough. He sighed, whom to get rid of? He was about to opt for the good old technique of eeny-meeny-miney-mo when there was a knock on the door.

'Come in!'

A still chastened-looking Gerald stood in the doorway. 'There's a person downstairs looking for you. I don't think he's a client.'

Annoyed at being disturbed in the middle of important decision-making, Cormac glared. 'I don't want your thoughts, Gerald, I want facts. Who is this person and is it business?'

Gerald disappeared for a minute then came back panting. 'He says he's . . .'

'Em, hello.'

Cormac's heart did a little flip. It was Michael. Though his overalls were pristine, ironed even, the poor boy looked tired. There were dark lines running from beneath his pale lashes to the sides of his nose and his hair was curlier and more dishevelled than usual. Cormac sighed. Dishevelled or not, he looked simply divine. Cormac jumped to his feet. 'Michael, my dear boy! Why didn't they tell me it was you! Come in, come in.' He beckoned him towards the armchair and gestured for him to sit down. Michael looked at him gratefully. Waving Gerald away, Cormac rushed round to the other side of his desk and sat, regarding Michael closely.

'Now, Michael,' he said in a voice that the

kindest of uncles would be proud of, 'something tells me that this is not a social call. Is there something I can do for you?'

Michael nodded. He looked miserable. 'I'm sorry,' he said, barely above a whisper. 'I always seem to be looking for advice from you.'

Cormac held his hands out the way people do when they get the rain they've been hoping for for weeks. 'And what else am I here for? Aren't we almost family?' He placed his hands palm down on the table and leaned forward. 'Now come on, tell me all about it. Is it . . .' He shuffled a bit in his seat, 'is it about your special person?'

Michael shook his head. 'Not really, well, not about who we were talking about before. It's about Monica.'

'Oh.' Cormac's voice fell and he sat back in his chair.

Michael stood up. 'Don't say "Oh" like that! It isn't fair!'

The boy looked completely distraught and a great wave of protectiveness washed over Cormac. He came around the desk and laid his avuncular hands on Michael's shoulders. 'My dear boy, please don't be upset. I didn't mean anything at all.' When Michael sat down he pulled his chair round to sit beside him. 'Now you tell me all about what's upsetting you and I will fix it.'

Michael looked at him gratefully. 'There's a horrible story going around about Monica.'

Cormac tried hard to maintain a solemn expression. 'Indeed. I heard.'

As if he'd just remembered that Father Sean was Cormac's brother, Michael reddened. 'And Father Sean.'

'Yes.' Cormac waited a minute for inspiration and when none came, took a leap of faith. 'And I don't believe a word of it.'

Michael's face lit up. 'I knew you wouldn't.' He looked at Cormac with such gratitude that Cormac regretted, not for the first time, that he did not have a shower installed in the office washroom when he had the chance. Then Michael's face darkened again. 'Aunty Bernadette believes it though. So does Imelda. They seem pleased even.' His voice became more and more animated. 'You should have heard the two of them! They were talking about her as if she was some kind of criminal and they wouldn't listen to a word. And she's not a criminal, she's the kindest, most caring person . . .'

'Oh dear,' Cormac said, and he meant it. 'What was it you wanted me to do?'

'Well,' Michael's cheeks reddened. 'I'm supposed to be working for Father Sean at the moment but I don't want to stay there. He acts as if Monica is the devil and Aunty Bernadette keeps saying that Monica is a bad influence.' Cormac was about to suggest that maybe there was a grain of truth in that when Michael added, 'And she's not, she's taught me so much!'

264

The cheeks reddened even more and the grain shrivelled and died. 'Did she?'

Michael said nothing. Cormac waited for him to elaborate and when he didn't spread his hands out in front of him and examined his splayed fingers. 'You don't just mean driving, do you Michael?'

'No.'

The foxy old tart! 'Do you mean things that might help you with your, how shall I put it, special person?'

Michael nodded.

'Is it like, em, techniques?'

Poor Michael. His innocence recently robbed, the boy didn't know where to look. Cormac rubbed his hands in glee. The thought of indulging in any technique swapping with Monica Moran really didn't appeal at all though his brothers claimed to have been very satisfied in their day. 'I take it your Aunt doesn't know?'

'No way! She'd kill me!'

Cormac smiled. 'Actually, Michael, I'm not altogether sure that she would.' Michael was about to protest but Cormac held up his hand. 'That's strictly between us though.' He leaned closer. 'Your aunt and I have a very special sort of agreement. You mustn't worry about a thing.' Michael didn't look convinced. Bernadette was obviously playing it straight with him for the moment.

'But why is she so mean about Monica?'

Cormac had a good idea why. The boy had obviously grown fond of the old slag over the past two weeks and Bernadette, like Cormac, wouldn't want to encourage that too much. He smiled at the thought of her. What a wise little thing she was! And all those years he spent thinking she was just a fussy busybody! 'Michael,' he said, putting his hand gingerly on the boy's knee, 'I think your Aunty Bernadette, in her wisdom, just doesn't want you becoming too fond of, you know, people who aren't going to be in your life for much longer.'

Michael looked distressed. 'What do you mean?'

'I mean, when you and your special person get together you won't need her around will you?'

Michael shrugged. 'Suppose not.'

'There you are then!' Cormac clapped his hands in glee. 'Problem solved.'

'But what about Father Sean's? I can't stay there. They'll just drive me mad!' His face contorted and two huge tears rolled down his cheeks.

Cormac's heart melted in sympathy. He reached over and pulled a tissue out of the box on his desk. As he did so, his eye caught the papers spread out there. Of course. He handed the tissue to Michael and smiled broadly. 'Michael,' he said, 'I think I have the very solution. I was working on it just as you arrived.' He knelt in front of the boy and gently lifted his chin. 'Michael,' he said, 'how would you like to come and work for me?'

Michael beamed. 'For you? Really? Have you a job for me? I'm not even qualified.'

Between his fingers the little chin quivered in hope. 'Oh Michael, my dear boy, I'm sure you're more than qualified.' He thought of Monica and all the boy will have learned.

And Cormac quivered too.

Father Sean put the letter down and sighed. The bishop was not pleased. 'Confident' there would turn out to be a perfectly reasonable explanation for the strange tales he had been hearing over the last twenty-four hours, for the moment he couldn't think what it might be. Sean couldn't either. How could he explain that all his life Monica Moran had been a scourge to him? Or that the fact of his being the only boy on the street, apart from Cormac, of course, who wasn't interested when she offered to show her knickers, was the single fact that made him most attractive to her? She just couldn't take no for an answer. He picked up the letter again and re-read it. 'Scandals the Church could well afford to do without . . .' he could do without them himself.

He was about to make some notes in preparation for his response when the noise stopped him. What was that wretched woman up to? She had arrived first thing this morning with two large bags of vegetables and greeted him with one of those expressions you'd give someone on learning that their favourite gerbil had just been eaten by the neighbours' dog. Since then she had been busy in the kitchen and all he could hear was chopping and whirring, all accompanied by some dreadful country and western caterwauling, most of it hers. If he heard one more out-of-tune request to *lay your blanket on the ground* he would go out there, wrap the blanket round her neck and when she was well and truly dead, he'd take great pleasure in laying her *in* the ground. And her sullen nephew with her – he'd gone off in a huff first thing this morning and hadn't been seen since. He slammed the letter back onto the desk. Enough already! He stormed out of his study and towards the kitchen.

When he opened the door, the sight that greeted him was enough to make him want to draw a line under this awful day and go straight back to bed. By the cooker Bernadette Teegan stood stirring her cauldron. She was jigging along to the tape recorder. At the end of every verse she would sweep her hips around so that her skirt flew out like an umbrella with two handles. Two thickly stockinged handles.

'Ahem, Miss Teegan?'

She spun around, leaving a trail of beige gloop on the cooker hood as she did so. 'Oh, hello Father, did you want something?'

'Yes, I did,' he was too tired and too fed up to

pull punches. 'I wanted peace and quiet. I wanted to get on with the task of running this parish but that is proving impossible. And do you know why it is proving impossible, Miss Teegan?'

He expected her to say, 'Why, Father?' so that he could then tell her exactly what he thought of the din and mess in his kitchen – but of course she didn't. She just smiled sweetly and laid her wooden spoon onto the spoon rest beside her. Then she crossed the kitchen and taking his arm, led him across to a chair. She patted him sympathetically on the shoulder. 'Of course I know, Father! Sure aren't you a man tortured by the nasty rumours that absolutely everyone is talking about? I mean, if you knew the number of people who asked me about it in the supermarket! And shall I tell you what I said?'

Did he have a choice?

'I said, don't you dare come up to me with your filthy stories about Father Sean hurling semi-clad women out of his car and then speeding off down the road! I said, how could you suggest he'd ever do such a thing? I said, I have worked for Father Sean for years and he has never, I said, never ever, not once –'

Perish the thought! He held up his hand. 'Thank you, Miss Teegan. I'm sure that brought home the point very eloquently.' He sat forward and laid his head in his hands.

Bernadette pulled up a chair beside him. She

clasped her hands together and took a deep breath. 'Actually, Father, I don't know what happened but whatever it was, I know it wasn't your fault. Really I do.' He didn't move. 'I know what she's like. She's not a good woman.' Still no response. 'She hunts men down and torments them. She had poor Father Barry nearly driven to his grave.'

Father Barry? Sean could remember Monica saying something about Father Barry. She'd started accusing him of something dreadful but them Sean lost his temper. He sat up. 'She mentioned Father Barry to me. I wish I could remember what it was.'

Bernadette reddened and stood up. 'I'm sure that wouldn't help the situation at all. She says terrible things about people.' She rushed over to her cauldron where the mixture had now bubbled to the top and was threatening to spill over. She picked up her spoon and began stirring vigorously.

'Miss Teegan, what is that?'

Bernadette beamed. 'It's mushroom soup. It's organic and completely free range.'

'Free range mushrooms?'

'Oh yes,' she said, 'I wouldn't use anything less. See?' She pointed to some paper bags on the table. 'I selected every one myself, no prepacked.' Then she gave a little happy sigh. 'Cormac and I love mushroom soup. We were just saying last night,

270

when we were having supper, that it's one of our favourites.'

Aha! Sean raised his eyes to Heaven in gratitude. At least that situation seemed to be chugging along nicely, very nicely in fact if they were having supper together. And when he had mentioned it to Cormac not three weeks ago, Cormac had dismissed it as nonsense. He smiled. 'So all the wedding plans are going smoothly, are they?'

'Oh yes, Father.'

'Set a date yet?'

Bernadette looked surprised. 'Goodness, no, I hadn't thought of that. I've been so busy with the other things: buy material for the dress; bake the bottom three tiers of the cake; write the guest list. There's such a lot to do!' She suddenly looked very worried. 'I do hope nothing goes wrong.'

'Why should it?'

'Well, you know, Father, one minute things are grand and the next, something happens and your whole world is upside down. Just like with you, now that Monica Moran is in town. I hope nothing happens to Cormac and I.' She turned back to her stirring.

For a minute Sean said nothing. He had the distinct impression she was trying to tell him something. Was it possible that the wedding would not happen? He thought of all the things that had been said to him about Cormac over the years and sighed. This was thin ice all right. Cormac's reputation was not the best for the brother of a parish priest, and with the present trouble Sean could ill afford any more gossip. He stood up. 'Miss Teegan, if there is anything I can do to help you in your preparations, please don't hesitate to call me. I'll have a talk with Cormac and let's see how speedily we can bring the event to pass.'

Like the winner of *Come Dancing* Bernadette spun around and throwing her arms around his shoulders, jumped up and kicked her feet backwards in the air. 'You'll do that? Oh, thank you Father, thank you. You really are the kindest.'

That was not the best minute for Michael to return from his ramblings. He opened the door and stood glaring at the two of them, white with rage.

'Aunty Bernadette! How could you!'

He turned his face to Sean. 'I don't need to ask how you could, Father. Sounds like you do that sort of thing all the time.'

Before either of them had a chance to explain, he unzipped his overalls and stepped out of them. 'Here,' he said, 'you can have these. I'm not staying in this house a minute longer. It's corrupt.'

'But Michael,' Bernadette dropped to earth and

straightened her skirt, 'you have work to do. You have to stay here.'

'No, I don't,' Michael picked the overalls off the floor and handed them to her. 'I have a new job.' He glared at Father Sean. 'And if you want to stay safe, Aunty Bernadette, you'd better get one too.' Then he slammed out of the kitchen and was gone.

Sean looked at Bernadette. Then he dropped back into the chair with a groan. How bad could it get?

Bernadette folded the overalls neatly seam-to-seam and smiled at him. 'Don't blame yourself, Father. They say when a woman is in love she has an effect on other men too.' He opened his mouth to protest but she waved him away. 'Some women become irresistible.' Then she giggled, 'We can't help it!'

Father Sean sighed. That bad.

Michael was livid. At first he refused to get into the car when Bernadette pulled up beside him on the road, declaring that he would rather get pneumonia than find himself in a car with a woman of loose morals.

'Fine so,' Bernadette said. 'I've no doubt you'll catch pneumonia all right but as for being in a car with a woman of loose morals, well there's little chance of that. She's inside in the hospital!' Then she pulled off and left him to it. Michael glared after her. See if he cared. Ignoring the wind nipping at the edges of his ears he kept his head down and walked. As he turned onto the main road the wind picked up and blew straight into his face. It caught his tee shirt and billowed it out like a sail. He was now so cold his neck was stinging. Suddenly, as he passed the layby, there was Aunty Bernadette's car. She was sitting inside reading her *Woman's Weekly*. She rolled down the window and peered out, looking surprised to see him.

'Michael!' she said, 'is it you already? You must walk very fast.'

'Can I get in, please?' The tops of his ears had lost all feeling.

'That's not a very good idea,' she said, shaking her head. 'You see, I'm about to pull off and if you were to be sitting in my lovely warm car when I did, you might accidentally end up getting a lift from me.'

The redness spread to his cheeks and the freckles stood in little peaks on his arms. 'I don't want a lift. I just want to warm up.'

Bernadette sighed. 'No, Michael. I will not tolerate anything but the truth. And the truth is that you are now cold and sorry that you have been so terribly rude to me.'

'No I'm not, I'm not at all!'

'Fine, walk so.' She rolled the handle and shut the window.

Michael knocked the glass. 'Don't go! I am.' She was lifting her toes off the accelerator slowly. 'I am cold but I'm not sorry for what I said in Father Sean's kitchen.'

Bernadette opened the car door and beckoned him in. When he stopped shivering she turned to him, eyes brimming with tears and her voice quivering with emotion. 'Michael, you have known me all your life to be a good and moral woman, haven't you?'

He shrugged.

'So what on earth are you talking about?' Before he had a chance to say, she continued, 'Because one minute I was making soup for my fiancé in his brother's kitchen and his brother was saying how he'd give us all the help he could so that our wedding would go smoothly and after the shock we all had yesterday I was so grateful I just threw my arms around his neck and suddenly . . .' She gulped. 'Oh Michael, how could you!' And she sobbed into the handkerchief she was holding.

'What! How'd it come to be my fault?'

Bernadette blew her nose loudly and stuffed the handkerchief into her pocket. She'd sighed deeply. 'You mustn't feel guilty, Michael, I won't have it.' She patted his knee fondly and turned the key in the ignition. 'Why don't we go home and have a nice cup of tea and a chat. You'd like that, wouldn't you? And I won't have you say another word about

275

what happened, you don't need to.' She flashed him one of her wrinkle-forming smiles. 'I know you're sorry.'

When they pulled up at the car park of Supasave Michael didn't think to ask why. He didn't imagine he'd understand the answer anyway. Nothing made sense. He had discovered his Aunty Bernadette (who was supposed to be engaged to Cormac Hegarty) in the arms of her parish priest (Sean Hegarty) only twenty-four hours after the same Sean Hegarty was seen pushing another woman out of his car and driving off. And Michael was being let off apologising? He sat staring ahead, trying to figure out at what stage of the proceedings the plot had been lost.

'Aren't you coming, pet?' Aunty Bernadette's silky tones caressed his earlobe.

He shook his head. 'I might stay here.'

'Ah no. Why don't you come inside while I choose something nice for our tea? You could go in and get yourself a coffee to warm up. Look, there's that nice O'Donnell girl in the cafeteria.'

Michael's heart lifted. Lucy! How could he have forgotten? Maybe he would go in and have a chat with her. That'd be the very thing. He leapt out of the car and followed his aunt inside. At the doorway he paused to check his reflection in the glass. Not bad. His jeans were baggier than usual what with all the lessons he'd been having and his appetite being so poor recently. He pushed his belt further over his hips so that the jeans wrinkled at the ankles and swept the floor the way Lucy's did. Unfortunately that made his tee shirt look huge. Aunty Bernadette always bought big so that he could grow into them. Damn! He pulled out the sides of his tee shirt and folded them over at the seams so that the shirt was tight across the front. It gave him a slim macho look. Then he held them down with his arms and, hoping he didn't look too rigid, went into the cafeteria.

Lucy was there. She looked nice. Her top half was all tight and her bottom all loose. What a sense of style. Michael could feel himself coming over all sweaty and was glad his arms were pinned to his sides. He sauntered over to the counter. Lucy looked up.

'Yea? Can I help you?'

Michael tried to speak but where his armpits were drippy, his mouth was dry. He held his arms even tighter to the sides and inclined his head towards the coffee machine.

'Large, medium or small?'

He felt affronted. 'Large, obviously.'

She shunted her gum to the other side of her mouth. 'Suit yourself.'

Michael watched her as she concocted the coffee. It was a huge machine, all hot and hissing, and he wanted to warn her to be careful not to scald herself. When she was finished she carried the mug over to the counter. It was bucket-sized. He'd be awake all night. While she rummaged below for some sugars he tried to take hold of the mug. No good. It was tall and the counter was high and if he tried to reach it his tee shirt would come loose. She threw three sachets of sugar on the counter. Michael didn't move.

'Two fifty,' she said, holding out her hand.

Michael paled. He had no money on him. There was a fiver in the pocket of his overalls but they were probably in the boot of the car. And Aunty Bernadette had the key. Damn, damn and double damn.

Lucy was looking at him expectantly and he was about to apologise for holding her up when she raised her eyes to Heaven and sighed impatiently. That did it. Something inside Michael snapped. He'd had enough of women being right and him being wrong and it not being his fault in the first place. Careful to keep the shirt tight over his chest he pressed closer to the counter.

'You'll have to wait for the money. I've given my wallet to my aunt so that she can do her shopping. She won't be long.'

'No money, no coffee.' Lucy blew a big bubble and let it snap on her lips.

Michael flared. 'Suit yourself. I'll go wait for her over here.' He walked, not too rigidly, over to an empty table and sat down. Bloody women. He slumped in the chair, legs splayed, and regarded himself in the dark window. He did look good – very James Dean-ish. Behind him he could hear Lucy clattering at the counter but his own head was in the way so he couldn't see what was happening. He was about to risk a quick peek when she appeared at the table. She put the coffee with the sugar sachets down and smiled. 'Here, you don't have to take offence. Pay for it later.'

Michael sat up, his heart pumping so wildly he was sure she could see it through his shirt. 'Thanks.'

Lucy pulled up the chair opposite him. 'You're Michael Teegan, aren't you?'

Michael's heart flipped.

'And you live with your aunt who works for the priest?' Her eyes were sparkling with interest.

She was interested in him! She cared! He nodded.

'And you have that woman staying with you, haven't you? The one everyone is talking about?' Now she was practically leaning across the table. 'The one who was fixing her knickers at the roundabout?'

Michael pushed the coffee away. She wasn't interested in him at all. She just wanted to gossip about Monica.

She picked up one of the sugar sachets and started to fiddle with it. 'I met her, you know.'

'So?'

If his tone was indifferent as he intended, Lucy didn't seem to notice.

'She came in here the other day and we had a chat.' She spilled the sugar onto the table and started to make shapes in it. 'I liked her.'

'I like her too.' The loneliness he felt when Monica was taken off in the car washed over him again. He wished she hadn't been asleep when he got to the hospital last night, all flat out on her back with her gorgeous breasts and tummy rising and falling and her generous bottom lip trembling as she snored . . . dammit, now he was sweaty again.

'My mam met her in the hospital. She thought she was real friendly. She even went back at visiting hour but they'd given her strong painkillers or something and she was asleep.'

Michael shrugged. 'It happens.'

'So,' Lucy cast an anxious glance at the women working their way slowly along the pastry display towards the coffee counter, 'what do you think happened? I bet it was him, they're all like that. My mam says you couldn't trust any one of them.'

Michael looked at her in amazement and smiled. Wow! She was the same age as himself and she was so wise! She smiled back and as they sat there he could feel a tapping at his heart. He knew what it was. He knew who it was. As Lucy's little square finger traced a spiral in the sugar, Michael could see Miss April, wise little Miss April with her trusty rock hammer, tapping away at that big tough mountain. He cast a quick sneaky glance at Lucy's top. It wasn't bad at all. It was well tight.

And there wasn't a washerwoman in sight.

CHAPTER 14

At nine o'clock the following morning Bernadette opened the presbytery door to find Cormac standing there. For a moment she didn't know what to say – he looked so debonair with his Cromby coat neatly buttoned, his shoes shiny and a very smart silk paisley scarf at his neck. She stood holding the door open and sighed. Eventually Father Sean's voice called from inside.

'Miss Teegan, if there isn't a reason for contributing to global warming, I'd appreciate it if you would kindly shut the front door!'

'Hissssss!' Cormac licked his finger and stabbing it in the direction of the voice, pretended he had burned himself. 'Someone's in a bad mood!'

Bernadette giggled. 'I don't think he enjoys being the talk of the town. The Bishop's summoned him and Michael isn't here yet.' She stood back to let him in and pushed the door to. 'I can't manage the boy on my own, you know, you really are going to have to take him in hand.'

'Bernadette!' Cormac fanned himself with his scarf. 'The things you say! What am I going to do with you?'

Bernadette could think of a million things. She clasped her hands together. 'Marry me – soon.'

'Oh I will, my dear, I will. And don't you worry about Michael. That's all taken care of.' Cormac let his coat fall from his shoulders and handed it to her. 'Hasn't he told you?'

She nodded. 'About the job? But Cormac, Michael's not got a clue about –'

Cormac patted her hand. 'He doesn't need a clue, he's got me to guide him.'

Bernadette's heart filled with joy. Cormac to guide him – what more could a boy want?

When Cormac came out of Father Sean's study half an hour later, Bernadette was frozen. Even with the front door closed there was a draught. Fortunately she still had Cormac's coat clutched tightly to her but her feet were like blocks of ice. Sean glared.

'Miss Teegan! Have you been standing here all the time?'

Bernadette shook her head. 'No,' she said. 'I moved around a bit. It gets very cold, you know.' She shook out Cormac's coat, ignoring the creases she had now squeezed into it and held it out. 'Put that on you, pet, you'll catch your death.' She eased it over his shoulders.

Cormac buttoned up, wincing a little at the

creases and a lot as Bernadette started to smooth them down with her palms. 'Please don't worry, my dear, I'm sure they'll fall out in good time.' And with a quick salute to Sean he was gone.

Bernadette and Sean watched him go. As soon as his Jaguar turned at the gate, they shut the door and Bernadette turned towards the kitchen.

'Miss Teegan.'

'You wanted something, Father?'

'Miss Teegan,' he looked uncomfortable. 'I would appreciate, in my own home, the opportunity to have conversations in private.'

Bernadette's cheeks reddened but she recovered quickly. 'And I don't blame you,' she said. 'Especially now that you are the talk of the town. You poor thing, it must be awful to be at the centre of scandal like that. Would you like a nice cup of tea?'

Sean raised his eyes to Heaven. 'No, I do not want a cup of tea! Honestly woman,' his face was red and he was tapping the hall table impatiently, 'don't you understand a word I'm saying to you?'

'Absolutely,' Bernadette tossed her curls. 'I know precisely what you're getting at.' She walked quickly to the kitchen. 'You don't want tea.' She stopped at the door and turned around, flashing him a coquettish smile. 'But would you say the same if I offered you a nice milky coffee?'

Father Sean went into his study and slammed the door behind him. Bernadette sighed, oh well.

But at least she knew why. She'd heard every-thing. Cormac was keen for the wedding to take place as soon as possible and Father Sean said he'd definitely facilitate that. She didn't hear the next bit because that was when her feet were cold and she moved but then she heard some-thing about her not working once she was married. She giggled. Poor Father Sean, what a sacrifice for him. No wonder he was in such a foul mood!

At ten o'clock Michael turned up. He offered no explanation for his lack of punctuality except to say that he would be finished in the spare bedroom by the weekend and would start at Cormac's Monday. He didn't want anything to eat, claiming he'd had a croissant in the cafeteria at Supasave. Bernadette frowned. Michael was usually a three Weetabix, two slices of toast and a boiled egg sort of person.

'Aren't you hungry?'

He smiled dreamily. 'No – Lucy put butter on it for me.'

Aha! So that was it. Monica Moran was right about Michael having a notion of Lucy O'Donnell. Oh goody. Not that the boy wasn't welcome in his own home but once she was married she really hoped that she and Cormac would have lots of private time together. The idea of having a third person earwigging on their conversations didn't appeal. People needed their privacy. If Michael was taken up with Lucy, that would get him out of their hair. She smiled fondly. 'That was kind of her. A nice girl, is she?'

'Uummm.' Michael stretched his neck out as if he was swallowing something that tasted lovely. 'She's very kind. She's nearly as kind as Mo . . .' His face reddened and he turned. 'Anyway, I better finish up here. Cormac arranged it all with Father Sean earlier.'

Bernadette nodded and said, 'I know,' through gritted teeth. He had been about to say Monica, she was sure of that. After all that was said he still believed that bloody woman to be some sort of heroine. She'd have to put a stop in it once and for all. 'Sit down a minute, Michael. I need to tell you something.'

Michael sat.

'Monica Moran was not kind to you. She . . . she used you.'

'How?' his voice was heavy with scorn.

'Well,' said Bernadette, 'what did she ever do for you?'

'She gave me driving lessons!'

Bernadette shook her head. 'She did not, Michael. We both know that.'

He turned pale.

Bernadette smirked. 'Do you honestly think I don't know what she was doing?'

He was so shocked looking now she thought he was going to faint.

'Driving lessons, my eyeball!' she said scornfully.

286

'All those hours and the car didn't move one inch forward!'

He said nothing.

'Well, it didn't, did it?'

He shook his head. 'It kind of rocked a little from side to side . . .' he offered in a weak voice.

'Hah!' She was triumphant. 'And what good would that be if you needed to do the shopping! Face it, Michael, the woman taught you nothing useful at all. All her talk of theory was really just icing. You need the real stuff, the nitty-gritty.'

He opened his mouth but she stopped him. She had him now. He knew they weren't proper lessons. The car couldn't have moved. The rotor arm from the distributor was still in the drawer in the kitchen, and until she replaced it that car wasn't going anywhere. All those wasted hours. She looked at Michael sitting there, pale and shocked looking as if he had been caught with his hand in the till. It wasn't his fault he couldn't drive. That woman took him in with false pretences and gave him false hopes. She didn't want to teach Michael to drive at all: she just wanted an excuse to sit in Father Barry's car and probably remember the way she had taunted the poor man in it till she drove him to distraction. And he'd have gone over the edge if he hadn't had Bernadette there to save him. A wave of pity for Michael washed over her. He was like Father Barry in so many ways, so trusting.

'Michael,' she said, taking his hand in hers.

'Don't be upset. People aren't always what they seem. You can think you know someone all your life and then they turn around and surprise you. Monica Moran had you out there in the garage, not to help you, but for her own gratification.' She leaned in close to him. 'Because she did seem to be having a nice time, didn't she.'

Michael nodded, the colour flooding into his cheeks and a thin film of sweat appearing on his forehead.

'There you are then. She wasn't doing it for you, she was doing it for herself because . . . she was enjoying it!'

Two beads of sweat broke loose and flowed freely down his face. He was watching Bernadette with the strangest expression. 'You really think Monica was enjoying it?'

Bernadette nodded. 'I can assure you, pet, that she was loving every minute of it.'

'Gosh. I don't know what to say.'

'Say nothing.' She patted his hand and stood up. 'Now you know the truth and so you are under no illusion at all as to what that woman is really like. Off you go and get on with your painting.' She pointed to a saucepan on the cooker. 'I have a lovely pot of mushroom soup there for the lunch and when we get home tonight, there'll be another surprise for you.' She flicked the tea towel at him. 'Off you go now and get on with your work.'

Michael stood up, shaky and confused. He

looked as if he didn't know whether to laugh or to cry. He left the room and she could hear his tread on the stairs, slow and shuffling as if he was in a daze. Poor boy. And he really thought that woman could teach him how to handle a car. Bernadette smiled to herself. Well, he was in for a lovely surprise. She suspected he was keen to drive so that he could take Lucy out. Monica was no help there. Bernadette would be. She'd teach him to be as good a driver as herself and tonight the car would start. On the way home she would tell Michael her plan. When he finished eating she would take him out to the garage and (having replaced the rotor arm before tea) show him how well she could handle a car. She'd have him parallel parking; she'd have him turning on a sixpence and best of all with one little turn of the key in the ignition, she'd get the car to start! Oh yes, she'd offer to teach him in one hour all the special techniques Monica had failed to impart in two weeks.

She couldn't wait to see his face. It was just as they finished their tea that she told him. 'Now Michael,' she said, 'do you remember I said there was a bit of good news for you? Well, here it is.' She put her hands in her pocket and took out the keys of Father Barry's car. She held them up in front of him. 'You know what these are, don't you?'

He reddened and nodded.

'Well, leave the dishes, you can do them later. Follow me.'

Michael stood. He felt dizzy. She wasn't going to make him confess to what had been going on in the garage was she? With every step the blood drained from his forehead, his face, his neck and by the time they reached the garage even his feet were numb. She opened the door and switched on the light. Father Barry's car sat there, looking embarrassed.

Bernadette turned and smiled at him. 'Shall we get in?' What? Get into the car with his aunt? No way. 'What for?'

Bernadette shook her head slowly as if explaining something to a dim child. 'For a special driving lesson of course.'

'But I don't need a driving lesson!' Now his palms were sweaty and he didn't know where to look. She couldn't really be suggesting what it sounded like she was suggesting. 'I've learned all I need to know.'

Dim, dim, dimmer. 'Michael, you've only skimmed the surface.' She opened the car door and beckoned him to get in. 'An hour in here with me and when I show you what I can achieve with a flick of the wrist, you'll really see how things should be done.'

Michael stood rooted to the driveway. It was true! He looked at his aunt in horror. She still had her apron on and her face, pink and shiny from the heat of the kitchen, was framed by a selection of multi-coloured sponge rollers. She claimed the steam made her curls flat and having flat curls was some sort of social gaffe that must never be committed in Catholic households. She was holding out the keys.

'Come on, Michael, don't delay. Unlike Monica Moran I don't like to hang around talking. We'll just get in and get on with it. Imelda will come in the back with us so that if I forget anything, she can remind me.'

That did it. The sight of Imelda's skinny legs disappearing into the back seat while her squeaky voice thrilled, 'Oh, isn't it cosy in here!' was more than he could bear. He'd read about stuff like this in magazines he wasn't supposed to know about and he certainly never thought it would happen in his own town, never mind his own garage. Leaving the two women twittering about how it was always nicer in an old car and you just don't get the same feeling in modern interiors he turned and took off down the drive at high speed. He didn't know where he was going and he didn't care.

When Michael arrived in the ward Monica was shocked at his appearance. In a couple of days he had aged weeks. His face was pale and lined and his clothes hung loosely and were damp. He looked as if he had run all the way.

'Michael! What's the matter?'

He flopped on the chair by her bed, panting furiously. 'Oh Monica!'

Wincing from the pain in her extremities, Monica

hauled herself up on the pillows. 'It's okay, pet. You're safe now. Tell me what happened.'

Michael's breathing calmed a little. 'I'm telling you – everyone's gone mad – it's not safe out there!' He looked around wildly. 'It's not normal – one day Tullabeg's a regular town and the next – everyone's sex crazed!'

I wish, Monica thought. She was on the point of making a joke but one look at Michael's face stopped her. She pulled her gown over her chest. 'I think you'd better tell me everything. Here, have a drink of water first.'

Michael took the beaker and downed it in one. Then he wiped the stray drops from his lips and began. 'Well, first of all, there's talk in the town that the reason you're here is because you were in the car with Father Sean and you weren't – you know – with all your clothes on, and he kicked you out of it.' He looked at Monica for confirmation.

She said nothing, only nodded to him to continue.

'Then Father Sean turns into a sex maniac and had Aunty Bernadette swinging out of him in his kitchen!' She must have looked surprised because his voice became more insistent. 'Honestly, I caught them. Then Aunty Bernadette gave me a lift home and said she knew exactly what we were doing in the car and that you were only doing it to please yourself and you didn't teach me anything useful at all.' He paused, looked apologetic and

292

whispered, '*I don't agree with that, I think you were great*'.

Monica smiled. 'You too, pet.' Then she leaned forward. 'Are you sure she knew exactly what we were doing?'

Michael frowned. 'I think so, yes. She said she knew we never moved an inch forward.'

'And what did you say?'

Michael hung his head. 'I think I told her we went from side to side.'

Monica fell back on the pillows and laughed outright. 'Oh, God love you pet, we did too! And what happened next?'

Michael looked around at the door. 'It was horrible. As soon as the tea was finished she took me out to the garage and said she was going to teach me what you failed to.' With each word his voice was rising. 'She said something about one little flick of the wrist. She even – she even said that Imelda would sit in the back in case she forgot something!' His voice broke. 'It was so horrible!'

Monica sat smiling at him for a minute. The eejit. She could imagine the scene. Bernadette had obviously found time to undo whatever she had done to disable the car and was now going to pretend that her ability to get the bloody engine to come to life was down to skill and not subterfuge. She waited till Michael's breathing was calm again before she said quietly. 'I think she meant that she was going to get the car going, pet.'

'Why?'

'So that you could actually drive it. If you remember, we didn't ever get it going – the car, I mean.'

In Michael's head the light went on and colour flooded his face. 'You mean, she was talking about a driving lesson where you actually learn to drive a car?' She could see the thoughts rushing around in his head and bumping into one another.

Monica nodded.

'Oh.' One of the thoughts got up and steadied itself. Michael took hold of it. 'And what about the other story, you and Father Sean?'

She pointed to the cage someone had kindly inserted under the blanket at her feet. 'Michael, I have a condition most commonly known as gout.' She chuckled. 'The affliction of kings – serves me right. It makes my joints and particularly my feet sore. I also have a broken toe. Father Sean was kindly going to give me a lift but I said I'd walk and when I was opening the door, my skirt caught on the handle and I fell out. That was all.'

Michael buried his face in his hands. When he raised it again there was such a look of gratitude and relief on it that Monica felt like crying. The boy was such an innocent. She cursed her aching bones. There was so much more she could do for him. She was tempted to push over in the bed and do some of it right now when he stood. He was glowing.

'Lucy was right!' he announced. 'She said you were nice and Cormac was right too. He said he didn't believe a word of it.'

Monica was spared further revelation by the sudden arrival of Kathleen O'Donnell at the foot of the bed. 'So you're awake,' she said. 'I see you have a visitor already. And who are you? Oh!'

Michael turned to say hello and as she caught sight of him, Monica noticed her staring. In the dim hospital ward lighting the resemblance to his father was marked. Kathleen looked as if she'd seen a ghost.

'Hello,' Michael said, 'and goodbye. I'd better be off.' He gave Monica a quick kiss on the cheek. 'I'll come and see you tomorrow. I might even drive!'

'You be careful!' Monica called as he disappeared then she turned to Kathleen. 'You look pale yourself.'

Kathleen was staring after him too. 'I've seen him before but . . . he reminds me of someone. Who is he?'

Monica smiled – perfect. If Kathleen could figure it out for herself, there'd be no need to say anything. 'That's Michael Teegan, lives with the priest's housekeeper the far side of town.' Kathleen's brain was ticking, Monica could hear it. 'Don't know who his parents were, he's an orphan.'

Kathleen's lips tightened. 'I bet he is.'

'And he's just rushing off to see his girlfriend. She works in Supasave, in the cafeteria, I think.'

There was a gasp and Kathleen stood up. 'Well,' she said. 'I'd love to stay chatting but I must be off. I have to, em, collect my daughter.'

Monica smiled understandingly, very understandingly. 'Of course you do,' she said. 'I think that's a marvellous idea.' Then she lay back. 'I think I'll have a rest myself. It's been a busy day.'

If Kathleen wondered what she meant by that she didn't stop to ask. With a squeak of soft soles on vinyl she was out the door and away. Monica lay back on her pillows and smiled. Perfect! Now she wouldn't have to worry about a thing. Kathleen would protect her daughter; she had sorted things with Michael; and even old Cormac was standing up for her.

Perhaps life was going to settle down after all.

In the Teegans' kitchen the following morning Bernadette and Imelda sat drinking cups of tea. On the table between them there were two pairs of knitting needles, some balls of wool and a pile of pattern books.

'Bernadette,' Imelda whispered. 'I think that is the most beautiful idea.' She picked up the top pattern book and gazed at the back cover wistfully. 'Really beautiful. Cormac will be so touched.'

'I hope so. And I'll have them on a little plinth so that they don't get icing on their bottoms because I've had another idea about what to do with them afterwards. She pulled out another book. 'See here? Lovely knitted cushions. My plan is to save the little figures and when the honeymoon is over . . .' she blushed, 'if it ever is, I will sew them on to a cushion for him. He could keep it in his office to remind him of our wedding day!'

Imelda clapped. 'Ingenious! I think it's really beautiful.'

Bernadette took Imelda's hand. Her face was serious. 'And Imelda,' she said, 'I want you to take the wool back up to Dublin with you tomorrow and knit them for me!'

'Really? Oh Bernadette, I'd be so honoured.' She looked around the kitchen. 'I can't believe how much has happened since we arrived here.' Her face darkened. 'But you know there's something else I must do before I get on that bus.'

Bernadette raised an eyebrow.

'I must go in and see Monica. I haven't been near her since she was admitted, I was too upset. But I brought her here for the fortnight's holiday and now I can't just go home and leave her without a word about what's happening.'

Bernadette fought back a snarl. 'I don't see why not.'

Imelda fiddled with her cup and saucer. 'There's every reason why not,' she said in a voice that, coming from anyone else, Bernadette might have found decidedly whiney. 'Monica hasn't a bad heart, not really, not deep down. Whatever she did, I'm sure she won't have meant harm.'

It *was* a whiney voice. Bernadette wondered how she hadn't noticed it before. She took the saucer and put it on the draining board. 'There are no excuses.'

Imelda straightened. 'Bernadette,' she said. 'You are a kind and wonderful friend and I look forward to having you as my sister. But,' she wrung her hands, 'Monica has been neighbour and friend to the Hegarty family all our lives. We grew up together. I know she got us into scrapes but she didn't mean to. And she has settled down ever such a lot in the last few years. She's only just lost her husband and whatever you think, she is still in her grieving period. They say you should never judge a person then and whatever she's done, I cannot pack my bags and abandon her.' Her voice had risen an octave and her cheeks were red. 'It wouldn't be right. It just wouldn't!'

Oops! Bernadette looked at her for a minute. She was quite like her brother Sean when her dander was up. He tended to have these moments of passion; moral outrage, he'd probably have described them. Bernadette frowned. She looked at the pattern book on the table. From the front page a knitted bride and groom looked up at her.

Don't lose Imelda's support, their little black woolly

*eyes pleaded. Don't leave us here unknit – not when
things are at such a critical stage, not when there are
no signatures on the dotted line.*

Bernadette thought quickly. 'Imelda, Imelda,
Imelda,' she said, shaking her head. 'What are you
talking about?'

Imelda looked confused. 'Monica. I want to let
Monica know what's happening and see when she
will be allowed home.'

'Of course you do.'

'It wouldn't be right to just leave her there.'

'It certainly wouldn't, I wouldn't hear of it!'

'But . . . I thought you said there were no
excuses?'

Bernadette shook her head. 'And there aren't.
It would be neither right nor Christian to leave
the poor soul abandoned in the hospital with no
one to care for her, no matter what she's done.'

'But?'

'Imelda Hegarty! Did you not tell me only half
an hour ago that your poor husband would be
wanting you home and you really should go?'

Imelda nodded.

'And did we not agree that I'd drop you over to
the presbytery so that Father Sean could take you
to the bus?'

'*Yes but –*'

Bernadette held up her hands. 'Then that's
exactly what you must do.' Before Imelda could
raise any objections, she continued, 'There is no
question, absolutely no question of poor dear

299

Monica being abandoned. Look here.' She opened the larder door and indicated some Battenberg cakes stacked in the corner behind the ironing board. As Imelda leaned in to look Bernadette did a quick count – another one was missing. Michael must have taken it. He was still clinging to the notion that Monica was worthy of his attention but Bernadette wasn't worried about that. Deep down he knew she was useless. Look at the way he reacted last night at the prospect of a proper driving lesson. He'd bolted, terrified. All the nonsense that one filled his head with had left him terrified to even get into the car. And he'd probably gone into the hospital to challenge her. Bernadette smiled. And he wouldn't go in empty handed. He knew Monica had gout but he wasn't intelligent enough to realise that a steady diet of cake wouldn't do it any good. Monica would, but she'd be so hungry on a hospital diet, she'd eat anything she could get her hands on. She put her arm around Imelda's shoulder. 'I've been sending in little treats with Michael,' she said. 'I didn't tell you because . . .' she lowered her eyes modestly, 'I didn't want you to think I was too soft but . . .' When she raised her eyes again there were tears in them, 'I just couldn't bear to think of her all alone in that bed with no one to care for her.' She dabbed at her lashes. 'I really couldn't.'

She turned Imelda round and gestured towards the kitchen door. 'Now you go and do your packing and let's get on with it. You have got plenty to do when you get home and I have plenty to do here, but on the subject of poor Monica, you must relax. I will continue to take care of her. I'll bring in her things and when she's discharged, I will personally see her onto the bus for the journey home.'

'Oh Bernadette, will you really?'

Bernadette smiled. In her mind's eye she could see Monica's huge backside disappearing into the darkness of the Dublin bus. She could hear the clink as her fare fell into the ticket machine and the whirr of the ticket being dispensed. Then the whoosh as the door slid shut and the glorious rumble of the bus starting up. One puff of diesel exhaust and that slut would be out of their lives for ever. Would she put her on the bus? Would she ever!

On the table behind her the little bridal couple clasped each other's hands in glee. Bernadette to the rescue. 'Imelda,' she said, feeling more sincere than she had felt for a long time. 'It would be my absolute pleasure.'

As Imelda went upstairs to finish her packing, Bernadette stuffed the wool and needles into a bag for Imelda to take with her. She kept one ball of each colour back. It wasn't that she didn't trust Imelda to do a good job, it was just that she knew nobody would do better than she could do herself. Once Imelda was away, she'd knit up a spare pair and have them on standby – just in case.

Opening the drawer to stuff the wool in, she saw her list of pre-wedding jobs and sighed. She still had the top three tiers of the cake, Cormac and Michael's suits, her dress and the invitations. And she'd have to talk to Cormac about living arrangements. No point in having two houses, one of them would have to go on the market. And then the bridal couple to knit and then the last job – her least favourite – go and see the slut. She couldn't get out of it now. Monica and Imelda were sure to get together once Monica went home and Monica'd be sure to mention it. She added it to her list. Ho hum, best to get it done sooner rather than later. She'd drop Imelda over to Sean's and say her goodbyes then she'd pop to the hospital and see Monica. And she would be as good as her word – she'd bring her a nice cake and maybe even a small bottle of port. That should warm her tummy and heat her aching toes nicely. Bernadette giggled. If her plan worked and a steady supply of port and Battenberg reached Monica, then there was no hope she'd be out of that hospital in time to wangle herself an invitation to the wedding. No chance she'd turn up and ruin everything. She took a pair of needles from the table and stuffed them into the drawer as well. Maybe she should bring the knitting with her to the hospital. Mightn't be the subtlest thing to sit in front of the patient, nimble fingers dancing through the stitches when Monica was crippled with gout but it couldn't be helped. No point in sitting there with her hands idle. She looked at the Battenberg disdainfully. After all, her hands were fine.

She could knit.

CHAPTER 15

After Bernadette dropped Imelda to the presbytery, kissed her goodbye a hundred times and elicited firm promises that she would be back as soon as possible, she bustled Michael into the car. She had, she informed him, undertaken to look after Monica in Imelda's absence and she intended to visit her straight away. Michael didn't want to go. Even though they had all lived together for a while he didn't want to be with Monica when there was anybody there. For some reason, even the thought of being with her made him feel shy. It wasn't as if he was doing anything wrong; it was just that being with her made him want to.

After another round of *goodbye*'s and *see you soon*'s and *won't it be lovely*'s to Imelda, they set off. Bernadette was full of the joys and talked endlessly about how great it would be after the wedding. As she slowed for the roundabout, she turned and looked at him seriously. 'Michael,' she said, 'now that things are moving quickly for me, have you given any thought to your own future?'

Michael shook his head. 'D'you mean next week or next year or what?'

'Any of them.' She took her foot off the brake and the car sped along towards Supasave.

'Well, next week I'll be painting in Mr Hegarty's office; next year . . . I might get a girlfriend and after that I haven't thought about it.'

'You should, it's important to have a plan.' She paused a minute as if she was making up the questions as she went along. 'I mean, suppose you didn't get a girlfriend. Or suppose you had one and you were a bit slow off the mark and she went and married someone else, what would you do then?'

Michael cast a wistful look at the supermarket as they drove past. Inside he could make out Lucy talking to someone in the cafeteria. It looked like one of those shelf-stackers. Huh! Cavorting with a shelf-stacker in broad daylight – what was she playing at? Bet Monica wouldn't cavort with a shelf-stacker.

'Well, what would you do?'

They were just coming to the infamous roundabout where Monica fell out of Father Sean's car. Michael felt a stab of jealousy. If he had a car and Monica in it, he wouldn't let her fall out. He folded his arms crossly. 'Then I'd be a priest. Oh!'

There was a sudden jolt as the car came to a complete standstill. Aunty Bernadette's hands were tight on the steering wheel and her knuckles white. She looked shocked.

'Michael Teegan! What did you say? Did you really say that you were thinking of becoming a priest?' Her eyes were glistening and he wasn't sure if he'd just said something very right or very wrong. While he waited for clues, two huge tears disengaged themselves and rolled down her cheeks. Damn, very wrong obviously. He was about to retract when she let the wheel go and placed one hand on his knee. 'Oh Michael, I'd be so proud of you.' She beamed at him through her tears. 'My Michael, a priest.'

Hang on a minute, he'd only mentioned it as a last option. He hadn't said it was definite. 'I only said I might, if I didn't get a girlfriend.'

Bernadette took her hand back. 'Of course. You don't need to commit straight away. It's just nice to know where you're planning to be, that's all.'

'I'm not in a hurry to go anywhere.' She shot him a daggers look. 'No actually, I want to get married and get a place of my own – or be a priest.' The daggers softened into feathers. 'That okay with you?'

'Michael,' she said, softly. 'That would be just perfect.'

Monica was sitting up in the bed feeling a lot better and hoping for a visitor. Since Kathleen saw Michael and heard that he had a girlfriend in Supasave she hadn't stopped to talk at all. Bernadette was fast-tracking a wedding to the country's biggest girl's blouse and Michael was on the road to ruin if Lucy's mother didn't get in there quick. She lay back on the pillows and sighed. And the two weeks in Tullabeg were up. There was neither sight nor sign of Imelda. Poor Mel, queen of moral outrage but she usually softened quickly. Bernadette had obviously been hard at work. Aul rip!

Suddenly there was a bustling at the ward door. 'Oh, my dear, how *are* you?' Monica stared in amazement as Bernadette scuttled across the floor, scanning the ward as she did so to ensure that her Christian charity was being witnessed. 'Lovely to see you sitting up looking so much better.' She dumped some heavy bags on the end of the bed at Monica's feet and plopped into the chair. 'Oops, sorry, did I hurt you? I heard you broke your poor toe as well.' The smugness was oozing out of her so thickly you could scrape it off and use it to lay floor tiles.

Monica gritted her teeth and counted slowly to ten before replying. 'Oh I've broken more than toes in my time,' she nudged the bags off the bed onto the floor. 'Usually it's hearts. How is dear Cormac anyway?'

It worked. By the time she had retrieved her handbag's spilled contents, Bernadette's face was pink. 'My fiancé is fine, thank you very much. He's busy with the wedding preparations: it's such a stressful time.'

'It must be. Any day now he'll be Mr Bernadette Teegan. Imagine that.'

Bernadette had whipped a pair of knitting needles and some wool out of the bag and it looked as if she was about to plunge them into Monica's heart. Instead, she took a deep breath and started to cast on stitches. She hummed to herself as her fingers did little jigs and reels through the wool and she appeared to have forgotten that Monica was there at all. Eventually she looked up. 'You don't mind me knitting, do you, only I have such a lot to get done – it's for the wedding you know. I'm knitting Cormac –'

'I thought his mammy had knit him already.' Monica smiled at her own wit. 'Cause he does look knitted doesn't he? All soft-bellied and full of fluff. Can't say he'd ever appeal to me really. I prefer real men myself.'

That did it. Like a Ninja warrior Bernadette shot out of the chair and wrapped her wool around the needles. She thrust them in to her bag and stood bristling at the side of the bed. 'How dare you!' she said. 'How dare you say rude things – about my fiancé! You're so jealous! I won't stay another minute!' With every staccato phrase she took a step backwards and Monica wouldn't have been surprised if she had taken a leap into the air and shot herself, Matrix style, into another dimension. But she didn't. She got as far as the door, gave a loud disgusted 'huh' and left. The sound of her infuriated footsteps had no sooner receded down the corridor than Michael appeared.

'Hello,' he said, 'Aunty Bernadette not here yet? She was bringing you in some clothes and stuff that Imelda left.' He held out his hands. 'I had to go and clean up. I'm supposed to be buying paint.'

Monica smiled. 'Good to see you, pet. Have a look under the bed for me. I think she left some bags there.'

Michael reached under and pulled out the bags. Monica's nightdresses and tights spilled from the top of them and he reddened. 'I think they're all here. Will I put them in the locker for you?' Without waiting for an answer, he let the silky clothes fall into his lap and very reverently lifted each one up and folded it onto the shelf. When he was finished he turned and smiled at her. 'They're lovely, they smell like you.'

Monica wanted to cry. He was lovely too, sitting there with his soft curls and his freckles jostling for space with spatters of primrose paint and a teenage uprising. She held out her hand. 'And what about you, pet? How are things with you?'

His face darkened. 'Not good. I was going to ask Lucy for a date last night but as soon as I got to the shop her mother turned up and said she had to go home. Then when I went this morning for my buttered croissant, her mother was there again. She didn't gave me a chance to talk to Lucy at all.' He leaned forward and whispered. 'You know, I don't think she likes me. She's very crabby.'

Monica shook her head. 'Oh dear, that's a bad sign.' She let Michael's hand go. 'Don't ever get too close to a woman, Michael, till you've had a good look at her mother. A really good look. Because a girl's mother is a girl's future.'

Michael paled. 'Lucy's nothing like her mother!' He was indignant. 'Her mother is short and scrawny and Lucy is . . . is petite and slim and anyway, her mother has straight hair!'

'Oh well, that settles it then.' Monica shrugged. 'I'm only pointing it out, pet. She's not the only girl in the world, that's all I'm saying.'

Michael looked horrified. 'Well, don't. I don't know why you're being so mean about her. You know how I feel and nothing you or her mother or anybody says is going to stop me!' He stood up, huffy.

Monica shrugged.

He pushed the locker door closed with his foot. 'Bye then.' He leaned over and kissed the air somewhere to the left of her cheek.

'Bye.' Monica watched as he left the ward, shoulders hunched and angry. Oh dear, that didn't go very well. She thought if she planted a seed about Lucy's imperfections maybe it'd flourish but it looked as if he might go off in the opposite direction. She pulled the blanket closer, feeling distinctly unwanted. A tear nudged the inside of her eyelid. It felt like it did the first time, nothing but rejection, and this time there wasn't a Father Barry to come rumbling up in his big old car to gather her up and make her feel wanted again. To hell with them all. She sniffed and wiped her nose on the blanket. This time she wasn't going to wait around for her white-collared knight in black serge. As soon as she could put a foot on the ground she was out of here.

Monica Moran was going home . . . again.

For the next week Tullabeg was a hive of activity: on the Bishop's advice Father Sean took a week's holiday in the west of Ireland to 'get away from it all'; Bernadette took the week off and buried herself in preparations for the wedding; Imelda phoned every day from Dublin to say how the knitting was getting on; Monica obeyed all the doctor's orders and improved rapidly; Michael painted the ceiling of Cormac's office in shades of heather and lilac; and Cormac developed wrist strain. Because Cormac held the ladder.

Michael couldn't believe his employer's consideration and attention to detail. He insisted that Michael come down the ladder every half hour for a rest. He offered to massage his hands if they felt stiff from all that brush stroking. He even took it upon himself to pop the odd Turkish delight into Michael's mouth to keep his energy up. By Thursday Michael was sick of Turkish delight but the painting was coming along nicely. He should have been pleased with himself but there was a cloud hanging over him that wouldn't go away. Cormac, ever attentive, noticed.

'You're not yourself, Michael,' he said, signing a sheaf of papers and handing them to Gerald with a dismissive wave.

Gerald looked Michael up and down with his usual contemptuous sneer. At the doorway he made a great show of navigating through the paint tins, cloths and brushes that Cormac had so thoughtfully provided.

Michael glared back. The office boys were so snooty; every opportunity they got they made some remark. But they were the least of Michael's worries. 'I'm a bit fed up actually,' he admitted.

'Oh, my dear boy, you must take a rest and tell me all about it.' Cormac held the ladder so that Michael could descend the three rungs safely.

Michael slumped on the bottom rung. 'Not much to tell really. It's just that . . . well, I dunno . . . I feel like I'm being watched all the time.'

'Watched?' Cormac looked around the office. 'Who's watching you? When?'

Michael sighed. What was point of talking about it? Cormac wouldn't be able to make Lucy's mother go away, she was everywhere. Every time Michael went in to the cafeteria she was there, sipping at an empty coffee cup, waiting to give Lucy a lift home. And Lucy didn't seem bothered. Most of the time she just looked at him blankly, blew bubbles in her gum and shrugged. The only time she seemed interested was when he mentioned Monica and even then her mother would appear at his side looking for more sugar. He sighed deeply.

'Come on, Michael, you can tell me.' Cormac was stroking his knee in that understanding way that always made you want to tell him everything. A bit like Monica really.

'I just feel so frustrated, so near and yet so far, that sort of thing. Do you know what I mean?'

Cormac nodded vigorously so that his fringe, which had always struck Michael as starting remarkably near the back of his head, bounced up and down.

'It's like you're there and you're the only people in the world and any minute now it's all going to happen and then –'

'Call for you on line one!' Gerald called up the stairs. Cormac ignored it.

'And then suddenly you're not alone and you've lost the moment –'

'*He says it's urgent!*' the voice called again.

'And then you're back where you started.'

'*He's holding!*'

'Oh for the love of God!' Cormac stood and patted Michael on the shoulder. 'I know exactly what you mean.' He made a grimacing face at the phone. 'There's no rest for the wicked!'

'That's the problem,' Michael insisted in a loud whisper as Cormac picked up the phone and listened. 'I haven't even had a chance to be wicked yet! What'll I do?'

313

Cormac covered the mouthpiece and mouthed in a stage whisper. 'Be patient, my dear, try to be patient. It won't be too long now.'

'It had better not be, I don't think I can wait much longer.'

Cormac issued some assurances into the phone and then put it down. His face was red and shiny. He took Michael's hands in his and looked into his eyes. 'Trust me, I know exactly how you're feeling. Sometimes the urge is so great that you think you're going to burst.'

Michael nodded.

'But you must be strong. Take comfort from the fact that I feel exactly the same way.'

Gosh – who'd have thought skinny Aunty Bernadette could inspire such passion?

Cormac squeezed Michael's hands even tighter. 'We must both be strong . . .'

But she must do.

'Soon the wedding will be over and our new lives will begin.'

What did the wedding have to do with it? How would Aunty Bernadette marrying Cormac make it any easier for Michael to seduce Lucy?

'Your aunt is coming over this afternoon to talk about invitations and menus and I promise you I'll agree with everything she wants. There won't be a second's delay on my part.' Cormac was nodding and smiling as if the answer to all the questions was in there somewhere. 'She wants to invite the whole town!'

314

Of course! Lucy was probably going to be invited to the wedding! When she saw Michael there in his suit looking suave and grown up she wouldn't be able to resist him. And as the bride's representative, it'd be his duty to dance with the female guests and as soon as he got Lucy into his arms and she got a feel of his rippling muscles, well, on his right arm from the painting anyway, she'd be putty – pure putty. They'd melt together and when everyone else was dancing he could sneak her outside and with the moon soft on their heads and the grass silky beneath their feet they'd . . . they'd . . . do the business!

'Of course!' he breathed. 'Invite loads of people and then nobody would notice if we slipped out!'

'You mean at the reception?' The red of Cormac's face had now spread to his neck and drops of sweat glistened on his forehead.

'Why wait?' Michael felt ecstatic.

Cormac picked a brochure off the desk and fanned himself furiously. He was gulping for air but he didn't look unhappy. When he got his breath back he tapped Michael playfully on the shoulder. 'Honestly, the impetuousness of youth. Couldn't you even wait till afterwards?'

In his mind, Michael could see the lines on Lucy's bra as it strained against her top. There was a rush of blood to his head. 'Nope,' he said, punching Cormac playfully. 'I couldn't. And I don't intend to either. As soon as the last speech is up, do you know what I'm going to do?'

Cormac shook his head. 'Tell me.'
'I'm going in for the kill!'

If Bernadette was keen to get on with the preparations, Cormac was even keener. As soon as they'd had a cup of tea and a few nice buns he suggested they get down to the business of arranging this wedding. Bernadette laid all her brochures and wedding planner magazines on the table and announced she would knit while he perused them. He barely scanned the guest list before nodding furiously and agreeing that she get the invitations out as quickly as possible. He had already sent his best suit to the cleaners and insisted that to get a new one made would take too long and anyway, he'd be out of it as quick as he could.

'Cormac Hegarty! What's gotten into you at all! You're like a . . . a . . .'

Cormac rubbed his hands together and growled softly.

'A great big pussy cat, that's what you are!' She put down her knitting needles and giggled. 'Honestly. There must be something in the water. You're like a wild thing, Michael's like a wild thing, and I don't know which one of you I should be keeping my eye on.'

Cormac took her hand. 'Soon, my dear, you'll be able to keep your eyes on the two of us at the same time.' His eyes misted over. 'Because we'll all be together, for ever.'

She picked the needles up again but her hands had gone all sweaty and the wool squeaked and stuck to her fingers. 'Would you go away out of that! You're such a romantic. I hope you're not going to say things like that at the wedding and make me blush?'

'I can assure you I'll be saying as little as possible at the wedding. I intend to have the shortest, quickest groom's speech in history!'

'Do you?' A short insignificant little speech wasn't what Bernadette was hoping for at all. It had taken her the best part of fifteen years to get Cormac's attention and now that she had it, she intended that the whole world be notified of her success. 'I'd hoped you'd have lots to say.' She arranged her lips into one of those pouts you see on the telly where the man's cruel heart is softened and he gives his beloved whatever she wants.

Cormac mustn't have seen that particular film. He dipped his finger in the speck of icing sugar on his plate and licked it. Bernadette stuck her lips out further and lowered her head. The looking-through-the-fringe bit was supposed to be very effective too but not in her case – damn those heated rollers.

'Everything I need to say I intend to say in private, and certainly not when the guests are listening.' He licked the sugar again then reached out to her. 'I mean, it's not really for an audience is it, my little partner in conspiracy?'

The feel of his sugary finger stroking her under

317

the chin sent ripples all the way from the top of her head to the tip of her reinforced tights. Bernadette nearly squealed out loud. 'Oh Cormac,' she breathed. 'Don't do things like that to a vulnerable woman –'

He picked up the guest list she'd left on the table and said, 'I wouldn't dream of it,' without batting an eyelid. Bernadette marvelled at his self-control. There he was, setting her on fire and then carrying on with the arrangements as cool as you please. He was the most remarkable man. As she watched, he read the names under his breath and nodded. When he got to the end he looked up.

'No Monica?'

Bernadette bristled. 'Of course no Monica. You don't want her to be there, do you? I thought you didn't like her.'

'I don't,' he said, 'that's why I'd quite like her to be there – witness my victory, as it were.' And then he tickled her chin again.

That did it. Bernadette's insides exploded and she shot off the chair into his arms. She didn't care if it was a big sin and she might spend eternity burning in the flames of hell – she was alight already. Here she was, all alone in the world for so long and now a cherished prize, his victory. She sighed as she leapt – all those wasted years, she wanted to bury herself in him.

'Ow! Geddof! What are you trying to do!' Holding her firmly by the arms, Cormac held her away from him. His face was red and he looked to be in pain. Letting go of her he bent over and rummaged between the swell of his chest and the greater swell of his stomach and when he sat upright again he was glaring at her accusingly, holding the pair of knitting needles with which she had almost, unwittingly, stabbed him. 'You nearly skewered me!'

Bernadette fell to her knees, mortified. She'd forgotten she had those in her hands. 'Oh Cormac,' she said, 'I'm so sorry. I didn't think. I was overcome for a minute and I just leapt up. It's all so exciting for me, you see.'

He lined the needles up together and handed them to her. 'It's exciting for me too,' he smiled, 'but we must exercise a little self-control so no more trying to kill me off with knitting needles.'

She nodded, duly reprimanded.

'And no more leaping up either. You gave me a terrible fright.' He took her hand and helped her up onto the chair again. 'After all, you don't want to go giving me a heart attack before the wedding, do you? That wouldn't be right.'

Bernadette's spirits lifted and soared again. A heart attack? She knew exactly what he meant. All that rummaging and fumbling that goes on when a fellow needs his heart tablets – and all before the wedding? It wouldn't be proper. She smiled demurely. 'You're quite right, of course. We must be patient and keep our instincts in check but . . .' she took the needles from him and rested the tips of them demurely on her lower lip, 'I want you to know that afterwards, as soon as the wedding's over and you feel your little heart start to flutter,' she sucked the needle, 'I'll know just where to go for your tablets.'

And then she started to work on the boots again, knit one, purl one, knit one, purl one . . . the rhythm of her stitches like a mantra . . . knit one, purl one. As she worked, the clicking of the needles calmed her raging soul. She pushed the memory of her near manslaughter to the back of her mind. It wasn't her fault anyway, she'd never have leapt up and almost stabbed her beloved if he hadn't mentioned that awful woman and suggested that she be invited to their wedding. She gave a deep sigh. Typical. She knew it all along. Monica Moran was trouble and victory parade or not, she was not coming to the wedding. She slid a smile across the table to Cormac who was sitting there looking slightly bemused.

No, Monica Moran was out of their lives for ever.

Monica wasn't just out of their lives; she was also due out of the hospital. All her good behaviour and self-denial paid off and the pain and swelling in her fingers and toes had subsided. The doctor gave her a long list of foods to avoid and issued firm instructions to get plenty of rest before she attempted to get the bus back to Dublin. The cold and confinement of the three-hour journey could set her right back. Monica listened to it all and nodded. Yes, Doctor, she'd do this: no, Doctor, she wouldn't do that. Yes sir, no sir, three bags full sir. Monica stifled a sigh. Three bloody bags full was the problem. When she'd gingerly eased herself off the bed this morning she'd noticed them, all stuffed under it. Bernadette must have come in and left the other bags when she was asleep. Even the Battenberg cakes were there. She sniffed. She'd been well and truly evicted from the Teegans and now she was being evicted from the hospital and she couldn't think where she was going to stay. She opened her vanity mirror and had a good look. How had she managed to get into this desperate state?

The face in the mirror wasn't the usual one at all. Three weeks in the sticks and the roots of her hair were coming out in protest. Her eyes were pale and lifeless and even the panda mascara had faded from her bottom eyelids in the heat of the hospital. Against the ward's sallow walls her lipstick looked garish and the edges of her lips ill-defined. She snapped the mirror shut crossly. This wasn't good enough at all. She wasn't going to face the world looking like this. So what she had nowhere to stay? She'd find a bed and breakfast somewhere.

She reached into the bedside cupboard and pulled out her make-up bag. Even that looked a bit sad and old. The mascara brush had gritty bits on it and the eye shadow dish had a bald patch in the middle. She snapped the bag shut in disgust.

'You okay? You look a bit fed up. I thought you were due to go home?' Kathleen called loudly from the doorway, her voice barely audible over the whirring of the floor polisher she was pushing. She switched it off and came over to the side of the bed, shoving the make-up to one side. 'Do you want me to tidy up this lot for you?'

Monica shrugged. 'You might as well bin it, it's all past its sell by date, like myself.' She felt the tears threatening again.

'Oh dear, are we feeling a little blue?'

Monica couldn't answer her. She knew if she said a word it'd all come tumbling out: Bernadette's pettiness; Imelda's leaving without even a message; Sean's high-handed misinterpretation of her intentions; and Michael's abandonment of her when she was only trying to do her best for him over Lucy. All the great jumble of emotions would just come tumbling out of her and on the top of all of it the one she hated the most – loneliness. Dammit, too late. Before she could think another thought two huge tears rolled down her cheeks. She hadn't even the will to wipe them away. She sat slumped in the bed, beached.

'Ah, what's the matter,' Kathleen inched onto the edge of the bed, one eye on the door lest a nurse come in and catch her. 'You can tell me.'

Monica hesitated. She could and all. She could tell Kathleen who'd tell someone else who'd tell someone else and then the world would know your business. Oh, what the hell. Maybe it'd be nice to have the world wanting to know your business. At least you'd not be forgotten for a minute longer. She glared at Kathleen. 'Well, if you must know my business, I'm lonely. That's what it is. I am due to leave this hospital as soon as they can be rid of me and I have to wait a while before I can travel back up to Dublin and I have nowhere to go and no one that wants me.'

'Aah, you poor thing.' Kathleen sounded genuinely sorry. 'No wonder you're blue. And being in this place doesn't help.' She looked around the walls, her nose wrinkling. 'Are you not going back to the Teegans'?'

'Fat chance. They have me marked down as public enemy number one. Even Michael hasn't been in for days.'

Kathleen's face darkened. 'I bet he hasn't. He's been hanging over the cafeteria counter at Supasave morning, noon and night making eyes at my daughter. He has me driven demented keeping an eye on the two of them.'

Monica sighed. 'He's still keen then?'

'Yep, not that it's done him any good.'

'Glad to hear it.' Monica lay back and shut her eyes. 'Not that there's anything wrong with the boy. He's a nice lad.' She opened one eye and watched Kathleen.

Kathleen reddened. 'Of course he is, it's just that he's, well . . .'

Monica put her out of her misery. 'I know what you mean. He's very young and what with not having a proper job and all, it wouldn't do for Lucy to get tied up with someone like that.'

Kathleen's face cleared and she smiled at Monica gratefully. 'That's right, he's too young. It wouldn't do. Quite right –' She stopped suddenly and appeared to be having a debate in her head. 'Tell you what,' she said eventually, 'I have a great idea. You need somewhere to stay before you go home and I need someone to help keep an eye on that fellow for me. Why don't you stay over at my place?'

Wouldn't that be a real dose of pepper up Bernadette's nose? Monica sat up and beamed. 'Do you mean it? That'd be great, perfect. It's only for a couple of weeks. I'll keep a close eye on things for you.'

Kathleen held out her hand and shook Monica's. 'Deal. I'll come by after my shift and take a couple of these bags for you.' Then she got off the bed and went back to her floor polisher whistling to herself.

Monica lay back on the pillows, relieved. That was ideal. She'd have a chance to talk to Lucy and maybe point out to her the various attractions Tullabeg had to offer that she might not be aware of. There was a very good-looking porter on the early shift. She might even get to see Michael and have a chance to say goodbye to him. She sighed. Dear Michael. Dear innocent Michael. He was young, impetuous and hot-headed but oh dear, when he concentrated . . .

She could feel the old familiar glow about her again. Slowly she slid down under the covers. Maybe the show wasn't over really. Maybe the fat lady had one song left . . .

CHAPTER 16

Under Bernadette's precise instruction, Michael's driving improved considerably. Stopping was a juddery affair but he was improving all the time and it was with great pride that he accepted Bernadette's invitation to drive her to the church on the day of the wedding. That way, she explained, she would make the transition from Father Barry's Volvo to Cormac's Jaguar and it would be most appropriate, didn't he think?

He wasn't sure but said yes anyway. Bernadette was so happy nowadays that all you had to do was agree with everything and then she'd go off and leave you in peace. She had already made her dress, sewing and embroidering late into the night and there were six tiers of cake, each to be iced in varying shades of some purple colour, in the scullery.

Poor Michael was nearly turning purple himself with the effort of trying to get near Lucy. It was bad enough before but now that Monica was out of the hospital and staying with the O'Donnells, he hadn't a hope. If it wasn't Kathleen hovering around the counter at Supasave, it was Monica answering the phone.

And when she did Michael didn't know what to say to her. It was odd. When she lived at his house, talking to her was like being wrapped into a big comfortable cushion where nothing you did or said was ever going to be criticised. But now it was different. He didn't know how to talk to her. He'd ring and she'd pick up the phone and she'd say, 'Hello, O'Donnells' here, can I help you?' in a bright cheery voice and he'd say . . . nothing. He'd put the phone down and sit there till the heat went out of his face and he stopped feeling . . . feeling, well, ashamed really. Silly, he had nothing to be ashamed of. He hadn't done anything wrong. Kathleen O'Donnell's face came swimming into his mind and he tutted crossly – chance would be a fine thing. And it wasn't as if he missed Monica or anything. She was the past and he didn't need her any more and anyway, she'd be going home soon if she hadn't gone already. He didn't care. He'd just get on with his driving and his life and forget about her.

He got his keys and was already halfway down the road before he realised what he was doing. Hey – he was getting good at this sort of thing! Maybe he should call in on Lucy. He didn't usually call at this time so her mother mightn't be posted on sentry duty yet. He swung the car into Supasave car park and pulled up just beyond a pile of cardboard boxes stacked by the back door. Ignoring the heap, he leapt out of the car and ran inside.

Lucy wasn't in the cafeteria. Damn, damn, damn! All that thinking about Monica was making him confused and he needed to get his head straight. If only he could see Lucy he'd be okay. In a panic he raced up and down the aisles – she wasn't there either. The need to see her was building up inside of him. Reaching the last aisle he rounded the corner by the frozen food and there she was, stacking the freezer.

'Whoa! Slow down, you nearly knocked me over!'

'Sorry.' Michael put out his hands to steady her but she didn't need it really. She was quite secure on the first step of her stepladder, her chest eye level with him. Her lovely chest with its 'Flirty Babe' written in spangly writing across the front all stretched and pulled and . . . he put his hands out anyway and held her at arm's length.

'What are you doing?'

'You might fall.' His voice sounded deep. He tried not to swallow.

Lucy blew a gum bubble and let it burst on her lips. As she scooped it back into her mouth with her teeth she looked from side to side. 'I'm hardly likely to fall from here.' She sounded like she might be laughing at him.

Michael could feel the air from the freezer turn

to sweat and stick to his back. She was so close. She was chewing and watching him and it looked as if she was about to blow another bubble. Michael could see her lips part and the pink tip of the gum swell above the crease of her tongue. This was agony! Pure, unadulterated, delicious agony! He watched the little bubble, mesmerised. In the yellow supermarket lighting the tip glistened and seemed to be winking at him, teasing him.

Go on, Michael, it hissed, its little sugary voice barely above a whisper, *do it. Bite me.*

Beside him the cold air from the freezer rolled across his face but he didn't mind that. It wasn't too cold for him. It was perfect. It was just the sort of air you'd expect to have rolling across your face if you were in a cold place – like up a mountain. And Michael was up a mountain. He was up a very high mountain and it was a rocky one and he was clinging onto the side of it and Miss April was there and she was clinging on too and if he didn't hold on to her tight the two of them might fall off. And all the time the pink bubble was growing bigger and bigger . . .

Bite me, Michael, it was saying bite me, do it now.

And it was getting closer and closer and if it got closer still he was going to have to open his mouth and . . .

'Excuse me,' a woman's voice cut in from somewhere outside his line of vision, 'do you think you could pass me a packet of fish fingers?'

In a second Michael's world fell apart. The mountain disappeared and he was back in Supasave with one elbow in the frozen peas and the other attached to the arm that was holding, very tightly, onto Lucy O'Donnell. Tearing his eyes away from his line of vision, Michael looked up to see Lucy watching him. Without shifting her gaze, she reached into the freezer.

'Eight, sixteen or twenty-four?'

'Twenty-four,' the voice said.

As if with a mind of its own, her arm reached in and pulled out a large pack of Birds Eye Fish Fingers. She passed them from one hand to the other and then they were gone and Michael was alone with her again.

'That was very efficient,' he whispered.

'Thanks.' She was whispering too.

'And it was a big pack and all.'

'Yeah.'

Michael's heart sang. She was looking at him as she had never looked at him before. She was looking at him as if he was a lovely bun and she wanted to lick the topping off him. On one side of her face the cold air was turning her cheek pink and her neat little sticky-out ear pinker still. He wanted to reach up and put his hand over her ear and warm it up but that would mean letting go of her and he didn't want to do that. He wanted to stay there, holding onto her and looking into her lovely face as it moved, ever so slowly, closer to his . . .

'Actually, no, the medium packet will be fine. I'll take the sixteen.'

Fit to explode, Michael glared at the woman. 'Oh for God's sake! Make your mind up!' He wrenched the fish fingers out of her hand and threw them back into the freezer.

The woman stared at him in amazement. 'Excuse me?'

Excuse her? He wanted to grab her by her streaky blonde hairdo and wedge her head into the nearest packet of frozen chips and screw her face into them until she was buried up to her neck! He wanted to . . .

Lucy reached across him and wordlessly handed the woman another packet. Then she grabbed Michael by the elbow and stepping off the ladder, ushered him up the aisle. 'Shush, will you! Do you want to get me sacked?'

Michael couldn't take any more. He stopped and caught her by the shoulders. 'Lucy,' he said. 'If you want to know the truth, what I really want to do is get you *into* the sack.'

She looked shocked and he wondered if he'd gone too far. Whatever, he couldn't turn back now.

'I know it's sudden and all – for you – but honestly, I think you're gorgeous. You're all I can think about. You're all I've been able to think about for ages.' From somewhere above the boxes, the faintest whiff of perfume swooped and brushed his nostrils and for a split second he thought of Monica. He looked around but there was nothing there but shelf upon shelf of washing powder. He shook his head. Not now Mon, please, not now.

Putt! Lucy let another bubble burst and holding her head to one side looked at him for a moment. Then she nodded. 'Okay.'

Michael was lost.

Lucy started to laugh. 'What're you looking so shocked for? It's your idea.'

'What is?'

Lucy raised her eyes to Heaven. 'The sack, Dumbo – you and me? You said you wanted to.'

'I do.'

'You got a car?'

Michael nodded.

'Fine then, okay.' She pointed to the clock at the front of the shop. 'I finish at eight and Mam's out. She's taking that woman to the bus. Do you want to meet me outside?'

Did he ever! Michael thought he was going to die of sheer joy right there in the washing powder aisle.

'Fine – see you then!' Lucy pulled a length of gum and bit half of it off. Before he realised what she was doing, she popped the half into his mouth. 'Make sure you're ready!' And she was gone.

Ready? Ready! Michael Teegan was never more ready for anything in his life. Lucy O'Donnell had agreed to go out with him, to stay in with him even and he was totally, absolutely ready. With a whoop of delight he jumped up and punched the air. Thank you good fortune, thank you lucky stars.

The whiff of perfume brushed faintly across his face and he calmed.

'Thank you, Monica.'

As he let his Jaguar purr to a stop in the car park at Supasave, Cormac was sure he could hear someone singing. He squinted to see who it was. After a minute, the singer danced out under the supermarket's security lighting. It was Michael. He had his arms and legs spread wide and appeared to be trying to shake something sticky off the ends of his fingers in time to his song. As the music gained momentum he flicked and shook until his hands disappeared in a haze of movement and he appeared frenzied.

'Michael!' Cormac called, 'are you all right? What on earth are you doing?'

Michael stopped and looked around him. 'Oh, hello! Yea, I'm fine. I was rapping.'

'Is that what it was?' Cormac found it hard to keep the fondness out of his voice.

'I'm so happy,' Michael hugged himself. 'Things are great right now and soon they're going to get better.' He pulled some car keys out of his pocket. 'Well, I'd better be off. Bye!' With a wave, he turned and headed for the car.

Cormac's heart did a wave back. That boy – such life, such energy! He hoped he'd be able to keep up. He shook his head. A tonic, that's what he needed. He'd pop to the pharmacy counter and get himself a good multivitamin tonic while he was here and that should set him up. Only a couple of weeks to go: he hoped that'd be enough time for the vitamins to do their stuff.

A waft of home baking assaulted him as he came into Supasave's yellow glow. From all around, a cover version of Abba's *Fernando* lulled harassed shoppers as they wandered up and down the aisles seeking inspiration for the tea. Cormac smiled contentedly. Michael was right, life was great. He picked up a basket and looped it over his arm. Where to start? Just as he turned into the first aisle he spotted Monica. She looked pale and a little dejected.

Almost despite himself Cormac felt a whisper of sympathy for her. 'Goodness, I didn't expect to see you here.' He glanced into her basket. One packet of Mint Imperials. 'Is that all, nothing fruity? You can't be feeling yourself.'

'I'm not,' she admitted, 'nor anyone else either.' She leaned in close and whispered into his ear. 'To tell you the truth it's getting me down. I'll be glad to get away from this place. I'm off this evening. Kathleen is picking me up from here and we're going to have a quick tea and then it's off to the bus and home. I just came in to get a few supplies.'

Cormac shifted his basket to his other arm. 'Me too – supplies, I mean.'

'Goodness, still having to look out for yourself and the wedding so imminent? Bernadette must be slipping up. I'd have thought she'd be looking after your every need by now.'

Despite her gloom she was trying to goad him; Cormac could see that. Well, he wasn't going to rise to it. Hadn't he just seen Michael and he in a frenzy of excitement at all the lovely things ahead of him? He pulled himself up to his full height and pushed back a stray lock of fringe. 'I'm sure she will leave no stone unturned.'

Monica tutted. 'Honestly, I can't believe you are going through with this charade, Cormac. I mean, it's hardly a marriage made in Heaven.' She looked at him seriously. 'What are you hoping to get out of it anyway, you and Bernadette Teegan? She'll be embroidering your underpants before the honey-moon's over.'

'She can do what she likes with them. Once the wedding is done I'll hardly have time to wear any anyway!'

'Cormac!' She looked shocked – she who prided herself on being outrageous. 'Well, good luck to you, that's all I can say. If Bernadette Teegan does it for you then there's hope for the rest of us.' She shrugged. 'I'd better finish up here. Kathleen is picking me up in fifteen minutes.' She gave him a cursory kiss on the cheek. 'Good luck to the two of you anyway,' and turned towards her trolley.

Cormac watched her move away, surprised. Fancy that! Monica Moran, always a step ahead of the game and she didn't know what was really going on! He couldn't quite believe it. 'Monica?'

She turned around.

'You're only pretending not to know what's going on, aren't you?'

She looked blank.

He glanced around to ensure they weren't being overheard and then whispered. 'It's not really her, of course.'

'What isn't?'

'That I'll be married to – after the wedding.'

'Hey?'

'It's all a set up.' He shifted position. 'It's really Michael.'

Now she was completely befuddled. 'You're really marrying Michael?' Her face started to wash over pink and she looked at him sympathetically. 'Cormac, pet, are there some tablets or something you're supposed to be taking?'

'Nooo!' She wasn't taking him seriously. She was back to her old trick of skitting him at every turn. Agitated, he pointed out the front windows to the car park beyond. 'You didn't happen to see Michael out there a couple of minutes ago, did you?'

She looked to where he was pointing. 'As a matter of fact, I saw him in here.'

'And did he seem happy to you?'

'Ecstatic.' Her voice was flat and she looked troubled.

'Ah ha! Well, there you are.' Cormac picked up a magazine and rolling it, tapped her smartly on the shoulder. 'That's because he has a lot to look forward to!'

'But Cormac, it's so wrong. It's immoral, unnatural.'

Since when did Monica Moran take up residence on moral high ground? Cormac felt hurt. She'd known him since forever, was one of the first people to recognise and accept him and despite their competition, he'd always felt comfortable with her. 'I can't believe you feel like that, Monica. I thought you respected me.'

Monica looked surprised. 'Of course I respect you. You're one of the most successful reprobates I know. Why would you think otherwise?'

'You said I was immoral, unnatural.'

'Not you. What's it got to do with you? I am worried about Michael.'

'But Michael's got to do with me. That's the whole point!'

Monica regarded him for a minute then shook her head. 'Hang on. I think we need clarification here. This has nothing to do with you. So, from the beginning: I am upset because Michael Teegan – for whom I carry a great fondness – is about to commit adultery.'

Cormac nodded eagerly.

'With his own sister.'

What was the woman talking about?'

Monica must have noted his confusion because she caught him by the elbow and ushered him down the centre aisle to the far end of the shop. Around the corner, where cold air blasted onto his delicate skin, she stopped and pointed to a young girl who was standing on a stepladder dreamily feeding bags of pre-packed carrots into tall freezers. 'Do you know who she is?' she whispered.

He shrugged.

'She's Lucy O'Donnell,' she said, 'daughter of my hostess, Kathleen, former cleaner at the presbytery, in Father Barry's day.'

What did any of this have to do with Michael?

'And daughter of the aforementioned Father Barry.'

'And?'

'Look at her. Doesn't she remind you of anyone?'

Cormac squinted at the girl. She was vaguely familiar.

'Her curly hair? The way her jeans could be hipsters if she had any hips to hang them on?' Monica sounded tetchy. 'Look at her ears, for goodness sake!'

Cormac pulled his glasses from his top pocket and slipped them on. He peered at the girl. Curly hair, skinny hips, protruding ears . . . but cute all the same . . . neat . . . oh my dizzy aunt! A cold wave of air hit him and it wasn't from the freezer. 'Michael!'

'Precisely. Michael. That young girl is the reason Michael is so ecstatic, Cormac. He's in love with her. And she's his sister.'

This was all wrong. Monica was all wrong. Michael was in love with him. He'd said so. He'd said so the very first time he came to visit him . . . *in the aisle at Supasave . . . the medicine aisle . . .* that was where he'd seen his beloved. Cormac's mind flashed back to that day. He'd been feigning flu to get out of having Imelda stay with him and he'd come here and just as he was making his way to the check-out, Bernadette and Michael came up and . . .

'Hello, Mr Hegarty, hello, Monica!' as if she sensed his presence, the girl turned and waved at them.

Her voice was in his memory too . . . *There you are, Mr Hegarty, if that lot doesn't cure you . . .* The girl was jumping off her ladder and coming towards them. She was glowing.

'Hello pet,' Monica said. 'You look happy.'

Lucy grinned. 'I am,' she said. 'Say nothing to my mother, will you, but I have a date tonight.' She winked conspiratorially. 'A hot date.'

'Anyone we know?'

Lucy pulled a stray wisp of hair and ran it coyly between her lips. She looked from one to the other as if she was considering letting them in on a secret. Then she shook her head. 'Probably,' she said, 'I'm not saying but –' she smoothed her creaseless tummy, 'he has a car!' Then she wiggled her non-existent hips. 'And you know what that means!' With a laugh that suggested she knew a lot more than her times tables, she ran off back to her shelf-stacking.

Cormac felt as if he'd been slapped. 'Her?' His mind was a babble of conversations as everything

Michael had said to him turned on its head. 'That's who Michael's been talking about?'

There were tears in Monica's eyes. 'I don't know what else to do. We can only hope he comes to his senses. He won't listen to me and I tried to tell you and I tried to tell Sean and I tried to tell Bernadette . . .'

Bernadette! Bernadette with her sugary fairy cakes and her embroidered violets and her tight curls! Bernadette with her neat pleats and her colour-coded marigolds! Bernadette in his kitchen, buttering his soup rolls and mashing the lumps out of his mushrooms and . . . A groan must have escaped his lips. He looked at his watch in horror. 'I'm supposed to be getting married in a week's time!' He looked at Monica. 'What are we going to do?'

Monica patted him on the sleeve. 'I don't know, pet,' she said. 'I've done all I can and I'm out of here on the first bus. And if you don't want to be mothered and smothered to death – I suggest you do the same – and quickly.'

With a last desperate glance at Lucy O'Donnell who was now fondling what could, in the right conditions, be a very attractive French garlic loaf, Cormac dropped his basket.

And ran.

Michael was still singing when he arrived back at Supasave at eight thirty. Lucy was standing out the front waiting for him. He opened the door and waved.

'Oi! Lucy! Over here!'

At first she didn't appear to hear him but then she turned and though he couldn't see her face he was sure it had lit up and there was a warm glow about her as she swept her way across the car park in her baggy trousers. She didn't say a thing when she reached the car, just looked it up and down. When she spoke she sounded a bit disappointed.

'This your car?'

'Sort of.' Michael wasn't sure if that was the right answer or not.

'It's a bit old fashioned.'

Obviously not. 'Well, it's not actually mine. I'm only using this one 'cause I was doing a job for someone, I have to leave it back.'

She ran her finger down the side of the front windscreen. 'Who owns it then?'

Damn! Admitting that he was intending a seduction in Father Sean's car was hardly a great warm up line. 'It's . . . em . . .'

She raised an eyebrow.

His spirits fell. 'It belongs to the presbytery.'

Lucy looked at him in amazement and then clapped her hands in delight. 'Wow! D'you really mean it? Making-out in a priest's car – that's *so* alternative.' She yanked at the door handle. 'Go on then, let me in.'

Michael leapt in and unlocked the passenger door. Lucy lifted the legs of her trousers, slid her bum across the seat and then she was there, beside him. Michael clutched the steering wheel to stop himself exploding in a great gush of delirious ecstasy and waited for his heart to slow sufficiently so that he could think what to do next.

Lucy looked at him. 'Aren't you going to start then?'

What! Here? 'In Supasave car park?'

She giggled. 'The car, Michael. I meant, aren't you going to start the car?' She was laughing at him again.

Michael huffed. 'I knew that.' He located the ignition, turned the key and the car purred into life, first time.

Lucy put her head back on the seat and closed her eyes. 'Go on then, where are you taking me? My mam is out till a quarter past nine. She thinks I'm going back to my friend's house and then getting a lift down. She said she'd meet me at the bus stop once the Dublin bus has left.'

All those details. Michael felt as if he was being blinded with science. If Lucy was being met by her mother at a quarter past that meant that they only had . . . dammit! Forty-five minutes! He pressed his foot on the accelerator and rode the clutch out of the car park as fast as he could. When he was learning how to do this sort of thing they took at least a couple of hours, to get up to speed and all, and now he was being offered only three-quarters of an hour to do the whole business! He didn't know if he was going to be able to manage it. Where on earth could they go?

Suddenly Monica's voice came into his head and he remembered a place she had mentioned to him would be a good spot. She'd said that maybe they'd go there for a practice if they ever got the car started. Thanks Mon. He shot down the road towards the trees at the edge of the park, sweating and praying furiously. Screeching to a halt between two huge beech trees, he switched the engine off and turned to look at Lucy.

Oh. She wasn't looking at all as he expected. Instead of sitting there with her eyes all misty and her lips delicately parted, she was snow-white and had her hands over her mouth.

'Whassup?'

'Mgunbe sck,' she muttered through her fingers.

'Eh?'

She lowered her hands. 'Sick, you gobshite!' she shouted. 'I'm going to be sick!'

'Bloody hell!' And in Father Sean's car that was due back tomorrow! He reached over and opened the door. When she didn't move he caught her by the shoulder and gave her a push. 'Not in here. Quick – get out!'

Lucy stumbled out of the car and leaning her hands on the nearest tree proceeded to throw up. He didn't watch. When she was finished she got back into the car. Michael said nothing. He sat staring ahead. She said nothing either. They sat in the dark for what seemed a huge portion of the allotted seduction time and eventually he knew he had to do something. He reached into the glove compartment and pulled out a packet of mints that Monica had insisted he keep in there for emergencies. Good old Monica.

'D'you want one?' He held the packet out to her.

Sulkily she took two. Swooshing them around her mouth for a minute she rolled down the window and spat. Then she leaned back in the seat. 'Well,' she said. 'Aren't you going to say sorry?'

'What for?' Even in the poor light he could see she was glaring.

'It was your fault,' she said. 'You drive too fast.' She rubbed her tummy. 'I always throw up when people drive too fast.'

Great. What was he supposed to do now? She's the one who made making-out an Olympic speed event and she had the cheek to complain he was going too fast? He felt like giving her another shove. He felt like this time shoving her right out of the car and driving off. He felt like . . . he caught sight of himself in the rear view mirror – Michael Teegan! What is wrong with you? There he was in the car, in the dark, alone with Lucy O'Donnell and she with her mouth all swooshed out and ready and he contemplating getting rid of her! He must be mad. He turned to look at her.

'Lucy?'

She said nothing

'Luthy?' he tried again, this time remembering to adopt a very slight lisp that Monica told him was often a good idea, igniting as it did an urge in most women to take men in their arms and mother them.

Lucy wasn't most women. She lifted one corner of her nose and looked at him scornfully.

Right. If not boyish charm, try the macho man offensive.

'Are you sulking?' he asked her.

She shrugged.

She was. He wondered how long she could keep it up for. He glanced at the clock on the dashboard. Only twenty-five minutes before she had to be at the bus stop! She had finished the entire packet of mints by now and was starting to examine her nails, biting off the jagged bits at the edges. Please God, don't let her be a good sulker. He cast around in his head for any instructions Monica might have left to cope with such a situation. There was nothing. There wasn't even a spare packet of sweets he could soften her up with. He reached in to see if maybe one had fallen out or something but the only thing there was his crumpled magazine. That was it!

'Lucy,' he said. 'I think you should give up working at Supasave.'

No response.

'I think you should travel. Go north somewhere and get a job up there. Somewhere cold.'

She stopped examining her nails and looked at him. 'Why?'

Steady now. 'Because you're beautiful,' he said

simply, without looking at her. He took the magazine out of the compartment and making sure to hold it in the shadow so she couldn't see the page, he turned to the centre spread. Miss April smiled up at him. 'You could be a model and people would pay hundreds of pounds to buy your photograph and just look at you.'

'But why up north?' She was leaning forward now and her voice had softened.

He looked at her as if he had just remembered she was there. 'Your skin. You don't want to go to a hot country where you'd get burned. You need to be somewhere where people can appreciate your beautiful milky skin. You could model and be on calendars and that sort of thing.'

She caught a strand of hair that had come loose from her ponytail when she was being sick and twirled it round her finger. 'But I might get cold!' she said, pouting. 'I might be fweeeezing!'

Bloody hell! Now *she* was lisping! Michael's palms were sweating and before he could stop her, Miss April slipped out of his hands into a heap at his feet. Abandoning her to her fate he launched himself across the gear stick and embedded his face in Lucy's. Kiss. 'Lucy, Lucy,' he moaned. 'You're all I ever dreamed about.' Kiss. He buried his face again.

Actually, not quite, a small voice floated up from the floor on the driver's side. Michael pulled back and looked around him in surprise. There was nobody there. Just him and Lucy.

She doesn't taste as nice as you'd hoped, the voice continued. She tastes of mint and yuck. She ought to taste of port and marzipan.

Michael shook his head. She tasted fine. He took a deep breath and dived. She tasted lovely; he wanted to consume her. With a clinking of teeth and a tangle of tongues that rivalled any mess Aunty Bernadette ever got her wool into, he stroked her face furiously till he could feel her ears grow red.

'Oh, Michael.' She was panting now and he hoped she wasn't going to get too hot and feel sick again.

He sat back. 'Are you okay, you don't want to get out again or anything?'

She leaned forward and wriggled out of her jacket. As she flung it over into the back seat of the car, the furry hood brushed his cheek like a caress. That did it – enough kissing. He was going in for the kill. Monica, Monica, he thought, I'll do you proud. And then he dived again.

As if on autopilot Michael's hand reached across and touched the lettering on Lucy's tee shirt where it strained across her breasts. For such a slight girl she was suddenly remarkably well-endowed. Michael smiled and shut his eyes. He liked well-endowed. He was brought up on it. Very slowly he wormed his hand underneath and started the long, glorious journey upwards. After only a couple of seconds his fingers met with something hard. It was long and swept across her side to a point in the middle. After that there was a dip and then another one. He was about to ask her what on earth she was hiding up there when the little voice started up again.

It's her ribs, stupid.

Ribs – of course. Well, ribs were okay.

She's got no glorious flesh to bury yourself in.

Yes, she has. Michael had felt the strain.

She's a washboard!

Would you please shut up!

Michael opened his eyes and locked stares with Lucy. He was on the threshold of the most wonderful moment of his life and the last thing he needed was a jealousy-crazed rock-climber trying to dampen his ardour. Under his shoe the magazine creased and crumpled and he shifted slightly so that he could catch it with his heel and mash it. He leaned down and kissed Lucy's tummy. She smelt of fabric conditioner.

He slid his hand, with more than a little difficulty – boy, was it a tight squeeze in there – across the top of her bra. She caught her breath and threw her head back in abandon. At that angle he could see her goitre, all pert and pointy, bobbing up and down in her neck, expectantly. Then he lowered his gaze to her chest. Even in the dark it looked amazing. Her bra was an acreage of pink lace that covered her breasts and cleavage completely. He could only guess at the wonders beneath. Shutting his eyes again, he pulled her top up to her neck and reached back to undo the hooks. With a click of relief, the bra sprang open and something landed on his lap. He ignored it. He rubbed his sweaty palms quickly on his shoulders and twiddled his fingers. Lusciousness of Lucy – here I come! He lunged.

Nothing.

Michael pulled his hands back and tried again.

Still nothing. Where her breasts ought to be there was nothing. What on earth?

Told you so, told you so!

He opened his eyes and peered at her in the darkness. Even in the dim light of the street lamp her ribs were visible and above them her tee shirt creased across her chest and wedged under her armpits, and in between – nothing. Michael looked closer. There were no breasts! He looked up into her face. If that were Monica he'd have scaled the Alps by now.

'Lucy,' he said, trying to sound casual. He swallowed. 'Lucy, where are your boobs?'

Lucy looked at him and her eyes widened. 'Oh hell,' she said, 'you haven't lost them have you?' She pulled her top down and started scrabbling on the floor at his feet. 'I've only had them two days. Damn. Where are they? I can't afford to replace them.' Her voice was muffled as she searched. 'Gotcha!'

Triumphantly, she sat upright again clutching something in her hand. Michael squinted. It was oval, about the size of a cigarette packet and looked worryingly like an uncooked chicken fillet. She held it out to him. 'They're clever, aren't they? Gel – d'you want a feel?'

A feel? Did he want to sit in a car with a semi-clad Lucy O'Donnell fondling chicken cutlets? I don't think so.

You'd have had more fun groping her goitre, wouldn't you?

Shaking his head he slid slowly back to his seat. As he readied himself to start the car he felt the magazine slippery under his shoe.

Should have stopped when you were ahead, that's what I say!

Will you SHUT UP!

Bloody Miss April! Bloody fake Miss April and her bloody fake smile and her bloody fake rock hammer! It probably wasn't even a real mountain! In disgust he grabbed the magazine from where it was wedged under the pedals. Ignoring the tearing sound as some pages came loose, he opened the door and flung it as far as he could into the trees. Then he started up.

'What's the hurry?' Lucy asked. 'I don't have to be back for fifteen minutes.'

'I'm taking you back now,' Michael growled. 'I'm going to leave straight away and drive very slowly, so you won't be sick.'

'But I feel fine!' She slipped the gel insert back into her bra and was sitting there, lopsided. Michael shot her a quick glance.

Washboard.

Gritting his teeth so tightly that he nearly bit himself on the forehead, he drove slowly to the edge of the High Street near the bus stop and leaning across her, opened the passenger door and motioned her to get out.

She pulled her jacket off the back seat and got out of the car. 'Thanks for nothing,' she said crossly. 'I could have gone to my friend's house and watched *The Bill*. She gave another cursory look inside the car. 'And you've lost my other insert!'

'Don't worry,' Michael said, pulling the door closed, 'if I come across it, I'll leave it at the counter at Supasave for you.'

She glared.

'Or maybe drop it in to your mother's. I don't want it anyway!'

She may have replied but Michael didn't wait to listen. He drove to the end of the road and parked there, tears of anger and frustration burning his eyes. At the corner the car stalled and a cacophony of horns assaulted him as a large coach pulled out around him towards the Dublin Road. Michael waved his fist at its tail lights. That's all he needed. The woman of his dreams turns out to be a fake and then he suffers road rage at the hands of a bloody bus driver. Who can you bloody trust? And a bloody Dublin bus driver at that.

Monica!

As if he was Saul on the road to Damascus,

Michael was hit by a blinding flash. The Dublin bus! Of course! Monica was going home on the Dublin bus! Monica who had never let him down; Monica who had tried to warn him and he abandoned her. In a flurry of panic he turned the key in the ignition and prayed for the car to start.

Up ahead the rear lights of the bus disappeared into the distance but Michael wasn't going to let them disappear for ever. Monica was on that bus. Dear, darling Monica with her gorgeous smells of port and marzipan. Monica with her wonderful swathes of flesh that a fellow could drown in and die happy. With a roar, the car burst into life and Michael's heart lifted.

Hold on, Monica, I'm coming, Monica. Hold on!

CHAPTER 17

As he closed his suitcase and started to haul it out to the car, Cormac was struck by the uncomfortable thought that what he was doing wasn't quite right. What nonsense! He left his case by the front door and went into the kitchen. There was still half a carton of cream and a couple of very nice pastries in the fridge and it would be folly to leave them there to go off. He filled the kettle and flicked the switch. He should have a mug of hot chocolate and a snack and then call in to the office and leave instructions on how to cope while he was away. There were no major jobs on at the minute – the boys would be fine. Cormac wiped his brow with his handkerchief and thanked his lucky stars he hadn't let them go. Imagine, he was on the point of cutting his staff when Michael turned up that day . . . He lowered the handkerchief to his eyes and wiped away a tear. Dear Michael, dear, dear Michael.

Behind him the kettle started to steam and Cormac watched it for a minute. It reminded him of something. He shut his eyes and recalled that evening in Bernadette's kitchen only a few weeks back when he had held her hands and asked her to collaborate with him in his claim to ill health. She had readily agreed: she would be his collaborator, his . . . Good Lord! That was it! His partner-in-crime! They were the words he used. She must have taken them and embroidered them and fuelled only by her own passion and imagination, succeeded in weaving a tapestry of ambiguity. He turned the kettle off and stood trembling. Why didn't he recognise it sooner, it wasn't his fault at all. He was just an innocent victim of someone else's plotting and desire. And to think how she had misled him over Michael! Holding the boy out like a carrot (he mopped his brow again) when all the while she had her eye on the real prize. He swept the kitchen with a fond eye – his Aynsley tea sets, his matching Portmerion cookware – that's what she was after. Cormac shook his head. You really couldn't trust women.

Taking the cream out of the fridge, he emptied the carton down the sink and put the cakes into a bag. There wasn't time to hang around a minute longer. He set the timer switch on his lights, activated the house alarm and took the bin bag out with him. Wouldn't do to come back to bad smells. One last check and he was away.

As he drove the rich voice of Luciano Pavarotti filled the car and he began to calm. All he needed was a couple of weeks away to let the dust settle and then he'd come back to pick up the pieces of his life. Sean might be a bit miffed but hopefully his latest scandal would still be sufficiently warm to keep him in check. Imelda might have a thing to say as well but she would be back in Dublin so it wouldn't matter. She had never approved of his lifestyle anyway. The only trouble spot was Bernadette. And he didn't know what he was going to do about Bernadette.

Up ahead, the lights of the High Street glimmered and at the end he could see people at the bus stop waiting for the nine o'clock coach to Dublin. He slowed as he passed them. Monica was there, standing guard over a pile of suitcases and he was tempted to stop and offer her a lift – he had room for a passenger. He sniffed. Behind him on the back seat was the soft leather travelling bag he had bought for Michael only two days ago and in it some lovely clothes and knick-knacks they were going to enjoy together. Maybe he should give Monica the bag, she'd surely find a use for it. He was indicating to pull in when the coach loomed up behind him, brakes screeching as it approached the stop. There wasn't room for him to stop as well. Bother. With a cursory wave in Monica's direction and without checking if she'd seen him, he pressed the accelerator and headed for the office.

After hours, the offices of Cormac Hegarty, Estate Agent were dimly lit. A soft glow warmed the reception area and the rest was generally in darkness.

But not tonight. As he purred to a halt Cormac could see a light on in his office. He opened the car door quietly and tried the front door. It was locked. Whoever was inside obviously had a key. Cormac frowned. There shouldn't be anyone there now. Should he call the Guards? Better not, that would only attract attention and Bernadette would be sure to find out and come and catch him. No, he'd deal with this one on his own. Feeling very brave he let himself in, picked an umbrella out of the stand and started up the stairs. There was a sound of paper being shuffled and someone moving about. He changed his mind and turned to go down. Whoever was in there might be hostile. It might be a big burly burglar type. Trying to avoid the creak on the third step from the top, he started to go down again.

'Mr Hegarty?'

The voice was familiar. Cormac turned to see Gerald Greeley standing at the top of the stairs.

'Gerald? What are you doing here?'

Gerald held out an envelope. 'I was just delivering this. I didn't want the others to read it so I was going to leave it on your desk.'

Cormac took the envelope from him and ushered him into the office. With a sigh, the boy sat on the chair Cormac indicated and even in the dim light of the desk lamp Cormac could see that he was upset. He looked at the envelope. It was damp.

'What's this, Gerald?'

Gerald sniffed. 'It's my resignation.'

Cormac raised and eyebrow. 'But why? Why would you want to resign? You're my best boy!'

'Not any more, I'm not.' He lifted his head and glared at Cormac sulkily. 'I work so hard for you – to please you and you don't even notice. I work much harder then the others and you don't say a thing except would I get another cup of tea for your painter friend!' He pointed to the ceiling, 'And look! He doesn't even do corners nicely!'

Cormac looked. Gerald was right. Although Michael had used masking tape he hadn't stuck it down properly and there was a wavy line all around the top of the wall. It was very sloppy really. He wondered how he hadn't noticed it before. He looked back at Gerald. The boy was obviously very upset. His face was streaked and he was wringing his hands and he looked so vulnerable. Cormac felt a warm glow flow over him. He reached over and took Gerald's hand in his.

'Oh my dear boy,' he said. 'Is that why you're leaving. Do you really think I don't appreciate all the work you do for me?' Gerald said nothing. 'Because I do.'

Gerald's hand twitched in his and there was the slightest squeeze.

'In fact,' the seeds of a truly wonderful idea were beginning to germinate and grow in Cormac's brain, 'in fact, I came here tonight hoping to find you.'

'What for?'

Cormac pointed out the window to where his car was parked below. 'Well,' he said, 'I've actually been thinking that you were looking rather tired and that you could do with a little time off.'

'You're sacking me?' Gerald's eyes were wide with dismay.

Cormac laughed, a big hearty avuncular laugh. 'Sacking you, my dear boy? Goodness no, nothing could be further from the truth. I couldn't do without you.' He slapped his hands on his knees. 'No, I was proposing that you take a short holiday, somewhere nice . . .' he caught Gerald's hand again, 'with me.'

In an instant, Gerald's face cleared and his eyes lit up. 'Oh, that would be wonderful! Thank you, Mr Heg –'

'Ah ah! None of that now!' Cormac stroked Gerald's palms affectionately. 'No need to be formal now, is there. Why don't you call me Cormac.'

In the car below the soft leather travelling case was no longer excess baggage. It had assumed a new purpose. It was going to be put to good use.

'Cormac.'

As the bus pulled out of Tullabeg Monica leaned her head against the window. In the large side mirrors she could see the lights in the High Street receding. Kathleen had promised to stay waving until the bus was out of sight but someone must have distracted her because she wasn't at the bus stop now. Nobody was. Monica heaved a huge sigh and tried not to cry. Isn't that a sorry way to end all the same – a dark and miserable night in a rural backwater and not a soul to care if you're coming or going? Before she could think another thought a tear escaped, flowed over the ridges of her waterproof mascara and plopped onto her breast. She didn't bother to wipe it away. There'd be more where that came from before the journey was done.

All around her the other passengers chatted happily – relishing the trip and the prospect of the city at the end of it. Monica didn't have anyone to talk to. For the last couple of days she had thought she'd be glad of that, pleased to get away from Kathleen and her incessant rabbiting away about *her* Lucy this and *her* Lucy that, and how Michael was such a fiend and her precious Lucy had to be kept safe from him. It was as much as Monica could bear. And then when the phone rang a couple of times and she answered it and nobody spoke but she knew it was Michael. His way of sniffing every so often was a dead give-away. But he didn't say a word. After the lovely times they'd had, when she was sure he had become genuinely fond of her, he'd cut her off completely. And now here she was, adrift on the Dublin bus.

As if in sympathy with her mood the windows of the bus started to steam up. Some of the condensation ran in small streams down the panes where it gathered on the dirty rubber seals at the bottom, ready to overspill onto her lap. The grimy remains of other peoples' muttered conversations. Great, just what she needed. She reached into her bag to get a tissue. She'd wipe the drops off before they landed on her – at least she could do that much to make herself comfortable.

Too late! As she leaned forward the bus swerved sharply and the water flicked across her chest, adding more marks to the one already there. Some bags fell off the overhead shelves and onto other passengers and there was a screech of brakes.

'What the –'

'Did you see that? Bloody lunatic!'

'Kamikaze *culchie*!'

All around her there was confusion. She'd had her head in her bag and didn't know what had happened, but by the sounds of it some eejit had tried to ram the bus. He was now parked across the road, blocking it, and the driver and two of the other men were getting out to have a word with him. Monica pulled her bag closer to her chest and waited. The wife of one of the men sitting opposite her was holding her husband by the elbow and threatening Hell and high water if he volunteered as well.

'You'll stay right where you are! There are enough other heroes on the bus without you getting yourself killed!' Her voice was already on the edge of hysteria.

Within a few seconds it appeared the man's decision to stay put was the right one. From outside the bus came the sound of shouting and struggling. Those sitting up front reported back that as soon as the car stopped, a mad-looking fellow jumped out and tried to scramble on board. He was clutching something in his left hand and shouting about needing to get back to what was real, about finding his destiny. A wave of fear washed over the passengers – a suicide bomber! Whatever he had in his hand, he wasn't letting go.

'It'll be a grenade,' the woman opposite announced with certainty. 'I've read about those types. Someone ought to ring the Gardai.'

From all around, people were pulling mobile phones out of bags and pockets and a variety of accounts was being fed into them to concerned friends and relatives. A long queue was building up behind the bus and when she looked back, Monica was sure she could see Cormac's Jag at the front of it. She lumbered to the back to get a better view. It was Cormac. He was sitting gazing adoringly at a young chap who appeared to be gazing adoringly back. The fellow from the office. Monica smiled. Cormac Hegarty, you fickle reprobate. Good luck to you.

At the front of the bus the action was hotting up nicely. A Garda car had arrived, sirens blazing and the Sergeant and a young Garda were attempting to talk the bomber into putting down his weapon. Everyone stayed quiet so that they could hear.

'Come on now, son. Just put it down and come quietly. You don't want anyone to get hurt, do you?'

The bomber muttered something. Monica strained forward to hear. 'Come on now, don't do anything stupid.'

'But I have to explain! It isn't real!' The bomber's voice rose over the heads of the passengers in front and hit Monica with full force. It was Michael!

'Michael!' She rushed forwards and pushed the others aside.

'Watch out, he's got an accomplice!'

As the husband opposite tried to grab her, Monica swung round and caught him off-balance with her chest. The man reeled back into the seat. Monica hitched her skirt and jumped down the high bus steps. The Garda Sergeant held up his hand.

'Madam, if you don't mind –'

'I do mind!' Monica was raging. Poor Michael was standing there, obviously distressed, surrounded by a bunch of lunatics. She held out her arms. 'Michael, pet, what's the matter?'

Michael lowered his arm and held it toward her. The Garda readied his baton.

'She was a fake, Monica. You were right all along. I did every thing you told me but look . . .' Very slowly he opened his fist and everyone craned to see. 'This was left in my lap.'

Monica looked.

'Careful now, we don't know what he's planning.' The Garda looked too but seemed no wiser for the experience.

'Not much if that's all he's armed with.' Monica threw her head back and laughed.

'It isn't funny!' Michael looked as if he was about to cry.

'It's them I'm laughing at, pet, not you.' She took the object from Michael's hand and tried to pass it over. The Gardai, the driver and the other men all pulled back. Monica snorted. 'Doesn't any of you know what this is?' She held it up for the other passengers in the bus to see. Every head was shaken in denial but a few cheeks reddened all the same. 'Well, aren't you all a credit to your mothers?' She leaned forward and whispered loudly. 'It's a boob,' she said simply. 'A little boob.' Then she shot a warning look at them. 'Just like the one you made here. Imagine the headlines. 'Bus Bomber Boob – Garda Mistakes it for the Real Thing!' She held her hand out to Michael. 'It's all right now, pet, I think that'll be an end to it. Do you want to go home?'

Michael shook his head. 'I want to come with you.'

'To Dublin?'

He nodded.

'For what?'

Michael smiled and took her hand. 'For ever, please.'

★　★　★

Even though the queue of traffic was now beeping and blowing enough to raise the dead, Monica could hear none of it. As Michael wrapped his arms, as best he could reach, around her, she could feel the warmth. All the drops on the sills that had appeared offensive a few minutes ago glistened like stars now and Monica's heart sang. Disengaging Michael gently, she ushered him up the steps into the bus.

'Hang on a minute, he can't leave his car here.'

Monica turned around. 'You take it,' she said. 'The keys will be in it.' She smiled. 'It belongs at the presbytery.'

The Sergeant looked doubtful. 'Maybe you should hang on a bit. Father Sean might have a word to say about this.' The young Garda leaned forward and whispered in his ear. The Sergeant's eyes opened wide and he smirked.

'There'll be no problem with him,' Monica said from the top step, 'and here, you could give him this as a keepsake!' She threw the gel insert at them and pulling her skirt comfortably over her hips, made her way back to the seat with Michael. As he wedged up against the window she wedged in beside him. 'A bit of a squeeze, pet, but at least you'll be warm.'

Michael beamed. In the harsh glow of the interior strip lighting his face was pale but as the driver got in and settled himself for the journey two bright spots of colour came into Michael's cheeks and he started to glow. And as the bus rumbled into life, Monica's hand slid onto his knee and the glow spread.

In the study of the Priest's house back in Tullabeg, Father Sean and Bernadette Teegan sat facing one another over a tray. Bernadette's face was ashen and Sean didn't look much better. For a full two minutes nobody spoke, and then Bernadette took a deep breath.

'When you use the word "gone", Father, what exactly is it that you mean?'

Sean shuffled the papers on his desk. 'I mean "gone" as in . . . you know . . .'

Bernadette glared. 'As in "not coming back"?'

Sean nodded. He picked up a piece of paper on which he had scribbled some notes. 'He said he simply couldn't go through with the wedding.' He glanced up apologetically. 'It's nothing personal, you understand –'

'NOTHING PERSONAL!' Bernadette leapt up and with a sweep of her hand sent the tray and its contents tumbling to the floor. 'The love of my life has jilted me on practically the eve of our – very public – wedding and you tell me it's nothing personal!' She placed a hand on either side of the table and leaned towards him menacingly. 'He's gone with her, hasn't he?'

Sean muttered something that sounded suspiciously like *I wish* and shook his head. 'Certainly not. Please believe me when I tell you there's no other woman involved, really.'

Bernadette fell back into the chair, sobbing. 'That's nearly worse,' she said. 'He left me for nothing then.'

Sean looked as if he were about to comment but thought better of it.

'And why didn't he call me to tell me himself? Is he some sort of coward or what?'

'He didn't stop to think it through. He just left and called me once he'd got there.'

Bernadette stood up. 'Well he needn't think he's getting away with it! If I can use your phone, Father, I'm going to ring Michael this minute to get up and we're going straight over there to have it out with him!'

Sean reddened. 'Em, I don't think that will be possible.' He motioned her to sit again. 'I don't think Michael is at home.'

'Of course he is! He doesn't have a job on so he was still in the bed when I was coming out this morning.' She cast a tearful eye towards the kitchen. 'Which meant I had to haul all those tiers into the car by myself . . .' The tear escaped and rolled down her cheek. 'All six tiers of wedding cake ready to be iced and eaten at a wedding that's never going to happen.' Then she threw back her head and howled.

Father Sean leapt to his feet and came around the desk. Seemingly unsure how to handle such a display of naked womanly grief, he placed a hand on each shoulder and tried to calm her. She shrugged him off.

'Don't bother,' she said crossly. 'You were never on my side anyway.'

He looked shocked.

'You knew how I felt about Cormac and you deliberately foisted that dreadful woman on me to try and tempt him away.'

Sean shook his head. 'Believe me, my dear Miss Teegan, there was never the remotest possibility that my brother would be tempted by Monica Moran, nor she by him.'

Bernadette felt a prickle of irritation. 'And why wouldn't she?'

'She's not . . . em . . . his type, as it were.'

'Huh, well he won't be anyone's type by the time Michael and I are finished with him!' Bernadette kicked the tray with her foot and prepared to leave the room. Sean stopped her.

'That was the other thing I had to mention to you. Please,' he shifted the scattered papers aside and sat her down, 'I've also had a message from Michael.'

Bernadette was looking at him blankly.

'He phoned me this morning, early.' His face began to redden. 'He's been up all night. He's in Dublin.'

'What?' Bernadette felt as if her world was spinning out of control. Michael in Dublin? Could that be why there was no noise from his room this morning? 'What's he doing in Dublin?'

Sean picked up the message pad and held it close to his face but it did little to hide the livid embarrassment that was suffusing his cheeks. He took a deep breath and read '*tell her I can't stay in Tullabeg any more. My destiny is here in Dublin and I have to find it . . .*'

Bernadette snorted derisively. 'That fellow couldn't find a pair of clean socks in a laundry basket, never mind find his destiny in a big city!' She looked at Sean. 'And what's this destiny supposed to be anyway?'

Sean turned the note over as if he hoped the answer might be written on the back. 'I don't know exactly. He said it happened all of a sudden. He was sitting in the car when suddenly he saw lights and realised that he had to follow them and so now he's in Dublin. He said he'll call you as soon as he gets settled.'

Bernadette frowned. 'And he was sober?'

'I think so, though he sounded very happy.'

Bernadette looked at the note. 'Lights? Sitting in the car?' She shook her head. 'What did he mean by that, I wonder?'

'I don't know about the lights but the car is the one I lent him when he was doing the painting. As far as I can work out he was sitting in Father Barry's car when he realised his destiny and –'

'Oh! Oh!' Before he could react, Bernadette leapt from her chair and flung her arms around his neck. 'Of course!' she was practically singing to herself. 'Of course! How perfect! How utterly, wonderfully perfect.' Then her cheeks reddened and she lowered her eyelashes, 'And even more wonderfully, perfectly appropriate.' When Sean didn't appear to be any the wiser, she caught his cheek and pinched it playfully. 'It's like Saul on the road to Damascus. Sitting in Father Barry's car when he saw the light? It's just too wonderful for words! Don't you see?' She threw her head back and tossed her curls. 'My Michael has gone off to Dublin to follow his true destiny.'

Sean looked completely lost. 'I don't understand.'

'I do,' she said. 'My Michael is going to be a priest!'

While Cormac and Gerald walked the pier in Salthill and Monica and Michael snuggled up together on the sofa in her sitting-room in Dublin, Bernadette sat in Father Sean's kitchen picking cherries out of the side of her wedding cake. The joy she had felt when she figured out Michael's cryptic message was easing off a little and a gnawing ache was taking its place. It was loneliness. Cormac was off on his adventures and Michael had probably signed up for the seminary already and here she was, getting to bite all the cherries. Alone.

She looked around his kitchen and sighed. Everywhere you looked there was wedding cake, sliced thinly, thickly, every way. She hoped it would freeze. It wasn't coming home with her again anyway. A sob escaped her. What was there to go home to? *She* didn't have a destiny.

From outside came the sound of a car on gravel and Bernadette looked up. It wasn't Father Sean's Corolla. She got to her feet and went to the window. It wasn't any sort of a Vauxhall, it was a Volvo, Father Barry's Volvo. Bernadette's heart quickened.

The car came slowly up the drive and stopped just in front of the window. As the sound of the engine died the driver's door opened and Father Sean got out. He looked bothered. Instead of shutting the door impatiently behind him as he usually did, he turned back into the car and started to rummage under the pedals. From her vantage point Bernadette could see that there was something wedged under the accelerator. It looked like a piece of paper, a magazine page or something. It was twisted on the pedal and Father Sean was trying to prise it loose. He fiddled around for a minute and eventually the paper gave way. Looking pleased with himself he smoothed it flat on his knee and then held it up for inspection.

For a minute he was still and when he lowered the page again Bernadette was shocked at the expression on his face. He looked horrified. His mouth had fallen open and there was a rush of livid red coming onto his cheeks. She yanked on the window catch and pulling it open, leaned out.

'Father,' she called. 'What is it? Are you all right?'

His mouth opened and closed but he didn't say a word.

'What is it you have there? Do you need me to give you a hand with anything?'

He crumpled the paper defensively and shook his head. 'Thank you, no, I'm fine.' He started to walk towards the back door.

Bernadette lowered the window and went over to open it for him. As he came in he had the paper clenched in his fist. Bernadette watched him as he struggled to take his coat off.

'Is there something you need me to do?' she asked him sweetly.

He wouldn't let the paper go and the effort of freeing his arm from the sleeve only made him more agitated and his face redder. By the time the coat was off he was sweating.

He was dripping and his face was red and outside on the drive the engine of Father Barry's car was still warm. Bernadette looked from the car to the remains of cake on the table, her plate still strewn with unbitten cherries. And then she looked at Father Sean's face and saw that it was agitated and he was still holding on to the piece of paper. She didn't know what was on it and she didn't want to know. It didn't matter. The world had gone higgledy-piggledy this morning – everyone had gone off and nothing was where it should be – except herself and Father Sean. And like Saul on the Damascus Road and Michael on the Dublin one, Bernadette suddenly realised her destiny. She looked at his face and saw that he was still very flushed. She gave a big sigh. Poor dear dependable man. She knew exactly what was wrong with him. There she was thinking that everything was different when in fact, things were really the same, the way they'd always been, the way they were meant to be. And to think she'd never realised he had a weak heart!

'Don't you worry about a thing,' she said as she approached him. 'I know just what to do.'

And in the crumpled up page in his hand, a skinny Miss April lost her hold on the mountainside and toppling, fell into a huge vat of suds and soapy bubbles.

And drowned.